UNRESTRAINED BEHAVIOR

The Pleasure and Risk of Choice

Book Three

Jerry Summers

CONTENTS

PROLOGUE

Wendy closes her office door, settles back into her chair, and ponders her intense, negative feelings toward Zach. Knowing she must keep her feelings out of her voice, she reaches for her trac phone. Quietly contemplating, she dials the direct number for Zach and exhales slowly when he answers.

"You don't know me, Zach," she purrs, "but we have some common interests, and I believe I would very much enjoy sharing some of my secret abilities and unique skills with you..." She hears his quick intake of breath and smiles, knowing this will be a meeting she truly enjoys. "I want to see you."

"Who are you?" he asks.

"My name is Monique," she replies.

He clears his throat. "When and where?" he asks huskily, and Wendy smirks.

"Where is your favorite place for..." she pauses and chuckles, "meetings like this?"

The appointment is set, and Wendy returns to her penthouse for the night to perfect her disguise.

As she toys with the black stilettos that she plans to entice Zach Rawlins with, she contemplates the change in direction her life has taken since the death of her brother, Mark. Remembering Mark's best friend, Sean's, description of finding Mark's body at the McCall vacation home, she shakes her head. Interesting, how Sean vomited when he realized Mark had been shot. It dawns on Wendy that she has seen far more death than Sean will ever see, or could ever imagine. Still, Wendy likes Sean and has become attached to him.

The attachment she has to Mark's widow, Bonnie, has also grown because of Mark's murder, and Wendy plans to continue to be of assistance to Bonnie in ways Bonnie will never know. Working behind the scenes is exactly how Wendy prefers it, and she chuckles as she realizes that is also the way she became such a close friend to Sean and Jessica. She smiles smugly, knowing their fledgling relationship started mainly because of her.

Wendy is proud, in a perverse way, of what her life has turned into. She is thrilled by her creativity in helping her domestic violence clients gain freedom from their abusers. She fantasizes about all the options available to her to continue to make abusers' deaths look like accidents or suicides. Her relationship with Mark was what led her to counseling victims of domestic violence to begin with, and she recognizes what an odd twist it is that his death is what made it possible for her to become (as one of her clients so aptly put it) a powerful angel of mercy.

Coming back to the present, Wendy stares at the provocative red-soled shoes. She's even more aware than usual of how twisted people can be and how simple it is to 'Spin' her 'Unmerited' favors to keep the FBI from investigating any more deeply.

She inhales sharply as the familiar rush of adrenaline from the mercy she is about to bestow on behalf of Zach's wife, Jill, becomes almost overwhelming. Wendy can't imagine not helping others when it is within her power to do so, so very easily. The fact that she enjoys it is simply an unexpected benefit.

CHAPTER 1

DEATH OF THE COUNCILMAN

After setting the appointment to meet Wendy at his favorite rendezvous restaurant, Zach Rawlins quietly places his City Council office telephone receiver back into the cradle wondering who this mysterious woman is that seems to know so much about him. His mind races as he considers many hopeful women and likely candidates, but he remains baffled because no one has purred at him the way she did, and he can't remember ever meeting a woman named Monique. "You'll recognize me when I walk in," she had said, "and if you don't, we'll never meet." The mystery of going to his familiar restaurant and waiting without knowing who to look for fills him with anticipation about this chance encounter. Zach checks his calendar, recognizing his own building excitement. He quietly sits back in his desk chair, and wonders if Monique had this mental build up in mind for him, knowing the next twenty-four hours would create a bittersweet agony that will demand release in its own way. He chuckles, wondering if this mysterious woman has any inclination of what his fantasies consist of or the precarious position she may be placing herself in playing these types of games with someone of his caliber.

Wendy is equally focused upon her upcoming meeting and knows full well what the anticipation would be doing for Rawlins at the moment. She is confident in her ability to recognize him, having stopped by the library to search the Los Angeles City records, the City website, and the City Council blog in order to locate and review photographs of Zachery Rawlins. She is amazed at how easy it is to find the necessary material on the internet she'll need to carry on an intelligent conversation with Zach tomorrow and smiles slightly, considering the thrill she is expecting and enjoying her own anticipation. She arrives at Jill's hotel in La Jolla promptly at six o'clock to pick Jill up for dinner, knowing the information she intends to uncover from Jill about her soon-to-be deceased husband is important for the night to go smoothly. Jill comes into the lobby looking refreshed, less haggard and forlorn, albeit somewhat tentative. She knows the hotel can't be cheap and is very grateful for Wendy's generosity in paying for the room. She voices her concerns about cost to Wendy, worrying that she won't ever be able to return the favor.

Wendy quickly puts her mind at ease. "Jill, I know what you must be feeling right now, but don't worry about it at all. This is what I do, and I do it because others did the same for me when I was in a similar situation. It's important to me to pay back the benefits I received from others who struggled before me, and before you." Wendy pauses and sees Jill begin to relax as she accepts that she needs help and that Wendy wants to give it.

Jill sighs. "You're right, I know. Thank you."

"Of course," Wendy replies, and explains further, "I have contacted Jessica Silva, who is more than willing to help with your clothing issue." Wendy takes Jill's arm and begins to escort her to the car. The story about Jessica isn't entirely true, given the fact Wendy has arranged with the store to have her credit card charged without Jessica personally covering the costs. It's her way of carrying on the tradition Bonnie started with her not so long ago, clothing a woman who needs to feel cared for.

Jill tears up, unable to believe the kindness Wendy is showing her, but Wendy is quick to point out she is only repaying the gift of kindness she received from others recently. "Just enjoy it while it lasts, and remember that your time will come to repay this debt when someone else is in a difficult position, and you have the resources to help. Then and only then will repayment be expected of you."

Jill sniffs and nods at this statement, and Wendy continues. "I have a four o'clock appointment tomorrow that will take a couple of hours. After that I'll pick you up again to go to Beauty Boutique Clothing for our shopping spree. If I'm going to be late, I'll call the hotel and ask them to notify you."

Jill agrees and says, "We can shop another time if it's more convenient for you."

Wendy insists. "No, no. Not necessary. I already arranged for this shopping excursion to occur after the store has closed in order to maintain your confidentiality." Jill starts to speak but Wendy gently interrupts, "All the details are taken care of. Let's just focus on having a wonderful dinner and try to relax for a few hours."

Jill sighs and reluctantly agrees. "You're right. It will be nice to have a decent meal for a change."

Wendy snorts. "What? The rescue mission cuisine isn't extraordinary?"

"Extraordinary, no," Jill chuckles, "but don't get me wrong. I was delighted to get the meals I did. Let's just say the food wasn't to the standards I've grown accustomed to over the last ten years."

"I bet it wasn't."

"It really wasn't bad; it was just a rather basic dining experience."

"Well, let's see if we can improve upon that just a little tonight, shall we?"

Wendy glances over to watch Jill's expression as they pull up to a funky little hole in the wall place and is amused with the slight look of apprehension on Jill's face. Wendy kills the engine and puts her hand on Jill's arm. "Relax. I know it doesn't look like much from the outside but trust me the food is fantastic and the interior is eclectic and, most importantly, private."

Jill sighs. "Am I really such a snob that you could see my hesitation?"

"Yes, as a matter of fact, you are!"

"Oh, Dear God, I need to work on my attitude."

Wendy laughs. "Oh, lighten up, you're fine. Everyone I bring here reacts the same way initially, but I have yet to have one person complain about the quality of the food or service."

Jill nods as they walk toward the restaurant. They enter and Jill looks around appreciatively.

The owner greets Wendy warmly, welcoming her back.

"Would you two prefer a group table for some interaction or a private space to chat?" she asks.

"A private spot would be most appropriate this evening, thank you," Wendy replies, and they are escorted to a booth tucked away from the fray of major activity. They order a nice bottle of red wine and settle in, studying the rather bizarre menu options.

"An eel cocktail? Do you have a different menu than I do?" Jill asks, grinning.

Again Wendy chuckles at her reaction. "Nope, same stuff on mine. Be brave. Everything on this menu is terrific."

"Well, if you say so," Jill says, "I think I'll try the wild boar in port sauce."

"An excellent choice. I'm going to have the roasted Bob White quail. You can try that as well, if you'd like," Wendy says and Jill nods. Their conversation is casual, and then Wendy says, "I know this may be a painful topic, but I need to gather some more information if I'm going to help you through this. How did you meet Zach, and what attracted you to him initially?"

Jill nods and takes a deep breath. "I guess I'd have to say I was attracted to his sense of decorum initially. We met at a cocktail party for my bosses 50th birthday. It was Zach's first date with Mindy, an office coworker of mine, and it became apparent pretty quickly that things weren't going well for either of them. Yet Zach was polite and remained attentive to Mindy, even while she was getting toasted and belligerent towards everyone. I think he recognized she was about to do something she would later regret and instead of allowing her to do so, he got her out of the party and took her home, probably saving her career with the company. I found it sexy, so I did a little snooping about him with Mindy. She told me she wasn't into him and asked if I wanted to meet him. I said yes, and the next time he called her she told him he wasn't really her type but a coworker was interested, so she gave him my name and office number. I was pleasantly surprised when he called me immediately."

"I see. Tell me about your first date?"

"We had coffee together, and he was attentive and charming with an edge of intrigue, but I sensed under the polite exterior he was a 'bad boy'," Jill replies, gesturing quotation marks around the term.

Wendy raises an eyebrow. "I'm intrigued by the way you are describing him, and I get the sense that he would be pleased by your impression of his bad buy persona."

"Oh, yeah, he thrives on the persona of a polite bad boy, and he'll tell you straight up that that's what the women he is interested in secretly crave," taking a big drink of her wine.

"Well, that definitely makes sense given the circumstances you find yourself in currently."

Jill nods. "The problem is, he's right. His fantasies were both enlightening and exciting to me, at least, until they took a turn towards the perverse. I found most of his desires and behaviors erotic and intense."

"Where did he cross the line from enlightening to perverse for you?"

Jill considers. "I guess when things turned violent I realized I was in trouble. He got off on strangling me, especially if I struggled, and that's just not okay with me."

"It sounds like it also didn't feel safe for you anymore," Wendy observes.

"Precisely. Then came the perverse requests that I have no interest in whatsoever. They are just too twisted, and I don't understand how they could be sexualized."

"I understand," Wendy begins, but the conversation is interrupted with the arrival of their food, and Jill's expression after her first bite tells Wendy this was an excellent choice for dinner.

Jill moans at the flavors infused in the port sauce. "I have never tasted anything so divine. I'm so surprised!"

Wendy smiles and says, "I told you it's fantastic food."

"I had no idea a place like this existed anywhere near Los Angeles."

"Well, it's not really near; it's a ninety-minute drive from L.A."

"It's one that I would make regularly for an experience like this one," Jill says around a mouthful of boar.

"I'm delighted you appreciate it," Wendy says, smiling.

"Oh my God, do I ever."

Wendy chuckles. "So, getting back to our conversation, what do you think happened to bring about his change from experimentation to perversion?"

Jill chews slowly. "Personally, I believe it was extreme success and political power. The more important he became within the power base of Los Angeles the more women were willing to tolerate his extreme behavior." She pauses, shaking her head, "Myself included."

"Have you considered what may have happened if you refused to cooperate sooner than you did?"

"Recently, yes, but in thinking back on everything I think he just would have left me sooner."

"Interesting. Why is that?"

"Wealth and power go together and either extreme is manageable on its own, but when you combine the two, often the result is an over-inflated ego and sense of entitlement within one's professional and personal life."

Wendy considers Jill for a moment. "You know; I find you to be very astute. Why do you think you missed the danger signs?"

"Oh, I don't believe I missed them. I chose to ignore them. Other than the way things were changing in the bedroom my life was picture perfect. I had an incredible home, a wonderful husband, I ran in all the right circles in town, I didn't have to work, and there was always plenty of money to do whatever I wanted to do."

"Do you think Zach will ever change his preferences, especially when he realizes he'll lose you?"

"No, I don't. Zach is all about Zach now, and if I no longer meet his requirements then unfortunately I'm no longer useful to him."

"But you're not an object! You're his wife. You're the woman who put him through law school and got him his first elected position," Wendy protests, pushing Jill to explain more.

"Yeah, so what? From his perspective, he provided me with all the comforts any woman would need or desire, and the least I could do was keep him happy in the bedroom. I haven't done that."

"He didn't actually say that did he?"

"Yes, he did, as he was throwing me out of the house and calling me a greedy, selfish bitch."

Wendy shakes her head. "I'm so sorry."

"Me too. Why all the interest in Zach?"

"Honestly, I'm fascinated by your case. I told you from the beginning I haven't dealt with the complexity of some of the issues you're facing, and I'm trying to wrap my head around Zach's personality, what drives him, and what has brought about the changes within your marriage and especially his personality."

"Okay, I understand. I firmly believe it was the subtle shift in power for him, personally and within our marriage. In the beginning, he had to rely on me keeping my job to support him while he attended law school, and he loved being able to have me quit work and stay at home while he provided for us. As I see it now, he eventually forgot how we got to where we were and began to resent me not working. Once he realized I had become dependent on him, the ultimate power shift occurred, and he saw me not as his partner but as his property. When I truly realized this might be the case it was too late for me because I had nothing of my own. In essence, I was trapped and if I wanted to keep my picturesque life I needed to mold and conform to his changed desires."

"So your participation in the changing sexual dynamics of your marriage wasn't out of desire, but obligation?"

"Sort of. Initially I was fond of the idea of sharing myself with another woman for the enjoyment of my husband. I was raised in a traditional home where you married once, for life, and you did whatever was necessary to keep the marriage together even during the bad times. As things began to get rocky for us in the bedroom, Zach wanted to start experimenting, and I acquiesced, viewing sex with another woman not as infidelity, but as entertainment for him. I was secretly pleased when Zach became jealous seeing me with another woman, even when he participated, and decided we didn't need to continue experimenting that way. Then, I was shocked when he suggested and enjoyed seeing me with another man. I think it relieved his guilt about his own infidelity. When things really got weird I decided enough was enough."

"Do you think there is a chance, no matter how small, that you and Zach can save your marriage and return to the earlier days when life was normal and good for the two of you?"

Jill shakes her head sadly. "Never. There has been too much water under the bridge, and his perversion has reached a level that won't allow him to be satisfied with me or any other woman. I believe he'll continue to decline into further perversion and the level of extreme behavior will become more severe as time passes."

"If that's true, the overall outcome doesn't look very promising for other women or Zach," Wendy says carefully.

Jill shrugs. "Probably not. It won't surprise me if he kills someone in a sexual rage or himself through a cocaine overdose."

"Well, let's hope it doesn't come to that."

Wendy orders another bottle of wine. "I'm sorry the conversation became so depressing. I think I've learned enough to make some sound judgments in your case. Should we discuss more pleasant topics?"

Jill agrees. "Yes, definitely. I need to laugh, and I really enjoy your company."

The conversation turns to the beautiful clothes Jill will be trying on the next night, how Wendy knows the designer and other eclectic restaurants Wendy can introduce Jill to. The evening is relaxed, uneventful, and very refreshing for both of them.

The next morning, Wendy gets up, pours herself some strong coffee, and contemplates what her day will hold. She turns her attention to her scheduled four o'clock appointment with Zach Rawlins. She walks into her closet and carefully chooses a black bra and panty set, then decides on a classy black dress with buttons down the front to the waistline and a slit up the back. Pleased with her selection, she decides to accent it with a big brim hat with a fish net face covering. She picks out a single strand of pearls and a pair of Christian Louboutin stilettos with the signature red sole to finish the image of sexual allure and power. She smiles, knowing after questioning Jill that Zach will recognize her immediately and be drawn to her chosen persona like a moth to a flame. She sets the outfit aside, deciding she will excuse herself from the office at lunch to come home and prepare herself for meeting Zach. Glancing back at her clothes, she pulls out jeans and a blouse for her morning at the office.

She spends the morning in session with some of her more normal clients and signs a few checks Mona has prepared for her approval.

As lunch nears, she begins planning her seduction of Zach. Thoughtfully, Wendy works through which mannerisms will be most effective to drive Zach crazy with lust. She goes back and forth between a head toss and piercing eyes or a softer more demure approach, and finally decides that, given his preference for violence, the piercing stare and sexual confidence combined with the show of power will work the best. As she works through the rest of her paperwork for the morning, she starts to role play possible conversations in her head. She's amused at how simple it is to control powerful men using their weakness for women with confidence and certain physical attributes. Mostly what a man like Zach Rawlins wants is for a woman to flaunt her sexual prowess while on his arm.

She rolls her eyes, thinking how pathetic men are as individuals. *If there is a man in the world that wouldn't fall for the appeal of a beautiful woman, I'd give my right hand to meet him,* she thinks, then concludes there probably isn't one. Lunch arrives before she knows it, and she checks in with Mona before she leaves for the afternoon.

"Everything will be fine here." Mona says, "Go do your thing."

"Thanks. I'll be picking Jill up tonight to get her outfitted at Beauty Boutique Clothing, so I just want to be prepared," Wendy says, and Mona waves her out the door.

She returns to her penthouse and heads straight for the bathroom. After multiple attempts, she finally feels she has the especially dramatic effect she desires for her eyes. She checks her watch, cursing her lack of ability with makeup, and is relieved when she sees she still has time to spare. She plans her drive precisely, planning to arrive at the restaurant five minutes past four o'clock. Getting the dress settled just the right way and her toes straightened out in the stilettos takes just enough time, and she turns on the GPS tracker on her cell phone and leaves it on the counter before locking up. She knows there will be calls made to her cell which, if tracked by the police, will indicate she had been in the penthouse all afternoon and solidify her alibi.

The drive is short, and she walks through the front door with an air of confidence.

"Hello, welcome," the hostess says warmly. "What can I help you with today?"

Wendy turns so the fishnet conceals more of her face and replies, "I'm here to meet with Zachary Rawlins, but it's been a while and I'm not sure he'll recognize me. I'll just check the dining area and see if he does, if that's alright?"

The hostess smiles knowingly. "Of course you can, miss."

Wendy simply nods at her and strolls into the open seating area of the restaurant. The hostess turns to watch her and, just as planned, Zach immediately stands up and heads toward her.

The hostess says, "I see Mr. Rawlins has noticed and is coming to get you, so I'll leave the two of you alone."

Wendy smiles at her covertly and replies, "Thank you." Turning, she greets Zach with an outstretched hand. "I'm glad you recognized me," she purrs.

"You told me I would. I'd have to be a fool not to," he replies smoothly.

As he leads Wendy to his table, he guides her with a hand on her back, allowing it to slide from her shoulder blades to the small of her back before they reach the table and he pulls her chair out for her to be seated.

"Thank you, Mr. Rawlins," Wendy says as she settles into the chair, "the level of class you exhibit is disarming."

He smiles at her. "I would hope so. Tell me, Monique, how do you know so much about me when I know virtually nothing about you? I don't believe we've ever met. You are a captivating woman, and I wouldn't have forgotten you easily."

She gives him a chuckle charged with sexual innuendo. "I would hope not. No we have never met."

"May I ask, then, what on earth prompted you to call me at my office?"

"Mr. Rawlins, the spiking community on the west coast is a growing but tight knit community for several reasons. First, every one of us who participate in it are driven and excited by fantasies broadly fitting into three categories: power, control, and humiliation. Second, given these categories, there is always a certain element of personal risk, and we must be careful who we allow into our group. Last, since certain aspects of our fantasies are actually, and unfortunately, illegal, there is a membership selection process that has been put into place."

Zach nods his understanding. "So you're here to determine if I meet all the membership requirements?"

"Yes, I most certainly am," she replies as she slides a foot up the inside of his leg, stopping at mid-thigh and sliding it slowly back down.

He clears his throat. "Then would you care to have a drink and lunch with me?"

"A drink would perfect, but I'll have to turn down lunch. Perhaps an appetizer? I have a different type of meal plan in mind if things go well with us today."

Zach gives her a slow smile and motions to the server. "I'll have a rum and coke with top shelf rum," he says, and then looks at Wendy.

"I'll have a dirty martini, please," she says, locking eyes with Zach. "The dirtier the better."

His gaze heats for a moment, and then he returns his attention to the server and orders an imported cheese platter and pâté. When he brings his eyes back to her, the heat in them has cooled. "Will that be suitable?"

She simply nods, and Zach waves the server away. They sit quietly, observing each other for a few minutes, until their drinks are delivered.

Wendy reaches for her martini and Zach catches her hand, pulling her forward across the table. "You still haven't told me how you found out about me, and that disturbs me a bit. Why don't you enlighten me, before we continue this little game?"

Wendy glances at her trapped hand and nods, once. "Very well. You met with a woman in Hillsboro recently and fulfilled a fantasy. She recognized your immaturity during this encounter as it pertains to a specific activity, so she prompted this analysis by contacting a friend and telling her what transpired. We gathered information about where you reside and what you do, and then I came to further evaluate you. The rating you received from your partner was 4 out of 5. She felt you were too impatient during your encounter, but liked your overall performance. Anyone receiving below 3 out of 5 is automatically eliminated from membership. In other words, you made it past the first round."

He absorbs the information and releases her hand with a caress. "And who is the mystery woman you 'report' to?"

"Oh, it doesn't work that way, for confidentiality reasons. Let me explain things a bit better. Your partner contacts a friend who makes contact with someone in your permanent residence area who ultimately does a little research then contacts you. That person just happened to be me in this area. This system has been established to shelter everyone. For example, if you or your partner were caught engaging in spiking what do you think the media would do to you as a city councilman and prominent attorney? The threat is just as large for any of us, since most of our spouses have no idea what we are in to. By keeping the contact between members limited, the most the media can uncover is three people: you, your partner, and her initial contact, who of course would deny any knowledge of her sexual activities. Likewise, if she got caught with someone other than you it couldn't be traced back unless she tells the media who all her partners have been, at which point we all deny it, leaving her the only one accountable." She pauses.

"So I'm only allowed to be involved with you and the one woman I've already met?" he asks, glancing around covertly.

Wendy smiles. "Not at all. If you have to travel, to the east coast let's say, and you're interested in a play date, you can call your partner here and tell her where you'll be. She can call ahead for you and let someone know you'll be coming to town. That person will ask for your rating and preferences and will contact an appropriate person for you that your partner doesn't know. This person will call your office and leave a message that goes something like, 'I understand Mr. Rawlins is going to be in Florida next week, and I'd like to get together with him if he can find time in his schedule. If he does, will you please have him contact me at this number by this date?' When you get the message and you don't recognize the name you'll know what is happening. Then when you call her she will say something like, 'I understand we have similar interests. When can we get together?' and you can work with her to set a place and time."

"What if my initial partner refuses to open these doors for me?"

"That should never happen. None of us have exclusive rights to anyone else and this is clearly understood from the beginning. Therefore, anyone refusing to assist someone else is immediately removed from membership."

"What if she really doesn't know anyone in that area?"

"Then she will tell you that and will check with others she knows to uncover someone for you. If you never receive a call no one was located and you're on your own."

"How will I know their likes are compatible with mine?"

She shoots him a look. "You ask."

He gives her another slow smile. "What things would you like to explore?"

She pauses, taken off-guard. "Very smooth. I am always interested in games involving control, power, and humiliation."

"The trifecta of this intriguing closed group. I'd like to know more. Specifically, what activities in those three areas interest you?"

She pulls the fish netting on her hat to the side, giving him a loaded look. "Spiking, because I like power. Autoerotic strangulation, because I like control. Golden showers, because I like humiliation. Just to name a few. I don't do bondage or whips."

The heat returns to Zach's eyes and he asks, "How is strangulation control for you?"

"I like being the one who strangles, and I also like being in control as to when someone stops strangling me."

"Your interests seem to be almost completely in line with mine. Where do we go from here?"

"That depends on you. Is there a place we could go to engage in our activities?" He nods, and she continues, "Then it depends on what your desires are at this time. I have some very specific rules."

"Care to elaborate?"

"Well, I won't engage in any type of spiking in a hotel. It's too easy to get caught, so if that's your fantasy today it must be done in a residence where we won't be disturbed. The strangulation and golden showers would be perfect in a hotel room. Also, these things are always better done in the bath or shower. I never do them in bed."

"In regards to the humiliation portion of your fantasies, do you prefer to humiliate or be humiliated?"

"I enjoy both. It just depends on my mood at the time."

"What about drug usage?"

She shakes her head. "I personally don't participate in drug usage, but I'm not opposed to others using. In fact, I do something very unique with cocaine that drives those who use through the roof. I'm always rewarded with incredible sex afterwards."

He looks intrigued. "Really. Do tell."

"Not so fast," she says with a sly smile, "that's a surprise reserved only for those I play with and enjoy."

"What if I told you I'm not sure you're for real and I want you to prove everything you have claimed to be interested in?" he asks.

"I'm prepared to demonstrate my skills right now, if you have a safe home we could go to. I'll rock your world," she promises, sitting back and pressing her foot firmly on his crotch to emphasize her point.

He shifts, pressing himself against her foot. "I'm in the middle of a divorce, my wife no longer lives with me, and I'd like to take you home right now and see if you are truly who you claim to be. I'm particularly interested in your cocaine trick today. How does that sound?"

She makes a slow circle with her foot. "Yes. I'll follow you in my car. But you should know I have a date with a girlfriend of mine tonight, so we only have about an hour and a half. How far is your place?"

"Twenty minutes, tops. That will leave us at least an hour." He smirks. "Can you truly rock my world in that timeframe?"

"Like you would never believe. My performance is to die for, rated 5 out of 5 by everyone I've ever played with. Let's go. You'll never be the same again."

He wraps his fingers around her ankle and murmurs, "Promises, promises," then gestures for the server to bring their bill.

Zach pays the bill quickly and escorts Wendy out to her car. The closer he gets to his house, the more excited he becomes. At a stoplight, he quickly lines and snorts some cocaine, and Wendy watches his head bobbing up and down through his rear window. She sighs and rehearses in her mind what is to come next. Glancing down at herself, she unbuttons the fourth button on her dress, exposing a bit more cleavage than in the restaurant just for good measure, and then follows Zach into his driveway.

CHAPTER 2

EXECUTION OF A BRILLIANT PLAN

Zach walks back to Wendy's car and opens her door for her. He smiles as she swings her legs around and leans forward, allowing him a brief glimpse down the front of her dress. She fusses with her purse a moment, pretending not to notice his more than obvious ogling. He offers his hand and helps her out of her vehicle, keeping a tight grip on her as they walk up the driveway.

As he escorts her into the house, Wendy is surprised by the warmth Jill has created in their home with her sense for interior design. She stands in the foyer for a moment, absorbing the atmosphere.

"Would you like a drink?" Zach asks, having already made his way to the kitchen.

She considers him a moment. "No, thank you," she says, then pointedly looks at her watch. "We have a little more than an hour before I have to leave."

Zach nods. "True. I'm fascinated by your comment about the cocaine trick. How does that work?"

She smiles at him. "Why? Do you have cocaine you would like me to use?"

"Yes, I have some. But I would really like to know what you're going to do with it first."

"Well," she says, tracing the kitchen counter seductively, "I would put on a latex glove, dip my finger into a little bit of water, and then

15

touch the coke, so it would stick. Then I would press my finger into your rectum. You'll get an immediate rush. But that's not the fun part. After that, I'll insert another finger and spread them, allowing room for a syringe, preloaded with some water and more cocaine, to fit and be injected into the wall of your rectum. While you experience the increased rush, I do a strip tease, leading up to getting the animal out of its cage and beginning my spiking routine. By the time I'm finished, you'll have reached your climax, and then I'll allow you to relax for a few moments before it's your turn to satisfy my desires."

Zach hesitates. "I'm not sure how I feel about becoming an intravenous user."

Wendy nods. "I understand. But this is something that you can do only when I'm giving you a spiking experience. Try it once. If you don't like it, you'll never have to do it again, but I have yet to find anyone that dislikes the effects."

He considers for a moment then says, "Why the hell not. I'm always willing to try new experiences."

Wendy smiles again as she follows him into his bedroom. "Good. You'll need to get some cocaine out and take off your clothes."

Zach pours some cocaine on a mirror on his nightstand then removes his clothes. Wendy does as she told him and administers the first round of cocaine. The second it is absorbed into his system he says, "Wow, what a rush."

"Alright, now a slight prick, then the cool flow of the liquid," Wendy murmurs.

As she starts the injection she smiles, knowing that instead of the water and cocaine, the potassium chloride in the syringe will take its full effect in less than ten minutes. After that, his heart attack will be over before she even finishes removing all of her clothing. She removes the syringe and her fingers and Zach takes a moment, then rolls over and sits up on the bed. Wendy begins a slow, sensual strip tease, watching Zach's increasing arousal intently. When she allows her dress to fall to the floor, exposing her matching bra and panties, Zach starts to masturbate. Wendy unclasps her bra and lets it fall to the floor, but keeps herself covered with her arms, biding her time. After a moment, Zach starts to rub his chest, and she notices he is beginning to sweat profusely. She ignores his signs of distress and continues with her strip tease enticements.

"Hold on a minute," Zach says, wheezing, "I don't feel right."

"That's just what happens with intravenous cocaine injections, baby. You'll be okay," Wendy says, exposing more of her breasts.

He shakes his head and stands up from the bed, clasping his chest and heading toward the bathroom. She stops her sexy dance, watching him stumble and then fall forward on the bedroom carpet. Silently, she starts to get dressed, knowing without even having to check that Zach Rawlins is dead. She takes a moment to scan the room to make sure nothing pointing to her being there is left behind. She double checks the capped syringe to make sure it is inside the latex glove and that both are in her purse. Checking herself, she makes sure all of her clothing is on, then glances at the scene.

Cocaine is still on the bedroom nightstand with Zach's clothes neatly stacked just as he left them. She surveys the room to make sure it looks like Zach came home, snorted some cocaine, and then was getting ready to take a shower. She considers her options and decides to go turn the shower on for added effect. Taking the other latex glove out of her purse, she turns the shower on and then walks out the front door. Once outside, she takes off the glove, wraps it around the other glove, and places the whole rolled up piece of evidence in her purse. She glances around as she gets in her car, then drives away smiling, completely unnoticed.

Wendy pulls into a fast food drive through, orders a quick meal of burger and fries, and then heads to a neighborhood park to eat in the sunshine. When she finishes her burger, she places the latex gloves and syringe in the bag with the other wrappers and throws the whole thing into the park's trash. She strolls around the park for a few minutes until she spots a group of teenagers playing basketball and listening to music. She decides to drop her trac phone nearby, knowing one of the kids will find it and use it until the minutes are gone. She chuckles, knowing that if the phone number is ever investigated any corresponding telephone calls won't make sense to investigators and the phone will quickly be eliminated as any kind of evidence. As she stands with the sun on her face she closes her eyes, basking in its warmth serenely, satisfied Jill will now be free from her demons and financially secure once again. Wendy opens her eyes, admiring how everything looks sharper; the grass greener, the sky bluer. She marvels at her ability to continue to conjure up unique methods of murder that won't implicate her, or anyone else for that matter.

As she makes her way back to her car, she wonders how long she can continue to be creative before she'll have to use one of her previous methods. She considers, trying to calculate the risks involved with repeating a similar pattern. Dismissing the risks with a shake of her head, she gets into her car for the thirty-minute drive back to the penthouse. During the drive she thinks about those she has helped to escape the trials and tribulations they were unable to overcome alone. A sense of accomplishment, profound satisfaction, and immense pride well up in her as she recognizes her lifelong destiny is finally being manifested through her performance as an Angel of Mercy for the downtrodden and abused. For a while she simply basks in the glow of her own success.

Before she arrives back at her house, she decides it would probably be a good idea to get rid of her hat and shoes, so she stops at a gas station in San Diego, fills her tank, and leaves her hat in the women's bathroom garbage. After returning to the condo, she breaks the heel off of one of her shoes and drops them down the garbage chute, knowing the dumpster will be emptied the next day. Satisfied she has tied up all of her loose ends she pours herself a glass of merlot and allows herself to feel the adrenaline rush of knowing she has successfully done it again.

Making her way out to the patio, she sits and gazes out at the Pacific Ocean, contemplating Jill's reaction when someone finds Zach's body in a day or two. Thinking of Jill, she suddenly realizes that time has gotten away from her. She quickly dresses in a business attire pantsuit, grabs her cell phone, and heads to the hotel to get Jill.

As she waits in the lobby, she checks her voicemail and texts, responding to Bonnie's text first, since it seems urgent. Wendy's reply lets Bonnie know she will call her later tonight to discuss the important pending business Bonnie needs to cover. Bonnie responds that any time prior to eleven o'clock would be fine.

Jill arrives in the lobby promptly and gives Wendy a big hug, then stands back and takes her hands, giving her a once-over. "Wow! I love what you're wearing. Where did you get it?"

"At Beauty Boutique Clothing, which is where we are headed right now. And Lora, who squared me away, is waiting to help you. Believe me, she is fantastic. You're going to look great."

"I can't wait to see what she'll come up with, because you look fabulous."

"Thank you. Let's go," Wendy says and guides Jill out the door.

Lora meets them at the door and invites them into the store.

"Hello! Nice to see you again Wendy," Lora says, kissing both of Wendy's cheeks. "And you must be Jill. I'm Lora." The two women shake hands, and then Lora launches into a bunch of style preference questions. Jill answers them all happily, and Lora says, "Okay, I've got some ideas now. You're a size four?"

Jill nods. "If it's a true four."

Lora bustles around, pulling clothing options, and hands Jill several high-to-low dresses in different colors. "These are the ones I'd like you to try first. Maybe the teal?"

Jill simply nods again and heads into the dressing room. When she comes back out, Wendy exclaims, "My God! You're gorgeous."

Lora watches Jill as she turns different ways in the three sided mirror. "What do you think?"

"I think it's terrific."

"Good, because it's a perfect fit for your body type," Lora says.

Wendy laughs and tells Lora, "Come on, anything will look good on a body like hers."

Jill feels herself blush for the first time in a long time and looks at the floor.

Wendy catches her reaction and asks, "Honey, why are you embarrassed?"

"Oh, I'm not. I just... I haven't had anyone compliment me like that recently."

Lora smiles and jumps in right on time. "Jill, you're going to be super easy to outfit, even without alterations. Your body is proportionally perfect." She pulls a few more outfits off the racks that include pants suits, blouse and pant combinations, and some more casual combinations. After about two hours, Jill has settled on several options. "These are all wonderful. But I need a couple of outfits for job interviews."

"Of course you do," Wendy tells her. "Don't worry. If you're going to get back on your feet, you'll need to have a fully functional wardrobe."

Jill nods. "Yes, but my point is, my priority is going to be getting a job, and if I get too far in debt I'll never get out. I should probably focus more on business attire."

Lora smiles. "You can get everything you've chosen and more, dear. All you've picked out today is fully paid for because you need them to get back on your feet. And speaking of feet, we don't have a huge selection of shoes but I think we can find one or two pairs here to get you through for a short while. We're trying to incorporate a shoe designer section into each store…" She trails off, disappearing, and then returns with shoe boxes.

Jill stands, stunned, as Lora matches most of the outfits with three pairs of shoes. With these additions, Jill is taken care of for a while. Lora removes the tags, bags everything for Jill, and sends them on their way.

"Thank you so much. Both of you," Jill says, and begins to cry tears of thankfulness as she leaves the store with Wendy. Wendy sits with her for a moment in the car, patting and offering tissues, and then Jill pulls herself together.

"Would you like to get a drink and some food?" Wendy asks, and Jill nods gratefully.

When they arrive at the bar, Wendy orders a margarita and Jill orders a whiskey sour. As they talk, Wendy keeps remembering the expression on Zach's face as she performed her seduction routine and wondering when the last time he had looked at his wife with that kind of lust in his eyes had been.

What a worthless pig, Wendy thinks, watching the light in Jill's eyes as she talks about her previous career, *I hope she doesn't make the same mistake on the next guy.* Jill keeps chatting and Wendy considers how long it will be before she gets the news of Zach's heart attack. She fervently hopes everything Jill explained about their financial preparations is correct, knowing that if it is, Jill will be set for the rest of her life. The thought pleases Wendy because she had a major hand in getting Jill back to her normal lifestyle.

Suddenly Jill stops midsentence and looks hard at Wendy. After a moment of silence, she asks, "How do you do it?"

"Do what?"

"Deal with people like me who have made complete messes of their lives. Doesn't it wear you down?"

"First of all those so called 'messes' aren't created solely by the people I work with, because they're the victim, not the instigator. Second, I do this work for those that are being victimized, not for myself. As a survivor, I understand the hopelessness each victim feels because I've felt it myself. The most frustrating things to me are seeing what needs to be done and not being able to convince the victim of the dangers of inaction, and also watching how our governmental and judicial systems provide more protection for the abuser than the victim. It's frustrating at times, but at other times it is the most rewarding work I could ever imagine anyone having the privilege of being involved with. It's not really a job to me, it's a way to give back. My challenge is to stay focused on the positives and not get bogged down in the negatives."

"It just seems like the need for someone like you is so immense, so I guess what I meant was, with all the demand, how do you maintain a balance in life and your sanity?"

Wendy chuckles. "Well, my sanity has always been questionable," she jokes, getting a genuine smile from Jill, but then adds, "Having been in a position similar to yours, I understand things that others may not. It's a passion in my life to help those who are walking the road I've already journeyed down."

Jill is quiet for a while, then nods. "Thank you again for everything you've done for me, Wendy. I now recognize my obligation to help someone else once I get back on my feet, and I promise I'll fulfill it as soon as I can."

"I know you will," Wendy says, taking Jill's hand, "and that is what makes it possible for each of us to become survivors despite our trying circumstances."

CHAPTER 3

THE DISCOVERY

Zachery Rawlins misses several appointments at his office the next morning and his staff leaves several call back messages. When he also misses several city council functions, the local police are notified and dispatched to check on him at his home. Since there is no indication of anything being amiss and his car is in the driveway, the officers leave a note on the door requesting that Zach contact his office, then notify dispatch that they were unable to locate him. The mayor checks with the chief of police shortly after and is informed of the officer's lack of findings.

Befuddled, the mayor says, "Well, Chief, please send someone out there again. If there still isn't a response, try his wife, Jill."

The chief agrees, and another officer makes the trip to Rawlins home. When the officer finds nothing has changed, Officer Irma Vasquez calls Jill who lets the call go to voicemail, fearing it's Zach using a number she doesn't recognize. Officer Vasquez leaves a voicemail, which Jill listens to quickly. Jill immediately returns the call. When Officer Vasquez explains the situation, Jill is concerned.

"Officer, Zach never parks his car in the driveway. The spare key is hidden under a fake rock near the front step. Please go check and see if everything is okay," Jill says, giving authorization for the LAPD to enter the house. "And please let me know what you find out."

The officers open the front door and calls out, announcing they are in the residence. They continue to announce themselves as they check from room to room. When they reach the master bedroom they can hear the shower running and call out again, still without a response, as they enter the master bedroom. The first thing they see is a white powder on the nightstand, then one circles the bed to find Zach's naked body on the carpet. They quickly check for a pulse and immediately recognize he is cold to the touch and deceased. The officer's radio for a supervisor, investigators, and the forensic team, then secure the residence.

Upon arrival, the supervisor is briefed and immediately telephones the shift commander who relays the message up the chain of command until the chief is briefed on the initial findings. The chief telephones the mayor with the information, and the mayor decides he will call Jill himself. When Jill see's the mayor's office is calling her, she immediately feels sick to her stomach but decides to answer the call anyway.

"Jill, I'm sorry to have to tell you this," Mayor Clifton begins, "the police found Zach on the bedroom floor in the master bedroom, deceased. From the initial findings it appears he may have had a heart attack. They also found what appears to be cocaine on his nightstand. They need to speak with you as soon as possible. Where are you?"

Jill is speechless for a moment. "I-I'm in San Diego. I have been for about a week now. Where do I need to go to speak with the police?"

He replies, "Don't you worry about a thing. Stay where you are and I'll have the police come to you. Where should I send them?"

She gives him the name of the hotel and her room number. "Have them come straight up please. I don't want to deal with any media just yet."

"Of course, Jill. If there's anything I can do, you know how to reach me," Mayor Clifton replies, and they terminate the call.

After they hang up, Jill immediately calls Wendy's office and explains to Wendy everything she was just told.

"Oh, Jill, I'm so sorry. Would you like me to come to the hotel and be there while you speak with the detectives?" Wendy asks, infusing her voice with concern.

"No, thank you. I don't want you tied up in this investigation and media frenzy."

Wendy pauses. "You know, I'll be pulled into it anyway because your room is registered in my name and paid for with my credit card."

"You're right! I'm so sorry. I'll do my best to keep your name out of everything, and I'll ask for the detectives' discretion. Hopefully I'll get some cooperation," Jill says.

"Honey, don't worry about it. All I did was to help keep you safe and your whereabouts confidential. At this point there is no need to keep your location a secret except for you to be able to hide from the press for a few more days. If you need me just call, and I'll be right there."

Jill huffs out a breath. "Thanks, Wendy. I really appreciate it, but you have already done so much for me. I'll handle the police."

❋ ❋ ❋

Jill answers the knock on her door to find Detective Briggs and Detective England, both of whom she has met before.

"Hello, detectives. Please, come in," she says, gesturing for them to make themselves comfortable.

"Hello, Mrs. Rawlins. We're so very sorry for your loss," Briggs says as the three of them settle in for a conversation. "I'm sure you've already heard about the situation, since you're so well connected. We need to ask you some personal questions. Do you feel up to speaking with us today?"

Jill takes a breath. "Yes, of course. Ask away."

"Where were you last night and today?" asks Detective Briggs.

"I've been in this hotel for five days. Prior to that I was in a Rescue Mission on South San Pedro Street for a couple nights."

The detectives exchange a look. "Were you and Mr. Rawlins separated?"

"Ya think?" she asks, somewhat bitter. "He kicked my ass out of our home and closed all of our bank accounts, leaving me destitute and homeless—" She stops and clears her throat. "Sorry. Yes, I'd say we were separated."

"I see. And where were you last night?"

"I was at dinner with a girlfriend from seven o'clock to about ten, and then in my room from then until now."

"What is your friend's name?" Briggs asks.

"Why is that important?" Jill counters.

"We'll need her to be able to confirm your whereabouts."

"Are you telling me I'm some type of suspect?"

"No, ma'am. This is standard protocol, and in circumstances where someone's cause of death is uncertain, we try to dot all of our i's and cross all of our t's. That's all."

"Well, I don't like what you're implying, and since I sent my husband to law school I know enough to ask you both to leave. When we talk again it will be with my lawyer present," Jill says, standing and walking to the door.

"Very well. What was your friend's name, did you say?"

She pulls the door open. "I didn't mention it. Good day detectives."

"Mrs. Rawlins, we may need to speak with you again. Can we reach you on your cell phone?"

"Leave your cards, and I'll have my attorney get in contact with you," she replies, and pulls the door open wider, obviously waiting for them to leave. As soon as they're gone, she calls Wendy.

Wendy listens carefully then says, "You should have given them my name. I would have told them we had dinner last night."

"Screw them. I didn't like their attitudes. If they want it, they can figure it out for themselves."

Wendy shakes her head, smiling slightly. "You know they are going to check on who is paying for the room and they'll probably be in my office in a few minutes. May I confirm you are a client and whatever information you have given them?"

"Sure, have at it. I just didn't like what they were implying."

"I understand, Jill. I just think we should make it easier on the fine men doing their jobs, not harder."

Jill sighs, agrees, and they hang up.

As Wendy is placing the phone back in its cradle, she hears the detectives come in and ask Mona if she is in.

Wendy calls out, "Just send the detectives in. I was anticipating their visit."

The detectives walk into her personal office and introduce themselves. "Do you have time to answer a few questions for us?"

Wendy simply nods.

"Thank you. Do you know Jill Rawlins?"

"Yes I do. But you already know that, since I'm paying for her hotel room, don't you?"

Both smile and nod in acquiescence.

"Yes, I thought so. I tell you what… Let me save you a lot of time and trouble. Mrs. Rawlins is a client and she has authorized me to speak with you both. I will confirm things she has told you, but I will not violate any confidentiality. My practice is counseling victims of domestic violence and sexual assault, and I'm paying for her hotel room in my name to maintain her confidentiality. I'm sure you both can fill in the blanks here. Jill and I had dinner last night from seven o'clock until about ten when I dropped her back off at the hotel. You can confirm this with the restaurant owner as well. She called me today after Mayor Clifton contacted her with the news, and again after she kicked you out of her hotel room, so I'm not surprised to see you here now."

The detectives take a moment to digest the information. "Thank you for being so straight forward, Ms. Stevens. How long have you been seeing Mrs. Rawlins?"

"A few weeks. She is a relatively new client."

"Why was she coming to San Diego for counseling instead of using a counselor in L.A.?"

"I asked her the same question, and she told me she had been referred to me by a couple of my previous clients. She didn't know who Zach had in his back pocket, so she came to me based on recommendations and because she didn't want to put his career at risk with any possible rumors."

"How long have they been separated?"

"I'm not able to answer that question directly, but I will address what my client told you to be correct or not. What did she tell you?"

"She told us you put her up in the hotel five days ago, and she was in the rescue mission for a couple of nights prior to that," Briggs says, checking his notes.

"That is the same information I received, and you already have confirmation for when I put her up in the hotel."

"What can you tell us about Mr. Rawlins? He wasn't your client was he?"

"No he wasn't, but I still can't tell you anything specific about him without violating Mrs. Rawlins' client confidentiality," Wendy replies.

"Then I guess we're done here. Thank you for your time, Ms. Stevens."

"You're welcome. If I can help in any other manner, please don't hesitate to call me."

"Oh, I suspect there will be follow up questions as time passes and additional information is revealed."

"Well, you know where I am, and I'm sure Mona has given you my card."

The detectives nod and turn to leave, but Briggs stops and turns back to Wendy. "One last question. Can you tell us why Mrs. Rawlins is so skeptical of law enforcement when all we are doing is trying to figure out what actually happened?"

"Well gentlemen, I suspect your questions about her whereabouts after what Mr. Rawlins has put her through pissed her off. She's extremely aware of the fact that she hasn't been anywhere near her home for the last eight days, and she has just been told her husband is dead. She is dealing with a lot right now and from my perspective you have just witnessed a normal reaction." Wendy pauses and shrugs, "Not to mention she was married to a very successful attorney and has a healthy view of how law enforcement and the criminal justice system really works."

"I see. Thank you for your input. We will be in touch."

"I'm sure you will."

As Detectives Briggs and England leave her office, Wendy contemplates their demeanor. She recognizes they probably aren't suspecting anything more than a cocaine induced heart attack and just simply needed to verify where Jill was given the fact she wasn't home and didn't report Zach missing. Given the explanation of Zach kicking her out of the house and closing bank accounts, Wendy is confident the detectives will verify everything with the financial institutions and find all is as it has been reported to them. Wendy's only concern is with the medical examiner's report, should they find the injection site. She reasons this isn't the type of situation that would warrant any type of intense scrutiny, but is still a bit apprehensive due to Rawlins' standing in the Los Angeles community. She quickly dismisses her concerns, reasoning it is precisely due to his standing in the community and the unwillingness to besmirch his good name that the autopsy will be routine. Since nothing should appear unusual due to the human body's habit of producing large amounts of potassium chloride at the time of death, everything should play out like she planned. Wendy sits back smugly, knowing the chances of detection are so miniscule that she isn't at risk. She closes her eyes and enjoys the all-too-familiar intense rush once again.

Detectives Briggs and Englands' next stop is at Mr. Rawlins' office to check his calendar. They immediately focus on his four o'clock meeting with Monique. They ask for and receive a copy of his calendar from his secretary, then head to the restaurant. The hostess there confirms Mr. Rawlins met, had drinks, and left with a stunningly gorgeous woman in her mid-forties.

"Do the premises have video of the interior or the parking lot?" one of the detectives asks.

The hostess shakes her head. "Unfortunately no, the premises aren't equipped with any closed circuit television."

"Thank you. May I confirm all of this with the manager?"

The hostess nods and hurries back into the office, returning promptly with the manager, who confirms everything the hostess told them. The detectives thank them for their time and decide their best alternative at this point is to wait for the autopsy results, reasoning that, since Mr. Rawlins was estranged from his wife, it wouldn't be unusual for him to be seeking the company of other women.

A couple of weeks later the official autopsy report is forwarded to Detectives Briggs and England, indicating the cause of death as a myocardial infarction. Additional notes after the cause of death indicate the white powder found on the nightstand, originally believed to be cocaine, was also found in Rawlins' nasal passages. It was confirmed to be cocaine through the toxicology, and visceral fluids determined his blood alcohol level was .043 with nothing else abnormal.

After thorough review of the results, they drive to the Rawlins' home. Jill is surprised to see them at her door, and before she can say anything, Detective England says, "Don't worry, Mrs. Rawlins. We're not here to ask you any questions. But we do have some information for you and would appreciate the opportunity to speak with you inside, if we may?"

Jill considers for a moment, then steps aside and motions for them to come into her home. They follow her into the living room and she asks, "Would you like some coffee or tea?"

"Coffee would be good. Thank you," Briggs replies, and England agrees.

When she returns to the living room with the coffee, Detective England begins, "Given the fact our last conversation ended with significant tension between us, we wanted to come by and give you the details of the medical examiner's report in person. Sometimes our job requires us to ask difficult questions that others find threatening or offensive and for that please accept our apologies. The report indicates Mr. Rawlins died from a heart attack. He had cocaine in his system and his blood alcohol level was .043."

"Was the heart attack caused by the cocaine?"

"We can't say specifically, but the common belief is that the drug certainly played a role."

Jill nods. "So what's next?"

"As far as the L.A.P.D is concerned this case is closed. Please accept our condolences for your loss."

"Thank you," she murmurs. "Um, when will I be able to get death certificates to provide to insurance companies, banks, and other financial institutions?"

"They are now available through the medical examiner's office."

"Oh, thank goodness. Then I can start to put my affairs back in order and move on with my life." She stands, "Is there anything else?"

Both shake their heads and offer her their hands. She shakes them, and the officers head to the door.

Briggs pauses and hands Jill his card. "If there is anything else we can do, please don't hesitate to call."

She smiles faintly. "Thank you, but I think you both have done enough."

They make their way to their patrol car, and Jill softly closes the door behind them, then calls Wendy to confirm her appointment that afternoon.

"Yes, I've got you on my calendar for three," Wendy says. "How are you doing?"

"We can talk about everything when I get there," Jill replies, then heads to shower and get ready before driving to San Diego.

Jill arrives to see Wendy promptly at three and sits comfortably on the couch.

Wendy is struck by how calm and put together Jill looks and asks, "How are things going for you?"

"Actually pretty well. The detectives investigating Zach's death stopped by the house before I left to come see you. The medical examiner's report ruled Zach's cause of death to be a heart attack. I guess he had a fair amount of cocaine in his system along with some alcohol. The death certificate is now available. I'll go pick up several certified copies tomorrow so I can get the bank to release our funds back to me." She shakes her head in disbelief for a moment. "His life insurance even paid off already, and I'm going to be just fine. I can repay you for the clothes and hotel."

Wendy shakes her head. "We discussed this already. You don't owe me a dime other than for the counseling services. How are you getting by without any money?"

"When I got back into the house I found my credit cards on Zach's desk, and apparently he hadn't cancelled them so I've been working off of our credit until I get access to our funds. That should be tomorrow after I get everything straightened out with the right people."

"That's terrific news. How are you doing with sleeping in the house and the bedroom you shared with him?"

Jill makes a face. "I am *not* sleeping in the master bedroom and won't until after it is completely remodeled. I just can't, so I'm sleeping in one of the guest rooms until then. It's a little strange being in the house without Zach, but I have a sense of peace about staying there. Every now and then memories come flooding back, some good and some bad. I guess it's going to be a process of letting go of what was and moving on with living here and now, but I have a great home and I'll just have to create all new memories in it without Zach. Honestly, I think I'm actually better off with him gone. That's sometimes hard to justify in my mind and at other times I couldn't be happier that he's dead." She lets out a bitter chuckle. "Does that make me a horrible bitch?"

"Oh, absolutely not. What you're experiencing are normal emotions and reactions that are all part of the grieving process. Your picturesque life had been so disturbed by Zach and his death came so quickly that you haven't really had any time to process the sea of emotions you'll need to work through. Just know that Zach's death has nothing to do with you and everything to do with his choices. The fact that his death provided for you in ways you never expected is simply a blessing in disguise."

"I guess so. It just all seems so surreal."

"Of course it does, and it will continue to seem surreal until all the loose business ends are brought together. Then, Zach's final arrangements will be made, and you'll finally get some sense of closure. Unfortunately, our time is up for today. Would you come back so I can see you next Wednesday at the same time?"

"Yes, perfect. Thanks again for everything you have done and continue to do for me," Jill says as they both stand and she gathers her things.

"Have a great week, Jill, and don't hesitate to call my office if you need anything."

Wendy watches Jill leave her office and quietly contemplates how different things would be without Wendy's benevolence. She sits down behind her desk, fiddling with a pen, until her thoughts are jolted back to reality with Mona on the intercom, "Bonnie is on line one for you."

"Thanks, Mona, I've got it," Wendy replies, and picks up the phone.

CHAPTER 4

SELECTION PROCESS

"What a pleasant surprise," Wendy says, "What can I do for you, dear?"

"Uhh, you can be here Friday morning so I can get Sean's and SERF's jets headed to Chicago to pick up Jim Bush and New York to pick up Skip Duran for dinner and interviews throughout the weekend. Can you stay in Marin until Monday evening?"

Wendy plops her forehead into her palm. "Shit. I forgot that was this weekend. What time on Friday morning do you want me to meet your pilot?"

"How about nine?"

"Great, as long as I can shower and get cleaned up at your place before the evening events. I certainly don't want to be uncomfortable all day."

"God forbid you have to look decent all day long," Bonnie scoffs with a chuckle. "So I'll assume you'll arrive in jeans and a T-shirt with your hair in a ponytail?"

"Pretty much, but I promise I will certainly look like a proper board member for your job candidates all weekend long."

"Thanks for that. I guess that's all I could expect anyways."

"How formal is the attire for dinner Friday night?" Wendy asks.

"A nice cocktail dress will be fine. Sean suggested sushi and Jessica has a fantastic place in mind in San Francisco," Bonnie replies.

"Sushi in a cocktail dress?" Wendy asks dubiously.

"It's very elegant sushi, and the reviews have been fantastic. I've checked with Jim and Skip and they both love sushi as well."

"Ugh. You have to know I love you for me to get dolled up and have sushi in a cocktail dress when I'd rather be in jeans sitting on the floor."

"We all make sacrifices in life dear," Bonnie says in a sing-song tone. "Thank you for your willingness to suffer at my behest."

Wendy giggles. "I'll see you Friday morning. I have a lot of work to get back to."

"Okay, see you then."

❊❊❊

Wendy meets Bonnie's pilot for the quick flight to San Francisco and as she deplanes Bonnie is waiting for her. They hop into the limousine for the short drive back to Marin County.

On the way, Bonnie asks, "Do you mind stopping by the Stevens Environmental Restoration Fund offices in Sausalito before heading to the house?"

"Not at all. In fact, I'd like to see the offices before we start interviews on Saturday."

Bonnie claps her hands. "I think you're going to love the space, and I am so excited to see this dream come true."

As they arrive at the Bridgeway location, Wendy is surprised at the subtle elegance of the facility. Viewed from the parking lot the building is rather non-descript, but once inside the view of the bay is phenomenal and the natural lighting provides a warm welcoming ambience.

"Wow, what a terrific place! Maybe I should relocate my counseling practice. I would love to work here."

"But you do work here! As a counselor to me and my staff," Bonnie replies with a grin.

Wendy makes a face. "You know what I mean. This place is fantastic, and what a wonderful corporate image for SERF."

"So you love it as much as I do?"

"Yes of course I do. Have Sean or Jessica been here yet?"

Bonnie shakes her head, looking out the window. "No, just Charlotte Evans, and she reacted about the same way you did."

"Why has Charlotte seen this place before Sean and Jessica?" Wendy asks, surprised.

"Just timing. I had lunch with her to let her know she has my support as CEO of Global Metal Refining. I wanted to bridge that gap, since we got off to such a rough start and it was just after I signed the lease. Charlotte is going to recommend Global Metal Refining transfer its financial support from Mother Earth Cooperative to Stevens Environmental Restoration Fund to the tune of one million dollars a year for the next nine years," Bonnie says, smiling.

"You never cease to amaze me with your persuasive powers," Wendy says, grinning.

"Well, let's just hope those powers hold out long enough to sign Skip and Jim this weekend," Bonnie replies, her tone shifting to slightly nervous.

"I'm sure if these two gentlemen are right for this organization they will be working here very shortly."

"I hope you're right. Now, let's get you settled before our hectic schedule begins," Bonnie says, taking Wendy's arm as they leave the building.

✻✻✻

As they arrive at the house Bonnie receives a call from Sean confirming the times Skip and Jim are to arrive and their hotel accommodations.

"Thanks, Sean, that's wonderful," Bonnie says.

"I'll also make sure my staff will get them settled in their hotels before bringing them to the restaurant," Sean replies. "The agendas for tomorrow are set and everything is in order. When is Wendy joining us?"

"She's here with me in the car. We'll meet everyone at the restaurant at seven. Will you please let me know if there are any last minute changes to the schedule?" Bonnie asks.

"Of course. We've got this covered though," Sean says.

Bonnie breathes a sigh of relief. "You're so great for pulling all the details together. Thank you."

"You're welcome. Jess and I will meet you at the restaurant at seven with Skip and Jim in tow."

"Terrific. See you then," Bonnie replies, and they hang up.

When Bonnie and Wendy arrive at Bonnie's house, Wendy slips into a bikini and heads poolside.

Bonnie stares in disbelief. "Do you ever stress about anything?"

"Absolutely. Why do you ask?"

"I'm frantic, worried about everything, and you're in a bikini soaking up rays by the pool."

"Why are you frantic? The high priced cabana boy just told you everything is under control and he'll let you know if a glitch occurs. Besides you are the one in control this weekend. Skip and Jim are interviewing for a job you're offering, not the other way around. Relax and enjoy the adventure."

"Only you refer to Sean Green as a high priced cabana boy, and I wouldn't advise letting him hear you refer to him in that manner."

Wendy smiles up at her. "You know me. I have no problem calling Sean on his bullshit. Besides, I bet he would get a kick out of it if I said it in private while sipping cocktails."

Bonnie rolls her eyes and flops on a lounge chair. "You're probably right, but I would hate to hear what he would call you my dear!"

Wendy chuckles. "I'm sure it would be something close to a bloodletting wailing wall that listens to everyone's problem, asks them how they feel about it, lets them solve their own issues, and then charges them outrageous fees."

"You two have a very weird relationship."

Wendy shrugs. "We just understand each other better than most, that's all. All kidding aside, I just want you to know how proud I am of you, and I'm sure Mark would be, too. I'm humbled by your willingness to establish Stevens Environmental Restoration Fund as a way of honoring his work and professional reputation."

Bonnie starts to cry and Wendy gets up and hugs her, allowing her to sob and release the pent up, stifled emotions. Together they hold one another with tears streaming down their cheeks, neither realizing in the moment the totality of the healing taking place for both of them.

After spending the afternoon together relaxing by the pool, Wendy and Bonnie arrive at the restaurant before everyone else. When Jessica arrives she is flattered to see Wendy and Bonnie looking gorgeous in the latest designs from Beauty Boutique Clothing.

"You two look fantastic," Jess says, beaming.

"Thanks to you and your fabulous designs," Wendy replies.

"Au contraire, it is the models the clothes are on that showcase the designs," says Jessica, hugging each of them.

Bonnie looks past Jessica and motions to Sean, Skip, and Jim to join the reunion. When Wendy turns to look at them she is immediately struck at how incredibly attractive the younger gentleman is and assumes Jim Bush is the amazing hunk of eye candy. Sean quickly introduces Skip and Jim to Jessica and Wendy, then makes sure he seats Jim next to Wendy at the table. When Wendy makes eye contact with Sean, he winks, and she mouths a *thank you* that no one else sees. He smiles, comprehending he is once again correct in his assessment of Wendy and her personal preferences.

Almost immediately Wendy becomes distracted by how amazing Jim smells. "Wow, you smell fantastic," she says, leaning closer. "What is that?"

Jim jerks his gaze to her, momentarily caught off guard. "I believe its *Mankind* by Kenneth Cole."

"Hmm. I like it. It's not only masculine but also subtle and appealing."

He smiles at her. "Thank you. I recently purchased it, and you're the first woman to comment on it."

Wendy cocks her head. "So do you always buy your fragrances to elicit comments from women?"

"Yes," Jim answers, then quickly says, "I mean no. I have to enjoy it as well."

"I see," she says, chuckling.

Bonnie and Jessica quickly exchange a glance then Bonnie says, "Skip, why don't you tell everyone about yourself and why you're interested in this particular chief financial officer position."

Skip nods. "Well, to start with, I always purchase my cologne to satisfy myself. But that's probably because I'm much older, and prior to my wife's passing I hadn't bought any cologne for quite some time." Everyone around the table chuckles, and Skip continues, "I'm sorry I couldn't resist the jab." Then he begins with a brief educational history, including his bachelor's degree in business, MBA in finance, CPA, certification as a forensic accountant, and ending with qualifications as an expert witness in magistrate, district, and U.S. District courts in forensic accounting.

"I've had an extremely successful career working for two separate fortune 100 companies as their chief financial officer," he says proudly, "I'm a widower, and my only child is attending Stanford University in Palo Alto. I don't get to see her as often as I would like to, and I don't like being away from her this much. I fully recognize it won't be long before she is off making her own life dreams come true, and I need to create my own life dreams again. So Bonnie, when you telephoned and explained what your plans are for SERF, who is involved, and the impact you want the organization to have on environmental mining restoration worldwide, I knew immediately this was an opportunity I had to pursue. I also suspect for at least the next five years it won't be as hectic or stressful as my current position. Also, I like the organization's mission statement, and I'd like to make a difference in the world through my participation in this startup endeavor. I know the organization is adequately capitalized so many of the initial start-up concerns aren't a factor in whether this company is successful or not, and that makes this a very appealing offer. Finally, I believe I have a lot to offer through practical experience and professional expertise." Skip stops, allowing the group to absorb all he has said. Then, he turns to Jim and says, "I suspect it's now your turn to answer the same question."

Jim smiles. "I suspect you're right. Let me begin with how excited I am to be considered for this position, but my goals are vastly different from Skip's. Unlike Skip, I'm single and hoping to distinguish myself as the premiere authority in the business development arena. I see this organization as providing a clear path for achievement of this career goal. I have a bachelor's degree in economics and a master's degree in political science. I have worked for three separate fortune 500 companies but never in the non-profit world. I have tremendous corporate resource connections, and I see

SERF as having the potential, with my help, to be the leading authority for corporate responsibility in the environmental realm. What better industry to accomplish that feat than the mining industry, which has had the reputation of raping and pillaging the environment for decades?" He turns to Wendy then. "I broke off an engagement, hence the new cologne. I dislike Illinois because it's so cold, and I'm an avid outdoor thrill seeker. I enjoy mountain biking, rock climbing, hang-gliding, and I want to get into spear fishing and free-diving, maybe even surfing. California seems to have all the opportunities for me to experience the things I thrive on. I work hard and I like to play hard."

There's a moment of silence as Wendy and Jim have an apparently silent conversation. Addressing the rest of those at the table he continues, "I see the possibility of making this business development position into a position I have always craved, and in doing so also establishing a niche not only for SERF but also my own career. In short, my professional goals are just as lofty as Stevens Environmental Restoration Fund goals."

"How so?" asks Wendy, slightly playfully.

He glances her way again. "Well, I want to be known and recognized for my innovation, creativity, and ability to achieve any goal set either for me or the organization. I believe that's also an important goal for SERF."

"What do you see as the most pressing goal facing SERF?" Bonnie chimes in.

"Branding, although I think Sean is much more suited than I to accomplish that segment. The most significant challenge I see in my realm of expertise is the immediate necessity to develop adequate, sustainable funding sources for SERF in order to have the impact the organization intends within the mining industry worldwide. The largest threat to that success, from my perspective, is time."

"How is time the biggest threat?" Jessica asks.

He turns his attention to her and explains. "In most instances time is on the side of the developing organization but, in this instance, the sooner SERF establishes an algorithm for developing sustainable funding mechanisms the greater the organization's approval ratings and impact for environmental restoration. The longer the organization takes to demonstrate its ability to attract corporate partnerships the weaker its impact will be. By establishing mutually beneficial corporate alliances within the mining industry separate from Global Metal Refining, we'll establish more credibility. With immediate credibility comes the ability to attract additional funds and demonstrates the viability and necessity for the organization's existence."

Jessica considers his answer for a moment, but Wendy interrupts. "But hasn't SERF already established its viability with the billion-dollar capitalization from Bonnie?"

"No I don't believe it has. I think it's demonstrated adequate start-up capitalization, but without the industry leaders rallying behind the cause the organization's sole survival would be dependent upon Bonnie's continued support and the sole support of Global Metal Refining, an organization in three of you at this table wield enormous control over. This is a great setup but, without mining industry corporate alliances, SERF could be viewed as a vehicle used by Global Metal Refining to avoid potential tax consequences in the United States. By establishing the corporate sponsorships, SERF demonstrates its viability and the necessity for mining industry practices to change worldwide."

While everyone is considering the implications of what Jim has said, but before anyone can continue the conversation, they are interrupted by the server arriving to take their dinner orders.

CHAPTER 5

INTERVIEWS

Bonnie clears her throat and stirs everyone out of their deep thoughts. "Shall we focus the rest of the evening on casual, fun conversation? We'll have plenty of time over the next two days for everyone to explore philosophies, experiences, and goals. Tonight is designed to allow everyone to get to know each other on a more personal level."

Jim chuckles. "My apologies for getting so passionate about my beliefs." He turns his attention to Jessica. "Tell me about yourself. I've researched Sean, Bonnie, and Wendy because of their association with Global Metal Refining. In comparison, I know very little about you and your company."

Jessica sips her drink. "I'm an open book. I grew up in Los Altos, then went on to earn a business degree from Dartmouth University and a graduate degree in fashion entrepreneurship and innovation from the London College of Fashion. I really enjoy fashion design, and started a small clothing company, Beauty Boutique Clothing, here in San Francisco. With help from Bonnie and SGM, we recently went international with a production factory in Brazil. Bonnie and I have been lifelong friends, and I met Sean through the insistence of Mark and Bonnie."

As Jim continues getting to know Jessica, Skip says to Wendy, "I know a little about you through your participation on the Global

Metal Refining Board of Directors, but do you have other business interests?"

Wendy smiles at him and replies, "I received my PhD from the University of California San Diego and have a private counseling practice in San Diego."

"Impressive. What type of counseling or clientele?"

"My practice is centered exclusively on victims of domestic violence or sexual assault."

"Wow, you must be an extremely tough woman to deal with those issues day in and day out."

Wendy inclines her head. "Not really. I do it for the victims. Nothing is more rewarding than seeing them become survivors."

Jim squirms in his seat a little, appearing uncomfortable, which doesn't go unnoticed by Wendy. She glances at him, "I don't analyze anyone who isn't a client, and everyone already knows that about me except you two, so you both can relax. I'm not psycho-analyzing either of you."

Skip chuckles. "But you are evaluating each of us."

"True, but only as far as your business acumen, not your mental health," Wendy replies with a wink.

"Well that's good to hear," Jim adds.

Dinner arrives and the rest of the evening is spent enjoying the food and saké, with light casual conversation. The agenda for the following days is given to Skip and Jim, and Sean tells them the limousine will pick them up at seven o'clock the next morning and drive them to the SERF offices in Sausalito. Interviews will begin at eight and will continue throughout the day, lunch will be catered, and then they will be on their own for dinner tomorrow. Sean promises them both they will back at the hotel by five-thirty. Turning to Skip, he asks, "Will you need a ride to Palo Alto for dinner with your daughter or is she coming into the city?"

"She's driving into San Francisco with her new boyfriend to take me to dinner, so I'll be fine, thank you."

"Very well," Sean says, and continues with the agenda, "Sunday morning you will be back at the SERF office until noon and then each of you will be taken to the airport for your respective flights home. On Sunday the dress is casual since you both have fairly long flights ahead of you."

After everything is in place for the next couple of days, the group enjoys after dinner drinks and then goes their separate ways.

Jim and Skip arrive in Sausalito on time. Bonnie gives them a quick tour of the facility and ushers them into the conference room for coffee, bagels, fresh fruit, and quiche. The facility is decorated in elegant furnishings and exquisite artwork yet still fully functional as executive offices.

While everyone enjoys a light breakfast, Sean presents an overview of Stevens Environmental Restoration Fund, its vision and mission statements, and the preliminary outline of SERF's first year goals.

"Clearly, these goals are merely an outline from which further discussions will be launched in each of your areas of expertise," Sean says. "Jim, Skip, you will each be interviewed initially by teams of Bonnie and Jessica, and Wendy and me. Then you'll both undergo individual interviews which should conclude the day. After you return to your hotel, the Board will compare and contrast notes, and by noon tomorrow each of you will know where you stand regarding your respective interviews. At that point, if appropriate, we'll give you details on the position offered, including the wage and benefit packages. We'll expect you to accept or reject any offer you may receive by the end of the work week. Are we all in agreement at this point?"

Both Skip and Jim acknowledge acceptance with head nods and the group breaks apart, with Jessica and Bonnie interviewing Skip first and Wendy and Sean speaking with Jim.

After the customary general questions, Bonnie asks Skip," How would you view your role of CFO at SERF?"

"Well initially, I see the need to establish transparency within our corporate donor relationships and ensure donors have a timely and accurate project management tracking mechanism of SERF's projects. This mechanism should focus on outlining funding deadlines, segment completion deadlines, and work progress in orders to allow corporate executives the ability to track onsite progress of restoration projects remotely, in as close to real time as possible. This would require end of the day, or end of shift, reporting if the project was around the clock. Monthly reconciliation reports need to be available on the first business day of each month with outstanding balances," Skip replies.

Jessica follows up by asking, "So do you see this as your role to complete or are you assuming a certain sized staff to maintain that type of program?"

"I would be primarily responsible for this procedure, at least until SERF has funded multiple restoration projects. Then a small staff would need to be hired. If the expectation criterion is set properly, this can be managed on Pacific Standard Time. However, as the international project expands, it will have to be dispersed by time zones, and then additional staff will need to be brought on in order to meet timely reporting deadlines for our international donors."

"Are you concerned about having to work around the clock?" Bonnie asks with a smile.

He smiles back at her. "There was a time early in my career when I would have been willing to come in at all hours to meet international deadlines. Nowadays I require a more definitive sleeping pattern, and that is precisely why I have never worked on the stock exchange."

Jessica looks at Skip and, in all sincerity, says, "I've reviewed your resume and I see you have always worked for fortune 100 companies, but have you ever been involved in a start-up company where systems and operational procedures aren't already in place and tested?"

He shakes his head. "No, I haven't."

"Can you explain to me how you view your particular skill set, experience, and accomplishments benefiting a start-up, then? And do you see the fact that you have always worked in established organizations with established cultures and practices hindering your ability to work within a fast paced, rapidly changing organization, with practically no established practices?"

Skip ponders the question for quite a while then replies, "Undoubtedly it will be more challenging in the beginning as we all settle into an evolving operational structure within SERF. I believe set traditions are not necessary, just like evolving practices aren't either. There are strengths and weaknesses in both structures, and I believe I can pull benefits from working with time tested established practices and also learn new skills in flexible, evolving systems.

Probably the most practical asset I bring to the table is balance. Ms. Silva, you and Mr. Green thrive in an ever changing environment and do so extremely well, but set patterns and established practices within organizations, especially within the financial arena, have tremendous power and perhaps could provide benefits not as established in smaller organizations. Let us not forget this organization is starting out as a billion-dollar firm that will need to bring some extra stability to the table from day one if it's to avoid a spiral out of control."

Bonnie and Jessica both nod, accepting that his answer is a good one, and continue questioning in a different area.

Meanwhile, Sean and Wendy are putting Jim through his paces. Wendy hits him with, "I understand you have a fairly good track record in business development with tremendous corporate connections. How do you plan on converting those business connections into corporate donors, raising funds for a start-up non-profit organization? Also, how much money would you deem, realistically, you could raise in one, three, and five years?"

"Excellent questions. Let me address each portion one at a time. First of all, I have built a powerful network of business people within the mining and mining supply industries. Through previous business dealings they have come to trust and, I believe, respect my business acumen, and as such I have a foot in the door most fund raisers don't. Secondly, through my various interactions with these executives, they have come to recognize I'm a man of my word possessing extreme integrity, so they know if I represent something as factual it can actually be trusted. Stevens Environmental Restoration Fund may be a new non-profit organization, but I would hardly represent it as a start-up organization—"

"Why is that?" Wendy interrupts.

Jim smiles. "I was working my way around to addressing that. Please, indulge me a bit longer. First of all, SERF is a non-profit spin off of Global Metal Refining, which is the largest corporate donor, currently pledging slightly over nine million dollars over the next nine years. Bonnie has capitalized this organization with one billion dollars of her personal funds to ensure its success. Very few start-ups start out that flush. It is also clear from its corporate roots within the mining industry that SERF isn't trying to prevent mining practices worldwide, but simply trying to ensure that after mining operations are completed the land is restored to its usefulness via environmental restoration. While the organization would oversee restoration projects and bear most of the costs for the restoration, it still partners with the organization having completed the mining in accomplishing its mission and goals. I believe these types of corporate and strategic alliances will make fund raising much easier for SERF than for an organization hell bent on eliminating mining. Finally, in light of all of that, I believe if I'm hired by SERF as its Vice President of Business Development, it should be realistic to raise in the neighborhood of twenty million the first year, thirty-five million in three years, and one hundred million in five years. Each time period would build upon the funds raised in the previous period, of course, and the organization's accomplishments will assist with that as well."

"So you are presuming a large portion of the funds raised in the first year will carry over into subsequent years?" Sean inquires.

"Absolutely. I would be looking for three-to-five year commitments from our corporate partners that would give us the ability to return to them for increased funding after several successful restoration projects have been completed."

"What would be your salary expectations?"

"I'm looking for a base annual salary of $450,000, plus 5% of the new funds I bring into the organization annually."

Wendy chokes on her water and sputters, "That's one million dollars in bonuses if you raised twenty million the first year."

Jim nods. "Precisely. And seven hundred and fifty thousand additionally, if I raised fifteen million from year two to three. But let's not forget that SERF would be receiving thirty-five million in that timeframe."

"Actually, that's not correct. SERF would benefit by thirty-two million, three hundred and fifty thousand after you have received your salary and bonuses," Wendy quips.

Jim represses a sigh. "Okay, true, but there is no such thing as a free lunch."

"What else would you expect in terms of benefits?" Wendy asks.

"Well, other than medical benefits, I'll need a substantial expense account and corporate credit card of course."

Sean interjects. "That's already been thought of. There would be an expense account and access, albeit limited, to the corporate jet."

This information seems to please Jim, and then there is a knock on the door as Bonnie pokes her head into the conference room.

"Time to switch?" she asks, and Sean nods. "Okay, I'll have Skip come and speak with you two now," she says, and disappears.

"Thank you both for your time," Jim says, shaking hands with each of them. He exits the room as Skip enters.

Sean, Wendy, and Skip concentrate on Skip's salary requirements, SERF's operational budgets, cost control measures, investments, and banking security protocols.

At the same time, Bonnie, Jessica, and Jim explore potential donors, fund raising strategies, SERF's top fifty targeted donor list, and Jim's expectations for the job requirements. The day passes quickly and, before anyone realizes it, it's time for Skip and Jim to return to their hotel.

Skip has dinner with his daughter and her boyfriend while Jim spends time at a downtown sports bar before calling it an evening.

Meanwhile, Bonnie, Sean, Wendy, and Jessica decide to discuss the day's interviews and candidates over dinner in Sausalito. Each of them is pleased with the quality of individuals chosen for the positions, so the discussion is centered on salary and perks required by both Skip and Jim. There are relatively few surprises, with the exception of Jim wanting greater access to the corporate jet then would be offered and Skip wishing to have greater flexibility with his working hours and vacation time. It is agreed upon by all that the requirements outlined by both candidates could be worked around and SERF would allow up to eight thousand dollars for moving expenses. Furthermore, since both Skip and Jim will need to sell their respective homes, they decide to guarantee the purchase of each property at ninety-three percent of the appraised value if not sold within six months of Jim and Skip beginning work full time in Sausalito. It's decided that the best way to handle the job offers would be to give the initial job offer to them both at the same time and discuss start dates, moving expenses, and the real estate buy-out for the relocation, then have Skip and Jim meet with the board individually to discuss their salary requirements and benefits packages. That being figured out, the four enjoy their dinner and some good wine before retiring to their homes for the evening.

The next morning, everyone gathers in the board room where Bonnie makes the announcement. "SERF is interested in hiring both of you for the respective positions you were interviewed. The initial benefits offered will be moving expenses and relocation real estate buy-out, if either of you wish to exercise the provision, six months after beginning your full time employment with SERF. Each of you will meet with the board for a formal offer regarding specific salary and benefits shortly after this, and I hope you will advise me of your decision by the end of this week. Now, on to the individual offers. Skip, please come with us."

After Skip and Jim receive their offers individually, each agrees to communicate their acceptance or rejection thereof no later than Friday morning. Sean and Jessica head back to San Francisco, but Wendy decides to spend the rest of the day with Bonnie before returning to San Diego in the morning.

As Jim sits in the corporate jet on his way back to Chicago, he ponders the offer received. While slightly disappointed that SERF countered his salary demand with a $375,000 base offer and 5% of funds raised, he also recognizes the additional benefits offered were ones he currently doesn't possess. He considers the offer for quite a while before deciding that he probably won't be able to find anything better.

Skip, on the other hand, is pleased with the $500,000 offer because it incorporates his flexible work schedule. He recognizes this will be a substantial salary reduction from his current position, but is content with the fact that it will also be an equally substantial reduction in his stress levels.

By Thursday evening, both Jim and Skip have communicated to Bonnie their acceptance of the job offers. Jim tells Bonnie he needs to give his two week notice at his current job, and then take a week to find an appropriate rental in Sausalito before starting at SERF. He requests the company jet be available to him for two separate trips to California within the next three weeks. Bonnie agrees and provides Jim with the name of her realtor to help him locate a suitable residence for the transition period.

Skip needs a month to complete tasks at his current position and requests an additional week for settling in after his move. Bonnie agrees to his requests as well, and offers the corporate jet to help Skip make the necessary trips to California in order to have easier access for locating transitional housing prior to purchasing his new home.

Bonnie spends the five weeks helping each of them make the transition out of their current positions and into their Stevens Environmental Restoration Fund positions. She also hires the additional people required for human resource manager, receptionist, and back office analytical support. Skip interviews and hires his personal secretary and two additional bookkeepers.

Upon the arrival of Jim and Skip, SERF is fully staffed and operational. From day one, both begin working at a fevered pitch.

Sean and Jessica are enjoying tremendous success with Beauty Boutique Clothing's international expansion. Even while starting to experience subtle competition from larger designers, both are ecstatic with revenue figures beyond each of their expectations, sales alliances internationally that are working well, and the press within the fashion industry being extremely positive. Their relationship continues to develop, as well, though at a slower pace than either would like. Career obligations keep them too busy to move quickly, and they're very happy they have a working relationship, as well, so they can spend a bit more time with each other.

Wendy on the other hand is becoming somewhat uneasy as Jill Rawlins, Kimberly Taylor, and Nancy Davis are renewing their personal friendships. Wendy recognizes the potential for any of them to share information that might cast suspicion on her, since each of their husbands are now deceased and each share a common connection to her. This is a development Wendy hadn't anticipated, and she is in the process of analyzing it when she receives an unexpected telephone call from Kimberly Taylor asking to meet with her at her office in San Diego the following week. Wendy schedules the appointment wondering why she failed to anticipate this potential wrinkle, and begins considering all types of potential responses. After a full day of working out all different scenarios in her head, she settles herself down by reminding herself to not anticipate the worst and take each challenge as it presents itself.

CHAPTER 6

FREEDOM OF INFORMATION

Kimberly Taylor arrives for her appointment, and Wendy is struck by how happy and healthy Kimberly looks; however, there is an underlying caution as she speaks that Wendy finds unsettling.

"You seem to be struggling to say something," Wendy says, gently. "What is it?"

Kimberly shrugs. "Well, I'm not sure how to tell you about it."

"About what?"

"I guess I'll just be blunt and let the chips fall where they may."

"Kim, this is not like you at all. What is it?"

She huffs out a breath. "Okay, I was having lunch last week with my good friend, Janet Parker, and her daughter Lindsay. During our conversation, I mentioned you had been counseling me during the divorce, and that you are counseling Nancy Davis and Jill Rawlins because of Arnold's and Zach's abusive behavior. I wondered out loud how difficult it must be for you dealing with Jack's suicide, Arnold's suicide, and Zach's heart attack in such a short timeframe..."

Wendy tilts her head. "I'm afraid I'm not following you."

"Give me a minute. Lindsay Parker is the local television news reporter who covered the botulism outbreak at the Bistro on Union Street and was one of the first reporters to find Jack at the Castaway Grill just prior to his news conference. Well, anyway, when she realized you were the domestic violence counselor for Nancy, Jill, and me, and two of our husbands committed suicide, she started asking all kinds of questions about you and your qualifications. I got the impression she was fishing for information about you."

"Well, dear, lot of people do that. What are you so worried about?"

"She made a comment that she was going to start an investigation on you," Kimberly blurts.

"But why should I be concerned about what a young news reporter does?"

"Wendy, she said she was going to send out a bunch of Freedom of Information Requests to the police departments around San Diego and the San Francisco to see how you fit into all these investigations. I think she is thinking you are somehow responsible for the suicides, and she told her mother she is dating one of the FBI agents who interviewed you a while back. Steve Davis. Do you know him? What's going on?" Kim asks, her speech getting more frantic.

"Oh, my gosh, Kim, please, relax. This is why I have malpractice insurance," Wendy says, placing her hand on Kim's.

"It doesn't bother you at all to be investigated by a news reporter who is dating an FBI agent?"

"Not in the least. People have all types of conspiracy theories these days, and I've done nothing out of the ordinary, so I have no reason to worry. But thank you for letting me know about all of this nonsense. Agent Davis is a charming young man, I'm sure I won't have any trouble."

"Whew," Kim says, visibly relaxing. "I thought this would be upsetting to you."

"Again, thank you for thinking of me. Did you come down to San Diego solely to tell me this or is there another reason?"

"I actually came down to help Nancy get her condo put together. She was able to sell the house and has moved into an oceanfront penthouse overlooking the San Diego harbor. It's beautiful, and she is so happy," Kim says, smiling and squeezing Wendy's hand.

"Good. I'm glad you're helping her, and it's fantastic to hear she is doing so well after Arnold's unfortunate death. Give her my best, and if there is anything either of you need, please don't hesitate to call me."

As Kimberly gets up to leave the office, Wendy gives her a hug and thanks her once more for her concern, wondering how best to prepare for the eventual fallout that will reveal the fact that husbands of several other clients have committed suicide or suddenly died. She isn't really concerned about any police investigation, but she is concerned the medical board may look into her counseling practices and they are always a major pain.

Mentally she examines each crime scene, considering any loophole she may have missed and knowing the freedom of information requests will eventually reveal she is a reporting party, other, or person of interest listed in several police reports. This causes her to wonder just how capable an investigative reporter Lindsay Parker truly is, and how she will approach Wendy with her findings.

"Mona," Wendy calls, and Mona pokes her head into the office. "Are there any more appointments scheduled for this afternoon?"

"No, not today."

"Oh, okay. Wonderful. Thank you."

She decides to take the rest of the day off and head home.

After arriving home, she pours herself a glass of wine, makes herself a light snack, then proceeds to map out every death she knows she is going to be found associated with in the police reports. She outlines her alibis and any challenges she can imagine might be encountered and rehearses her possible responses. After she has the best responses firmly arranged in her mind she destroys her outlines, shredding them, and dropping them into a mixed bag of garbage to send down the garbage chute of the building.

Next she decides to head to the library to do a little research on Lindsay Parker, because she doesn't want that to be discovered in the browsing history of her computer.

She quickly discovers Lindsay could be a nuisance having earned double bachelor degrees in criminal justice and English and master's degree in journalism from San Francisco State University. Wendy watches several investigative reporting segments Lindsay has done in her brief career and then studies closely her exclusive food series on Jack Taylor and the Bistro scandal. Wendy is impressed by the thoroughness of Lindsay's research and the competence of her reporting. She makes a mental note when Lindsay contacts her to be extremely careful in their discussions.

Next, Wendy decides to swing by the office and speak to Mona about Lindsay. She explains to Mona she expects Lindsay to contact the office in a couple of weeks and begin fishing for information and instructs Mona to be very careful during any telephone conversations they may have.

"Kimberly warned me about it when she was here earlier. Lindsay is investigating my counseling practice due to the recent suicides of Jack and Arnold and Zach's heart attack," Wendy finishes.

Mona rolls her eyes. "So she's trying to bring your counseling skills into question?"

"That's exactly what I think she is going to do, so we just need to be cautious in what we say to her."

"This is such bullshit. Why are reporters always picking on the counselors who deal with domestic violence victims?"

"Sometimes people, especially reporters, don't understand the cycle of domestic violence and just need to be educated, sometimes they are threatened by the fact that there is a necessity for individual counselors to specialize in this field, and sometimes they think the counselor is the problem. Whatever this case may be, we have been warned this reporter is targeting me for some reason, so let's just stay vigilant and be careful in our interactions with her until we know what her angle is and where she is coming from."

"No worries. I've got your back, always," Mona says with a fierce grin.

"I know you do, but it never hurts to get a heads up so we're not surprised. Is there anything I need to take care of before I head to the beach this afternoon?" Wendy asks.

"No, but check your calendar for tomorrow morning. You have a new client coming in. His name is Michael Prichard and his domestic partner is starting to get a little abusive."

"How so? Did he mention anything specific?" Wendy asks, reviewing her schedule for the next few days.

"Nope, other than that he writes screenplays and lives in La Jolla."

"Interesting. I'm not seeing him here. When is he scheduled?"

"He's your second appointment at ten o'clock. Now go to the beach and relax or give me the afternoon off to do so!"

Wendy smiles and waves as she heads out the door, reassured that when Lindsay starts probing around she'll not get any information she can use against Wendy. She stops by the penthouse, grabs her bikini, and heads to her favorite stretch of beach to enjoy the afternoon relaxing and reading a new book.

The next morning, Mike Prichard comes into her office promptly for his ten o'clock appointment. He is a polite and gracious man in his mid-forties, attractive and tan with a flair for the English language and an understated air of sophistication. As he introduces himself to Wendy she thinks, *Wow, what kind of person would be abusive to such a kind soul?*

She motions for him to have a seat then asks, "Would you like a cup of coffee or tea?"

"That would be great. Coffee, please, black."

Wendy has Mona bring in a fresh pot of French press coffee and two scones with a little honey. Mike accepts a cup of coffee and politely declines the scone.

"What brings you in today, Mr. Prichard?"

"Please, it's Mike. Well, I'm a bit troubled by the way my relationship is progressing with my partner, Kenneth. You come highly recommended by several people I've spoken with, and I need some advice."

Wendy sips her coffee and nods. "Go on."

"I had been single for quite some time, but recently became involved with a younger man."

"How much younger?"

"Kenneth is 37, so nine years younger than I am. We've been together for almost a year now, and he moved into my home here in La Jolla a couple of months back. There have been minor disagreements over his cat and my dog. My dog chases the cat, and it irritates Kenneth. I've explained they are just playing with one another, but he is convinced my lab is going to kill his cat, which is just ridiculous. Hercules loves cats and is really gentle with them and always has been. Kenneth is also deathly afraid of water because he doesn't know how to swim, but he doesn't want to learn, and that's somewhat problematic because I have a pool and I like to spend my days lounging by it, swimming and writing. Kenneth wants to fill it in with soil and landscape, which I absolutely refuse to do, but I did get a cheap bubble cover that floats on the surface to appease his irrational fears about water."

"Okay. So far what you have told me are minor adjustment issues every loving relationship goes through."

"I understand that, and thought so myself, but there is so much more."

"I'm sorry I interrupted you. Please continue."

"A couple of nights ago, I was balancing my checkbook and found there had been several thousand dollars removed without my knowledge. When I asked Kenneth about it he became outrageously hostile and unpleasant. Eventually he told me he used the funds to purchase his new vehicle. I have always paid all the bills because I make substantially more than Kenneth, I have never asked him for any money, and we have always maintained separate financial accounts, but after I shared my PIN with him, he removed thousands of dollars from my account to purchase the vehicle and doesn't intend to repay me. I told him I didn't appreciate the dishonest way he went about taking the money and that if he didn't repay it, I would report him to the police. He began threatening me physically. I told him if he had asked me for a loan I would have been willing to lend him the money he needed. He began slapping me at first then he punched me in the stomach and side and broke two of my ribs. I told him to stop or leave. He stopped, but a few hours later he had several of his friends come over to the house, and they threatened to kill me if I continued to complain or call the police. Since that time he has been emotionally abusive and I'm afraid for my safety in my own home."

"How many individuals are living in the home currently?"

"It's just Kenneth and me."

"Are you physically afraid of Kenneth or the combination of Kenneth and his friends?"

"Normally, I would say it's his friends that concern me. But his actions and my two broken ribs do have me frightened."

"Has there been, or is there currently, illicit drug use occurring in the home?"

"Absolutely not! I don't believe in drugs. I've seen too many terribly brilliant and successful people ruin their lives with drugs. Although I do enjoy a good Brandy old fashioned sweet, every now and then."

Wendy considers this for a moment. "Does Kenneth know you have come to see me?"

"No, I haven't told him yet."

"How do you think he will react when he finds out?"

"It depends on his mood at the time, but I think he will probably become physical," Mike replies quietly.

"Then you certainly don't want to tell him until we can work out some type of safety plan for you."

"Well, I'm probably good for a couple of days. I have to be in Los Angeles early tomorrow and the next day pitching my most recent screenplay to two separate movie producers. Tonight Kenneth and I are going out to dinner and a movie, but it will be an early evening because I have to get up early to commute into L.A."

Wendy nods and gets out one of her business cards, flipping it to the back. "So you'll be back in La Jolla Thursday evening then?"

"Yes, that's correct."

"Okay, why don't we schedule to meet again? Does Friday morning at eleven work for you?"

Mike thinks for a moment, then nods. "That will be fine. Kenneth will be working."

"Perfect. During that appointment we'll develop a safety plan for you," she says, writing on the back of the card.

"Wonderful. Thank you for your time, Ms. Stevens."

"Please, call me Wendy," she says, and stands to shake his hand. Then she hands him her card with Friday's appointment written on the back. "If you need anything for any reason before our appointment, call the office number on this card and my answering service will get the message and notify me immediately."

He nods. "I'll keep that in mind. Good day, Wendy."

As she watches Mike leave her office, she thinks, *what an absolutely classy gentleman.*

CHAPTER 7

WHAT A TANGLED WEB

Wednesday, Wendy walks into the office mid-morning and quickly realizes it's going to be one of those days. Mona immediately asks for an extended lunch in order to get some personal running around done, and Wendy agrees, slightly unhappily, that she can go if she's back by two. The phone continues to ring off the hook, like Mona says it has been all morning, so in order to help out, Wendy grabs the next line. The male voice on the other end asks to speak with Wendy.

She represses a sigh. "This is Wendy."

"You don't know me, but I found your card in my house so it's apparent my partner has been to see you recently and I'd like you to meet you in person."

"Who am I speaking with?" she asks, now on guard.

"My name is Kenneth Quan. Mike Prichard would be your client," the voice answers flatly.

"I'm sorry, Mr. Quan. I can't speak with you about anyone who may or may not have come to see me or who may even have my card in their possession—"

"Listen bitch. I can't come to see you because I'm looking for my cat right now, and if I don't find it soon I'm going to kill the fucking dog that's been harassing it, but I want to meet you before I decide if I'm going to let Mike continue to see you or not. If you're unwilling to meet with me, you might as well cancel Mike's appointment with you on Friday because he won't be there. So, as I'd guess you're not going to say no, stop by my house for about fifteen minutes. If you ring the door bell and I don't answer it, walk around to the south side and come into the backyard. I'll be there searching for my cat."

"Mr. Quan, again, I cannot speak with you. I'm sorry you lost your cat. Have a nice day."

When she hangs up the telephone things have calmed down some, and Mona takes one look at her and asks, "Who the hell was that?"

Wendy clears her throat. "Mike's domestic partner, Kenneth. He wanted to meet with me, but I told him I can't without authorization from Mike."

Mona laughs and shrugs. "Why are people so stupid in this business?"

"It's not just this business it's in every walk of life."

"Yeah, you're probably right. Can I head out for lunch now? I promise I'll be back at two o'clock."

Wendy nods. "Sure, go ahead. If the phone gets any crazier I'll just let it ring through to the service and have them take messages. You can deal with them when you get back."

Mona sighs. "Fair enough. Why don't you lock the door behind me on my way out so you can get some billing done before your two o'clock appointment? That's the next important thing on your list today."

Wendy nods and follows Mona to the front door of the office, then watches her drive away in her blue Jeep Cherokee. Wendy stands very still for a moment, then decides to go speak with Kenneth. She leaves her cell phone on the desk, transfers all calls to the answering service informing them she is in the office doing some billing and needs to focus unless it's an emergency, then leaves the office.

After reviewing the file Wendy drives the short distance to Mike Prichard's home, rings the doorbell and, when there is no answer, she walks around back calling out to Kenneth. When she sees him she is surprised by his physical appearance. He is a slender man of about five foot five inches, and she guesses he weighs about one hundred fifty pounds.

Kenneth glances at her and gives her a condescending smile. "I thought you told me you couldn't talk to me."

Wendy shrugs. "I can't, and what I'm doing is not appropriate, but our call was disturbing."

"Which part? The fact I wouldn't let Mike ever see you again or that I was going to kill his dog?" Kenneth asks.

"Both actually. Did you find your cat, and did you kill the dog?"

"The answer is not yet to both."

"Well that's a relief. Would you like some help searching for the cat? We can talk as we look."

He sizes her up. "Well, you're off to a good start, I suppose. Why not. My cat's name is Jamie, and if you scare her off, we're going to have a serious problem."

As they search for his cat under shrubs and in trees, Wendy gets increasingly angrier with Kenneth remembering his threats to kill Hercules, breaking Mike's ribs, refusing to allow Mike to see her, and his belligerent attitude. Suddenly a thought occurs to her. She rolls her eyes, wondering why she hadn't thought of it sooner. She walks to the edge of the pool at the deep end, only a few feet from Kenneth, and suddenly gasps, "Oh, my God! Is that Jamie?" Pointing toward the bottom of the pool, she twists her face into a mask of horror.

Kenneth rushes in next to Wendy, yelling, "Where?!"

As he bends forward at the waist, straining to focus on the bottom of the pool, Wendy quickly slips her shirt over her hand, cups Kenneth's ass, and instantly shoves as hard as she can, sending him sprawling head first on top of the bubble wrap in the pool.

Kenneth panics as he begins to sink, and the more he struggles the more he becomes entangled in the unsecured pool covering. Wendy watches silently, with a small smile on her face, as he struggles and sinks to the bottom of the pool. She waits until Kenneth stops struggling and there are no more bubbles rising to the surface of the water. Suddenly, a line from a Laura Croft movie pops into her head.

"No more bubbles," she murmurs, "you have to let him go!" Smiling, she returns to her car and drives back to her office, energized by the magnificence of her spur of the moment planning and excellent execution. Once again, she senses the thrill of committing a flawless murder that can only be assumed to be an unfortunate accident. Invigorated by the thrill, she quickly completes her client billing and places it on Mona's desk, then begins to retrieve messages from the answering service just before two o'clock.

Mona returns to her duties promptly at two, and Wendy is on the phone scheduling additional appointments. Mona has just settled back in behind her desk when Jill Rawlins walks in for her appointment.

Wendy hears Jill come into the office as Mona greets her, and walks out to get her. "Jill, come on back. How are you today?"

"I'm good! Actually, I'm better than good."

Wendy smiles at her. "Go on."

"Well, most of my friends have reached out to me and, now that they realize I'm not angry with them for not supporting me when Zach kicked me out of the house, we've been able to reestablish our friendships."

"That's terrific to hear. So what are your plans now that everything has settled down in your life?"

Jill's face lights up. "Well, I'd like to spend about a year travelling throughout Italy, Spain, and various parts of Europe, drinking fine wine, eating fabulous foods, sightseeing, and journaling my excursions through my photography. I've always wanted to pursue my passion of photography in hopes I can exhibit my work in a high class gallery someday. I don't know if my work will be good enough to do so, but I'm going to give it everything I've got for the next year."

"What a wonderful idea! So when does this adventure begin for you?"

"Next month! I have a friend house sitting and I'll be back in a year, so I want to settle my bill with you today when we are done."

Wendy nods. "Perfect. You can do that with Mona as you leave, and there is no sense in wasting any more of your funds, as you seem to be feeling much better. But I have to insist that I get a personal invitation to your exhibit, wherever it may be, and I guarantee I'll be there."

Jill beams, her eyes filling with tears. "Wendy, thank you for everything you have done for me."

"Oh, stop that or we both will end up crying," Wendy scolds good-naturedly.

"Of course, you're right. I'll send photos and letters throughout my journey, because without you none of this would have been possible for me."

Wendy walks Jill out to the front office, you have absolutely no idea just how big a hand I had in your current position...

"Mona, Jill would like to settle her bill. Also, please schedule her for an appointment thirteen months from today," Wendy says, giving Jill a big hug.

Mona makes a small noise and gives Wendy an extremely perplexed look.

"Goodbye, Jill, and good luck," Wendy says, then turns and walks back into her office chuckling. Jill takes the time to explain Wendy's strange request to Mona before leaving the office and heading home to begin her new chapter in life.

CHAPTER 8

AFTERMATH

Thursday evening, Mike arrives home from Los Angeles around seven o'clock expecting Kenneth to greet him with eager anticipation about his business meetings. Instead, Hercules is the only one to welcome him back.

Mike walks farther into the house and sees the French doors leading out to the deck and the backyard are open, so he assumes Kenneth is out back.

"Kenneth, I'm home," Mike calls out. "I'm going to put my stuff in the bedroom and change and then I'll come out with you."

He gets no response and finds it strange, so he places his stuff on the couch and heads out back. As he walks toward the French doors, he sees that the pool is uncovered and thinks it odd, but figures Kenneth probably had a party while he was out of town and didn't get someone to cover it again before they left.

"Kenneth?" he calls, as he starts out of the house onto the back deck. Something doesn't look quite right, and he realizes he can see some of the blue bubble wrap is still in the pool. He gets closer to the edge of the pool and more bubble wrap becomes apparent, as does the implication behind what he's seeing.

Rushing to the edge, he is horrified to see a body entangled in the cover, resting on the bottom of the pool. Running back inside the house, he yells again for Kenneth, then he grabs his cell phone off the kitchen counter and dials 911.

The operator immediately dispatches both paramedics and police to his home then asks, "Sir, do you know who is in the pool?"

"No, but I'm jumping in right now to get whoever it is to the surface and shallow end on the stairs," Mike replies.

Before the operator can respond that he shouldn't disturb the scene, she hears a splash. "Mr. Prichard, please respond," says the dispatcher, and continues trying to get Mike to respond. Suddenly, the operator hears Mike scream.

"Oh, no! Oh, God, no!" Mike cries as he drags Kenneth's body to the stairs. He checks for a pulse but finds none, and attempts to drag Kenneth out of the water onto the patio but is unable to because of all the weight.

Mike hears a noise and jerks his gaze from Kenneth's body to see paramedics rushing to help him. As they haul Kenneth's lifeless body out of the water, one of them tells Mike to tell the operator they have started CPR and will be transporting Kenneth to the hospital. Mike numbly does as he's told, and the operator tells him the police are now arriving.

"Mr. Prichard, you'll need to provide the police with some information later on. As of right now, please give us your information and the name of the person you found in your pool."

Mike begins giving information to the dispatcher, but is interrupted.

"Please speak with the officers on scene, sir. They'll take it from here."

"Oh, sorry. Thanks," Mike says, and hangs up the phone.

He watches helplessly as the paramedics attempt to get a pulse. One of them shakes his head, and gestures for another to use the Automated External Defibrillator, but they get no response. They load Kenneth onto a gurney and prepare to transport Kenneth to the hospital.

"Wait, can I ride with him?" Mike asks, grabbing one of the paramedic's arms.

"No, sir, I'm sorry," replies the paramedic, who looks at the officer and briefly shakes his head.

The officer picks up on the cue. "Sir, I will drive you to the hospital. There just isn't enough room in the ambulance while the paramedics are working on Kenneth. Why don't you change into some dry clothes and we'll be right behind the ambulance, okay?"

Mike nods and rushes inside as the officer and paramedic share a look, privately understanding the outcome at the hospital.

While Mike is changing the second officer who has been taking photographs all along continues documenting the backyard and sketching the scene, but wraps up in time to leave with the other officer and Mike. When they arrive at the hospital, the nurse escorts them to a private office where the patrol officers begin getting a statement from Mike.

"You are under no obligation to answer any of my questions, Mr. Prichard. Do you mind covering the basics?" the officer asks.

"No, go ahead," Mike replies, pacing the floor.

"Okay, then. When did you find Kenneth in the pool?"

"I arrived home from L.A. at about seven o'clock, dropped my bags in the living room, and walked outside, expecting to find Kenneth doing something in the backyard. When I saw someone in the pool I immediately grabbed my cell phone and called 911. As soon as I knew help was on the way, I jumped into the pool and tried to drag him out of the water. It wasn't until then that I realized it was Kenneth. I got him to the steps and, and tried to get him out of the water but—" He pauses, obviously struggling with reliving the moment, then clears his throat. "I wasn't able to because there was too much weight. About the time I realized I couldn't get him onto the patio the paramedics got there and helped me get him out of the water."

"You said you dropped your bags?"

"Yes, I'm sorry, it's all blurring together. I left Wednesday morning and spent Wednesday night and all day Thursday in L.A. I stayed at the Ritz Carleton on West Olympic Boulevard. I had two business meetings to attend; one Wednesday and the other Thursday."

"What type of meetings? What do you do?"

"I'm self-employed. I write screenplays, and I was pitching my latest work to two different producers on those days."

"So you stayed in L.A. rather than driving back and forth?" the officer asks, making a note on his handheld pad.

"Yes, the meeting on Wednesday was for dinner, and the one on Thursday was an early morning breakfast."

"I see. Are you and Kenneth living together, and is he your partner?"

"Yes, on both counts."

"How long have you been living together?"

"We've been together for almost a year and he moved into my house about four months ago."

"How would you describe your relationship?"

"It's good. We're going through the normal adjustments when two people start living together, you know, normal stuff."

The officer raises an eyebrow. "Like what?"

"Well, for instance, Kenneth is deathly afraid of water and doesn't know how to swim. I love the pool and use it all the time. He wanted me to fill it with soil and landscape, and I refused. But since he is so irrational about the pool, I got the cheap bubble wrap cover so he wouldn't be so nervous about it."

"So Kenneth is afraid of the pool?"

"Yes, that's why I can't understand how he got in it," Mike says, looking extremely perplexed.

"What do you mean?"

"He was completely irrational about it. Like he thought it would grab him and pull him in. He usually stayed at least two feet away from the side of it, so I just can't imagine or understand why he would have gotten close enough to fall into it."

The officer nods. "Mr. Prichard, I'm going to need to ask you some very personal questions, and I apologize if they seem rude or insensitive, but they need to be asked and answered."

"I understand. Go ahead."

"Does Kenneth drink or do drugs of any type?"

"He drinks alcohol, but doesn't use drugs."

"How can you be so sure?"

"Really? He's my lover, and we have been together for nearly a year. We have been living together for four months. I think I would know if he did any type of drug. Besides I would never be with anyone doing drugs. I've seen many talented friends ruin their lives with a combination of drugs and excessive alcohol consumption."

The interview is interrupted when Doctor Montgomery, the attending emergency room physician, knocks on the door then enters the room.

He makes brief eye contact with the patrol officer, then turns to Mike. "Mr. Quan was just pronounced dead on arrival. I'm sorry, Mr.

Prichard, we did everything we could. Can we call anyone for you? Do you know Mr. Quan's next of kin?"

Mike looks stunned and sits down heavily in one of the office chairs. Realization dawns on his face, and he begins to sob burying his face in his hands for several moments before he takes a few deep breaths and looks up at Dr. Montgomery. "He has a brother in town, but I'll call him myself."

"I'm very sorry for your loss," the doctor says.

"Thank you," Mike replies, his voice thick. He turns to the officer. "Can you take me home after I say good bye to Kenneth?"

"Yes, of course. I'll be right there with you."

Dr. Montgomery tells Mike, "Once the nurses have the room cleaned up and safe they will come and get you."

Mike nods mutely.

Shortly after the doctor leaves, a nurse appears and walks Mike in to view Kenneth. When he is done saying his good-byes, he turns and tells the patrolman he is ready to go home.

As he gets into the patrol car, Mike asks, "What should I expect next?"

"Well, since this was an unattended death, additional investigation will need to be done. There will be an autopsy, and by the time I get you back to the house there will be two detectives there who will probably want to speak with you. They will ask for access to Kenneth's records and belongings."

"What if I say no? I see no reason to do so, I'm just curious."

"Then they will probably get a search warrant for his personal records."

Mike nods. "Well, that won't be necessary. They can search anything they want to."

"This is all just standard protocol in situations like these," the officer says.

"I understand."

After that, there is very little said during drive back to the house, and the car is quiet except for the occasional radio traffic between dispatch and the patrolman. When they arrive, Mike is introduced to San Diego Police Detectives Preston Adams and Beau Rogers. Mike is surprised to see Beau Rogers, whom he recognizes immediately as an inspiring actor who had been to at least one audition Mike assisted with for one of his screenplays.

Beau is in his mid-to-late thirties with a rugged complexion and a perfectionist complex. Nothing is out of place in his appearance, and not even the hair on his head lacks symmetry. Preston Adams, by contrast, must be in his early fifties, slightly overweight and, set against Detective Rogers, has the juxtaposed appearance of a slob with a wrinkled and stained shirt. Detective Rogers takes the lead since he has had prior contact with Mike.

"Mr. Prichard, we're here as a matter of protocol to investigate the death of Mr. Quan. We've already been thoroughly briefed by the patrolman and will try not to repeat any of his questions," Rodgers begins.

"I understand, Detectives. Thank you for your empathy but it's okay. Ask me anything you need to know. I want to help everyone understand what happened, especially me."

Beau replies, "Thank you. We understand you were out of town and you found Mr. Quan in the pool about seven o'clock tonight."

"That's correct. Please, call him Kenneth."

"Okay, I can do that. Would it be possible for us to examine Kenneth's room and cell phone?"

"Yes, of course. Kenneth was my partner, so we shared the master bedroom. His personal belongings are on and in the nightstand on the right side of the bed, and mine are on the left. Kenneth's clothing is all on the right side of the closet, mine are on the left and, you have probably guessed, he has the right side of the bathroom sink and medicine cabinet."

"Do you mind if we go search his personal belongings?" Beau asks.

"Not at all. Do you need anything else from me?"

"Not at this point, but we may have some additional questions after we are finished."

"No problem. I'm going to make myself a drink. Would either of you gentlemen like a coke, bottle of water, or coffee?"

Both detectives politely decline and walk into the bedroom to begin their search. Kenneth's cell phone is on the nightstand, and Detective Adams jots down the telephone numbers Kenneth called or received calls from beginning Wednesday morning through today, then photographs the phone.

In the drawer of the nightstand, Detective Adams finds the business card of Wendy Stevens with a Friday appointment scheduled for eleven o'clock. He shows the card to Beau.

"Isn't this the same counselor who was at the hospital with that Davis woman whose husband wacked off to porn, then blew himself away with the shotgun a while back?"

Beau thinks for a moment. "Yeah, I think you're right. She was the domestic violence counselor, right?"

Preston nods. "Don't let me forget to talk to Mr. Prichard about this in more detail."

When they finish searching the bedroom they walk back out into the living room to speak with Mike.

Detective Adams sits down and asks, "How was your relationship with Kenneth going?"

Mike looks a bit perplexed. "It was fine. Why?"

"Was Kenneth seeing a domestic violence counselor by the name of Wendy Stevens?"

"No, I saw her on Tuesday and have an appointment to see her tomorrow at eleven. How did you know about her?"

"I found her card in the drawer of Kenneth's nightstand, and I have to admit I'm curious why, if things were fine in your relationship, it would be necessary for either one of you to be seeing a domestic violence counselor?"

"Well, apparently he must have been snooping through my personal belongings while I was out of town. How rude. Anyway, I had asked several people I knew about finding a good domestic violence counselor and was referred to Ms. Stevens."

"Again, why was it necessary to seek out a domestic violence counselor if everything was fine in your relationship with Kenneth?" Detective Adams presses.

Mike lets out a sigh. "About a month ago Kenneth and I had some issues that reached farther than just adjustment to living together," he says, and summarizes what he had told Wendy a few days before. "After that happened, I made an appointment with Ms. Stevens to ask for her advice."

"Why is there a call from Kenneth's cell phone to Ms. Stevens on Wednesday morning?"

"I have absolutely no idea. Perhaps that question is best directed to Ms. Stevens."

"So he made a connection to a counselor you claim to have been seeing, and now he is suddenly found dead in the pool you say he was deathly afraid of getting near?"

Mike glances up at Adam sharply. "Detectives, am I under arrest?"

"No, sir, you are not. We're just having a discussion."

"Well, I don't like the tone this conversation has taken so I think you both need to leave now while I call my attorney."

"May we take Kenneth's cell phone?"

"No, you may not. Don't you need a warrant or something?"

"That is probably the cleanest way of handling it if you won't let us take the phone."

Mike sniffs. "Then I suggest you go get one."

"We'll do that. I must advise you not to alter the phone in anyway because that might be considered tampering with evidence."

"I'm not going to touch it. It will be in the drawer of Kenneth's nightstand when you come back with your warrant. Good evening, gentlemen. I'm sure you can find your way out."

Detective Rodgers represses a sigh. "Very well, Mr. Prichard. We will be in touch."

"I won't hold my breath," Mike replies, tossing back the rest of his drink as the detectives leave him.

CHAPTER 9

FOLLOW UP

Wendy walks into her office Friday morning at nine o'clock to find Detectives Adams and Rogers seated in her waiting room with fresh coffee.

She looks surprised, but greets them. "Hello, Detectives. I need to get myself some coffee, but you're free to move into my office and have a seat."

After retrieving her coffee, she walks in, sits down behind her desk, and asks, "How can I help you today?"

Detective Adams clears his throat. "Do you know Kenneth Quan?"

"No, I don't know him. Why?"

"Because your card was found in his bedroom nightstand."

She gives him a confused, mildly amused look. "So, do you investigate everyone who has one of my cards in their nightstand?"

He raises his eyebrow. "Only when they're dead."

"Oh, I'm sorry to hear that about Mr. Quan, but I fail to see how it's my concern."

"Can you explain why Mr. Quan telephoned this office on Wednesday morning?" Adams asks.

"As a matter of fact I can," Wendy replies, but stops.

Adams waits for a moment, then says sassily, "I'm listening."

"Well isn't there a follow-up question?" Wendy retorts with equal amounts of sass.

Adams stares at her for a moment with his mouth hanging open, then sighs and shakes his head. "Ms. Stevens, we can do this the easy way or the hard way."

"You can do it whatever way you wish."

"Why are you being so difficult with us?"

"I didn't realize I was being difficult, detective. I've answered every question you've asked me and, I'm sorry, but I don't particularly like cops. From my perspective too many of you are dishonest."

"I'm sorry you feel that way. I'll try to be more specific. Why did Mr. Quan call you Wednesday morning?"

She grins at him. "Very good detective. Mr. Quan telephoned my office around eleven, told me I didn't know him, that he was one of my clients' partners, and wanted me to stop by the house and introduce myself to him so he could decide if he would allow my client to continue to see me. I told him I couldn't speak with him without my client's authorization. The man, who identified himself as Kenneth Quan, then told me not to expect my client to make his eleven o'clock appointment today."

"I see. What else did he say?"

"Nothing that I recall."

"Are you sure?"

She thinks for a moment. "Well, he did say something about his cat missing and killing the dog that was harassing the cat if he didn't find it soon. Wait, no, my mistake. He very charmingly said he was going to kill the *fucking* dog that was harassing it."

"Anything else?"

"No. Why?"

"Are you sure?"

"Yes. Why?"

"I'm just making sure there isn't any misunderstanding here, like we've had previously."

"I'm sorry, did I miss part of this conversation? What misunderstanding do we have?" Wendy asks innocently.

"Well, I asked you about Kenneth Quan, and you told me you didn't know him when in fact you did."

"Well, detective, you asked me if I knew Mr. Quan, and I answered the question correctly. I don't know him. I have never met him and I have only had one very short telephone conversation with the man. I hardly think that qualifies as knowing someone. Now if you had asked me if I knew *of* Mr. Quan, then my answer would have been misleading and untruthful. So you see, you asked the wrong question for the information you were trying to uncover. It's basic English."

Detective Adams bites the inside of his cheek to keep from chuckling. "Well, then I stand corrected and I'll be much more specific from now on."

"Wonderful, thank you."

"Why did Mr. Prichard come to see you on Tuesday?"

"That is confidential and without a release from Mr. Prichard I cannot disclose anything about any of our discussions. Did you happen to get a release from Mr. Prichard?"

Adams doesn't bother to repress his sigh this time. "No, we didn't."

"That is unfortunate. Is there anything else I can help you with?"

"Not at this time."

Wendy stands up and motions the detectives towards the door. "In that case, thank you for stopping by. In the future, it's best to make an appointment, because my schedule fluctuates drastically from day-to-day and I wouldn't want you to have to wait hours to see me. I'll assist in any manner I can, if you need anything later."

After they walk out of the office, Preston Adams turns to Beau. "What a bitch! She is the reason I hate dealing with counselors."

Beau laughs. "That may be so, but it was funny to watch your reactions, especially when she told you it was basic English. How did that make you *feel*, with your English degree and shit?"

Adams gives him a dark look. "It pissed me off, that's how it made me feel. Especially because she was correct."

"Well if it helps any, you handled it well. I don't think I would have been so gracious."

Preston shakes his head. "Well, what do you say we get some breakfast, then camp outside her office. When Mr. Prichard walks out, we can hit him up for a release and if we get it then we go back in and shove it down her smart ass little throat?"

"Wow, she really did piss you off didn't she?" Beau asks tauntingly, then shrugs. "I'm game and I've got your back. Besides it will be great entertainment, even if nothing else comes of it."

✳✳✳

Mike walks in for his eleven o'clock appointment looking tired and weary. Wendy offers coffee which he gratefully accepts and sits down.

After a moment, Wendy opens the session. "Is anything wrong? You look exhausted and bit out of sorts. How was Los Angeles?"

"Los Angeles was great," Mike says, but there's no conviction in his voice. "Both producers liked what they saw, and I'm expecting one or both to make an offer by next week."

"That's terrific, but it doesn't sound like you feel that way."

Mike shrugs. "We won't need to work on a safety plan any longer."

"I was afraid of that. Detectives Adams and Rogers came by this morning asking me a bunch of questions about Kenneth. They mentioned something happened to him. What's going on?"

"It's awful! I got home yesterday and found Kenneth tangled up in the pool cover on the bottom of the pool. He was dead on arrival at the hospital."

"How horrible for you. I'm so sorry."

"So why were the detectives here to see you?" Mike asks quietly.

"Well, Kenneth called me on Wednesday, demanding that I go to the house to meet him or he wouldn't let you speak with me again. I told him I couldn't talk to him without your permission. Apparently he was looking for his cat and was mad about Hercules harassing it. He said it he didn't find his cat he was going to kill the dog... Oh, my God, is Hercules okay?"

Mike nods. "Yes, Hercules and the cat are both fine. He would always threaten things like that but I never felt he was serious. I think the cops suspect me of killing him."

"Why on earth would you say that? You didn't, did you?" Wendy asks calmly.

"Of course not. It's just that they found your card in Kenneth's night stand and figured I was the abusive one because you're a domestic violence counselor. When I explained to them that Kenneth had been abusive they pointedly brought up the fact that now he's dead," Mike chokes off and takes a moment to pull himself back together. "At that point I told them to leave the house or arrest me."

"That explains why they were in my office first thing this morning. I told them I couldn't speak with them without your consent and asked if they had a release from you. When they didn't we discontinued out conversation as well."

"What should I do?" he asks sadly.

"Did you tell them everything you told me about your relationship?"

"Yes."

"Then I think you should sign this release and let me speak with them. My policy is to only confirm or deny what you have told them, but with the release you authorize me to answer any and all of their questions. Since our conversations have been so short and I can't tell them anything you haven't already told them, I think it will look good; and it's always good to cooperate with the police during an investigation."

Mike looks at the release Wendy hands him and signs it. Handing it back to her, he asks, "Now what?"

"I want you to relax. Let's continue counseling for a few more sessions because I want to work with you on the issues that allowed you to get into an abusive relationship in the first place. Hopefully if we address them now, you'll never find yourself in another situation like this again. After a few more sessions you can determine if it's worth continuing or if it's best to discontinue counseling all together."

"That sounds good to me."

"Good. Why don't you tell me how you're handling this?" Wendy asks.

"I think that's a good idea," Mike says, and continues talking about his feelings and perceptions.

Wendy looks out her window and notices the detectives driving into the parking lot. As she sits feigning interest in Mike's conversation, she wonders what they're up to now and skips through a bunch of possibilities. None of them ring quite true until it suddenly dawns on her that they knew Mike was coming in for a session this morning, and they are probably going to try to get a release from him to allow her to speak with them.

As the session progresses, Wendy attends to what Mike talks about and suggests some good points for the next session, then clears her throat. "Mike, would you do me a favor?"

"Sure. What is it you need?"

"I have a feeling the detectives will be in the waiting room when we finish and will ask you to sign a release. If I'm right, I would really appreciate it if you would tell them no and walk out of the office. That way I can speak with them about disturbing my clients in a place that is supposed to be safe for them. I'll present them with your release and tell them what they want to know, but they need to understand that staking my clients is inappropriate."

"You got it. Detective Adams pissed me off last night anyway."

Wendy smiles. "Perfect."

Wendy explores several areas about Mike's life and past relationship choices, why he was single for so long, and why he was attracted to Kenneth before time runs out for the session.

As they are finishing up, Mike notices the detectives getting out of their vehicle and heading for the door.

He motions to Wendy. "Well, you're right. The detectives are coming toward the office now."

"Well, let's make sure we have some fun with them, shall we?" Wendy asks, and Mike smiles.

"Absolutely."

They get up and head to the outer office reception area to find Detectives Adams and Rogers walking through the front door.

Wendy looks at them and smiles. "To what do I own two visits from San Diego's finest in such a short time span?"

"We are actually here to speak with Mr. Prichard. May we use your office for a moment, Ms. Stevens?"

"Sure, go right ahead."

Wendy sits down in the reception area and listens intently, trying to hear if Detective Adams is requesting Mike to sign a release. She doesn't hear much, but finally hears a fairly loud refusal, and then watches Mike walk out of the office. He gives her a wink on his way out. Both detectives come out of her office and start heading towards the door as well, but Wendy asks to have a brief word with them before they leave. Preston shoots a quick glace to Beau as they head back into her office. She closes the door behind them and asks them to be seated.

"I'm just curious gentlemen. What makes you think it is okay for you come into my office to harass my client and disturb the confidentiality I hold so dear with him?"

"It's not like that, Ms. Stevens. We came to get the release you require in order to speak with us," says Detective Adams defensively.

"And did you get your release, detective?"

"Uh, no we didn't."

"Well, as I believe I said in our previous meeting, next time I would appreciate you calling before just showing up. Believe it or not, I can and will assist you, if you will pay me the common courtesy of a heads-up. For instance, you failed to get a release from Mr. Prichard because I have already gotten one for you. What would you like to know?"

"What are you talking about?"

Wendy hands him a copy of the release. "Surprised, detective?"

Adams shakes his head, folding the copy of the release and tucking it away. He then relays what they have been told by Mike.

She thinks for just a moment then nods. "Yes, it sounds like everything he's told you is accurate, and I can confirm it if you need. Mike thinks you're going to arrest him because you think he killed Kenneth. I asked if he drove back to the house during the time he was supposed to be gone, and he assured me he was in L.A. the entire trip. I told him if he was being truthful he has nothing to worry about."

"If, in fact, he's telling the truth he will be eliminated as a person of interest."

"So I didn't overstep my bounds by attempting to ease his mind?" Wendy asks, looking concerned.

"Not at all. Would you be willing to answer a few more questions from us, since we've had a chance to consider some follow-up questions from our earlier discussion."

"Sure, go ahead."

"Thank you, Ms. Stevens. May I call you Wendy?"

"Absolutely, I don't really care for formalities."

Detective Adams reiterates his initial conversation with Mike and asks if there was anything missing in the statement to the police.

"Yes, there is. What he told you is exactly what he mentioned to me with the exception that Kenneth was always irritated with Mike's dog, Hercules, for chasing his cat. Mike explained to Kenneth multiple times that Hercules loves to play with cats and would never harm one. He has always been very gentle."

"And?"

"Kenneth didn't believe Mike."

"Alright, thank you. We discussed the telephone call you received from Kenneth on Wednesday morning earlier where you refused to speak with him without Mike's consent."

"Yes, I remember."

"After you hung up, what did you do for the rest of the day?"

"Well, I helped with the phones until Mona left the office around eleven thirty. She recommended I lock the office door, and I notified the answering service I would be doing client billing and not to disturb me unless there was an emergency. I returned any calls after I was finished with the billing."

"So you didn't leave the office?" Adams asks, making a note of that fact.

"Not from eleven-thirty till after three. I finished my billings, put them on Mona's desk, and began returning calls at around one-thirty, I think. I had a client come in at two for about an hour, and after that I can't remember what time I called it a day, but I know I left the office sometime shortly after Mona, so maybe she has a more specific time."

"Was anyone else here?"

"I was alone while Mona was at lunch, but other than that she was here or I had clients. Why?"

"Since you were one of the last ten outgoing calls on Mr. Quan's cell phone we just needed to verify your whereabouts. It sounds to me like the only time you didn't have someone with you was the two and a half hours you were in the office alone."

"That's correct. Well, and after Mona left for the day. I can make copy of my weekly calendar for you if you wish?"

"Thank you, but that won't be necessary at this point. If we need further clarification after the medical examiner's report, we can always come back and get it, correct?"

"Absolutely. I'm always here to help, detectives."

"Well, then I think we're done here today," Adams says, standing up.

Wendy shakes both of their hands as they get ready to leave.

Detective Adams stops in the doorway, turns, and says, "Thank you for your assistance with Mike. I apologize for not respecting your relationship with your clients, and I won't make that mistake again."

"That's quite alright. Next time I wouldn't be as polite," she replies with a wink.

He smiles. "I understand. Thank you again for your cooperation."

CHAPTER 10

COURTSHIP

After the detectives leave her office, Wendy sits behind her desk analyzing their conversations and wonders if they suspect her story isn't true in any way. After a few moments, she decides they won't find any flaws. She goes over the details in her head one more time, just to be sure. She drove the back roads to Mike's house so as not to be picked up on any street surveillance camera. Mike's house and driveway are situated in a manner that provides maximum privacy, and she didn't see any other neighbors arriving or leaving so unless someone saw her from inside their home she doubts she attracted any attention at all. She decides if confronted with evidence that she was, in fact, at Mike's home, she'll claim she lied because her behavior was unethical and she feared professional sanctions.

Mona watches Wendy from the doorway for a few moments before she clears her throat and startles Wendy back to the present. "Excuse me for the interruption, but there is a smoking hot guy in the lobby asking for you, and he smells wonderful."

Surprise creases Wendy's forehead. "Oh, really? Just who is this wonderful smelling man?"

"I don't know. He wouldn't give me his name. All he would say is that you will recognize him when you come out to meet with him."

"Well that's horseshit! Go see what he is selling before I come out to meet him."

"Already asked. He says he isn't selling anything except maybe a good dinner invitation."

"Well, now I'm intrigued. A dinner invitation from a great smelling, smoking hot guy. Okay, I'm coming."

Wendy walks out of her office and makes eye contact with the mystery man. She begins laughing.

"Mona, I'd like you to meet Jim Bush. Jim is the Vice President of Business Development for Stevens Environmental Restoration Fund."

Jim shakes Mona's hand and they exchange greetings. As Jim turns back to Wendy, Mona waves her hand in the air behind him, like his handshake burned it, and mouths, "Damn! He's hot!"

Wendy represses a laugh with effort, then turns her attention to Jim.

"I'm in town speaking with some of Mark's contacts on behalf of SERF, but I'll be flying back to Sausalito tomorrow after my breakfast meeting. Since I'm in San Diego for the evening and it's your town, I'll buy dinner if you show me a good place to eat. What do you say?"

Wendy smiles at him. "What kind of food do you like besides sushi? I should probably warn you, my tastes in dining aren't nearly as sophisticated as Sean, Jessica, or Bonnie's."

"I'll take that as a yes then. I'm in the mood for a really different type of dining experience, as long as the food is good."

"Then I have the perfect place. So yes, I'll have dinner with you tonight. I'll drive and bring you back here to your car later. Mona, would you please call the place I took Jill the other night and see if you can get us a reservation on such short notice?"

Mona snickers, picks up her phone, and works some magic to get them a reservation in thirty minutes.

"Thank you, Mona," Wendy says, then turns to Jim. "The restaurant is a short drive from here, but you can buy me a drink before dinner after a day like today."

"Fair enough. Do I need to keep this tie on or can I lose it for dinner?"

"You can definitely get rid of it. Actually, lose the jacket, too."

He raises his eyebrows. "If you say so."

Wendy smiles and turns to Mona. "Please lock up and go home. Today has been enough for both of us. Have a great weekend."

Mona just gives her a wink as Wendy walks out of the office with Jim.

Wendy watches Jim's reaction when she pulls into the restaurant's parking lot and smirks when she sees him twist uneasily in the passenger seat of her car. She ignores his reaction initially and gets out of the car, watching through the corner of her eye as his uneasiness turns to apprehension.

As they get closer to the front door, Wendy stops and says through her laughter, "I've been watching your reaction this whole time, and I suspect you're wondering what the hell you've gotten yourself into. Trust me, this place is fantastic and the food is divine, even though the external appearance leaves much to be desired."

He chuckles. "If you say so."

"I promise this experience will not be disappointing," she says playfully.

His eyes lock on hers. "I'm going to hold you to that promise."

After a moment, Wendy clears her throat and keeps walking toward the door. "I thought you had an adventurous spirit."

"I do. I just don't relish the thought of food poisoning."

She rolls her eyes. "Just reserve your opinion until after the meal."

"Fair enough."

Wendy opens the door and as soon as they walk in she is greeted by the owner.

"Welcome back, Wendy. And so soon! I love it." She glances over at Jim and gives him a once-over. "I guess you would like a private spot tonight?"

"Perfect. Jim, this is Rachelle. She owns the place. Rachelle, this is Jim."

"Very nice to meet you, Jim," Rachelle says, shaking his offered hand.

"Jim was quite apprehensive when we first drove up," Wendy says, grinning at him.

"Well, let's see if we can calm your fears with good food and excellent service," Rachelle says. "Follow me."

She seats them both in a very private booth tucked away from the hustle and bustle of the main restaurant and takes their drink order.

"I'll have a crown and coke, please," Jim says, and looks to Wendy to order hers next.

She goes for the shock value, making eye contact with Jim and keeping it. "I'd like Sex on the Beach tonight, please."

Rachelle observes Jim squirm and blush slightly, she gives Wendy a sly wink. "I'll get your orders up right away."

Jim looks around the restaurant and is amused by the strange décor. The combination of picnic tables pushed together for a group dining experience, plush leather booths along the exterior walls, and a full open bar at the opposite end of the restaurant makes the vibe welcoming and comfortable.

The artwork is oddly sophisticated with quality local artist impressionist work displayed, offset by funky pieces of pottery and Native American artifacts. As he studies the surroundings, he recognizes that this odd mixture of designs works well. The restaurant is rambunctious yet cordial at the group tables with sufficient privacy in the booths. He decides he likes it. As he turns his attention back to Wendy, he realizes she's been studying his reaction.

He clears his throat. "This is definitely a unique dining experience."

"That's what you told me you wanted. But if this is too much, we can have one drink and go somewhere else."

"Not at all. You asked me to trust you and that's what I intend to do."

"Thank you. I think you'll find this experience to be not only unique but also delightful."

"How can it be anything less? After all, I am having dinner with you."

"Awe," Wendy says, smiling, then makes a face, "Gag me with a spoon."

He laughs out loud, and just then their drinks arrive.

Wendy offers a toast, "To wonderful company, conversation, and delicious food."

Jim raises his glass and his eyebrow. "Perhaps I need a spoon of my own to gag on."

Wendy laughs, enjoying that he also indulges in sarcasm.

They both look over their menus, and when Rachelle returns to take their orders Wendy orders filet mignon with the huckleberry reduction and blue cheese crumbles, and a side of fresh vegetables. Jim decides to try the pan seared dorado with wild rice and a Caesar salad.

Rachelle repeats the order back correctly, and Jim says, "Yes, that's right. Also, what type of oil is the dorado seared in?"

"Coconut oil," Rachelle replies, making a final note on her order sheet.

"Perfect. Thanks."

Wendy gives Jim an inquisitive look.

He shrugs. "I'm highly allergic to peanuts, so I wanted to make sure the fish wasn't seared in peanut oil. By the way, if you're ever with me and I look like I'm dying while grasping my throat, I probably am and you'll need to stab me with my Epi-pen. I always carry one, and it's always either in my left jacket pocket or my left front pants pocket."

She stares at him. "Just how severe is your allergy to peanuts?"

"Extremely," he replies, sipping his drink, "my throat will swell shut in less than two minutes without administering the Epi-pen."

"Thank you for letting me know. I think I would have freaked out if you reacted and I didn't know about the food allergy. Are you allergic to anything else?"

"Nothing that I'm aware of besides peanuts."

They chat for a while, and then order a second round of drinks.

Wendy asks, "So, you said during our little meet and greet in San Francisco that you were recently single?"

"Ah, yes. Brenda and I had been in a relationship for just over a year when she decided we needed to get married and have babies because she wasn't getting any younger."

"How old is Brenda?"

"She's thirty-three."

"Oh, well, that's fair. Why the break up?"

"Well, I'm not ready for children now and don't have any reason to believe I'll ever be ready. My career is of primary importance to me and has to be my focus. Brenda told me I was selfish, and she wasn't going to wait around for me to grow up. Then she gave me an ultimatum: my career or her." He shrugs.

"You chose your career?" Wendy laughs.

"Yes. So maybe I am selfish."

"Or maybe you know what is important to you and you stuck to your life goals. Maybe she's the one being selfish by demanding you change. Were your goals consistent from the start of your relationship with her, and did she know them?"

"Oh yeah. I was very clear on my position about work and life goals."

"Then professionally speaking, I don't think you're being selfish and it's her issue."

He simply grins at her for a moment. "Well, that's good to hear. What about you?"

"I haven't been in any type of relationship for over ten years now."

"Really? Why is that?"

"Like you I've been pretty focused on my career, and from what I see, most relationships have significant issues."

"Ah, I see," Jim says. "But you see the worst in relationships, and you can't judge everyone's actions in the same manner you judge your clients' circumstances."

"That's true, but every relationship has the potential to develop into the type of circumstances my clients find themselves in on a daily basis."

"And yet not every relationship becomes abusive. You've become stilted and need to allow yourself to become vulnerable again with someone who earns your trust. As long as you keep people outside the walls you've built, you'll never be able to trust anyone again."

"That's a little harsh don't you think? Besides, I'm not sure I want to let anyone that close to me again. They are the ones who can truly hurt you."

"That's absolutely true, but that's also where the greatest joy is found. With someone you can share your joy and pain, success and failure, dreams and fears, you know they truly understand and support you regardless of where you land on the spectrum."

Wendy sits back in her chair. "True. But I'm happy with my life, so why do I need to risk the hurt?"

"Because without risking vulnerability you'll never know the riches of joy."

At that moment, dinner arrives, and Wendy clears her throat and says, "Yes! Let's eat. I'm starving."

Jim sits there looking into her eyes. "We'll finish this discussion over dessert," he says finally and reaches for his fork.

She breaks eye contact, glaring down at her plate. "As far as I'm concerned, it's already finished."

"Oh, but it's not," Jim counters quietly.

Wendy doesn't respond, taking a bite of her filet instead, and savors it as it melts in her mouth. She is instantly in food heaven, and can tell by Jim's expression that he pretty much feels the same way about his dorado.

Jim swallows his first bite, looking absolutely stunned. "You were absolutely right about this place. This is fantastic. And to think I would have never come inside based on the look from the outside."

"Here. You have to try a bite of this filet," she says as she puts a bite on his plate. He does the same for her with his dorado as she continues, "This place is well-known among the locals it caters to, and unless someone introduces you to the place it's a well-kept secret around here."

"I can see how it could be. Thank you for sharing this with me tonight."

"Well, thanks for inviting me to dinner."

"Honestly, I hate eating alone. Besides, I wanted an opportunity to speak with you on a personal basis. There is one thing you'll learn about me very quickly. I am brutally frank and always say what I'm thinking, and sometimes people take that as me being cocky and arrogant," he pauses, and Wendy interrupts.

"It's not bad. I only see it as somewhat cocky. So tell me, how is the fund raising going for SERF?"

"It's going very well, and I believe the thirty million we're shooting for in the first year will be reached in about ten months if things continue going as they are currently. But I didn't ask you to dinner to discuss SERF."

Wendy pauses for a moment, deciding whether or not she should ask her next question. She isn't sure if she really wants to hear Jim's response, but then thinks, *what the hell? Go for it.* "So then why did you ask me to dinner?"

"From our very first meeting, I have been attracted to you both physically and intellectually. I wanted to see if you are attracted to me as well."

"That's certainly not what I expected to hear."

"Really," he says, much more statement than question. "I think you were hoping that was the case, but it scares the hell out of you at the same time."

She snorts. "Okay, now I see why people consider your bluntness arrogance."

"I don't think you believe that either. Look at it from my point of view. You asked me what cologne I was wearing the very first time we met. That's not something most board members would ask a job applicant. You also asked the most penetrating and potentially damaging interview questions, which makes it seem like you want to know more about me. Look, I wasn't sure I should pop into your office and ask you out, but I risked it because I believe getting to know you, regardless if we date or not, will be well worth the risk of looking foolish to you. Also, if I didn't think you had at least some curiosity about me as well, I would have never attempted anything as risky as asking you out."

She sits for a moment in silence, eyebrow raised, then says, "I didn't realize this was on official date."

He grins "Yes, you did, and it's scary for both of us. But here we are. So the question now is, will there be a second date?"

"Just how do you see a dating relationship developing between us given our respective positions with SERF?" Wendy asks.

"Well, you're a board member, not my boss. I would suggest we keep this our secret until we know whether or not this is something either of us wants to pursue on a more than casual basis. I would like to see where this goes without any real expectations, other than getting to know one another."

"Where do you anticipate this is going to lead us?"

"At the bare minimum we'll become better acquainted as business professionals. On the other hand, perhaps we become friends, or perhaps we become intimate and date seriously. I'm open to any of the possibilities, but it's my hope this can develop into a serious relationship. I wouldn't be so vulnerable with you otherwise. It's my hope you will trust me enough to become vulnerable with me, as well, but if not, I'll respect your decision as long as you can do the same for me. There is absolutely no pressure here, and if you tell me tonight you can't, won't, or aren't interested in the same thing, I'll accept it and we will have had a great dinner. Then we'll just be business associates and friends."

Wendy is quiet for a long while. "That certainly is a lot to digest," she finally says. "I find this to be very promising and believe I would like to get to know you better personally. The fact that I'm willing to even consider any of the possibilities with you, beyond just a professional relationship, scares me and excites me at the same time. You need to know that if we date, I'm not going to be an easy person to get to open up to you. You'll need to be very patient, or we might as well just decide to be business associates to begin with. I don't want to be pushed, and I don't want anyone to know we are dating, either in my office or at SERF, understood?"

Jim nods. "Absolutely. I promise to be discreet as long as you do."

"Perfect," she says and fiddles with her fork. "Can we please talk about anything less personal now? This is starting to give me a headache."

He smiles and switches topics instantly. "What's your favorite dessert on the menu, and would you like to share one? I don't think I can eat much more."

"I think the prune cake is the best."

"The what?"

"Prune cake," she pauses, gauging his reaction, then chuckles. "I know. I had never had one either before I started eating here, but trust me it's great."

He shrugs and says with a wink. "Very well. I haven't been disappointed so far."

After little shivers of anticipation squirm through her, Wendy catches Rachelle's eye and motions her to come over to the table.

"What else can I get for you guys?" Rachelle asks.

"We'd like a prune cake. And he thinks I'm crazy," Wendy replies.

Rachelle laughs. "I know, it sounds disgusting, but if you like prunes you'll love it."

Wendy nods and adds, "With some whipped cream, too, please."

"Of course! I wouldn't think of serving it any other way."

When Rachelle arrives with the dessert, Jim looks at it with apprehension. "It's certainly not what I expected."

"Just try it," Wendy chides.

He sighs and takes a bite. Both Wendy and Rachelle recognize the pleased and surprised look on Jim's face.

"This is really, really good!" he says, scooping another bite onto his spoon.

Wendy and Rachelle exchange a smile, and Rachelle leaves them to it.

They finish dessert and Wendy drives Jim back to his car. They both get out and stand chatting for a few minutes. She thanks him for a wonderful evening, and they discuss when he will be back in San Diego, and also when she will be in Sausalito again. When Wendy opens her car door, Jim steps in and gives her a slow, gentle, extremely sensual kiss goodnight. They break apart and he holds the door for her, then closes it, gets into his car, and drives to his hotel.

Wendy drives home and considers all that happened this evening. Jim's perceptiveness about her frightens her, yet at the same time, it is strangely comforting. His kiss caused feelings and sensations within her she has suppressed for so long she wondered if they would ever return. She also quickly realizes there are solid reasons for her not to trust anyone, and frankly it would be easier for her to keep things that way. At this point, she's frustrated. She knows that, in all reality, she longs for the type of companionship Jim described over dinner. His incredible kiss brought all that to light for her tonight, and she has no idea what she intends to do about it.

CHAPTER 11

RESULTS

At first the initial request results were disappointing given the theory Lindsay had formed based on what she'd stumbled upon, but now things were beginning to offer more credibility to her hypothesis. The Freedom of Information Act (FOIA) requests sent to the McCall Police Department, the San Francisco Police Department, and the Los Angeles Police Department all returned with no results. However, Oceanside Police Department listed Wendy Stevens as an "other" in the overdose death of Harder Gould, and the San Diego Police Department listed Wendy as an "other" in the Arnold Davis Suicide, as well as Kenneth Quan's accidental death by drowning. San Diego also had her as a "reporting party" in the suicide of Gayle Baxter. The request sent to the Federal Bureau of Investigation was declined, citing an on-going, open investigation.

Lindsay snickers, knowing she'll be able to get her FBI boyfriend Steve Davis to slowly tell her what she needs without having to worry about being denied information due to the pending investigation. Lindsay decides to pursue her plan with Steve tonight, then quickly sends requests for copies of all police reports listing Wendy Stevens from the appropriate agencies.

That done, Lindsay telephones Steve at his office and waits impatiently for him to pick up.

"Davis," he says when he finally comes onto the line.

"Hi, baby. Instead of going out for dinner tonight, how about you just come by my place for a home cooked meal and some quality entertainment?" Lindsay says, letting the end of the question dangle in temptation.

Steve stammers on the other end for a moment, then regains his composure. "That sounds fantastic. What should I bring?"

"How about your handcuffs?" she purrs.

"I can definitely do that. In fact, it would be my pleasure."

"Yes, sir, it most certainly will be!"

"What's for dinner?" he asks with a smile.

"You are, my love."

"Stop it," he growls. "I'm at work, and you're making it very difficult for me to concentrate at this moment."

"Oh, okay, party pooper. We're having chicken cacciatore and a mixed salad."

"And what's for dessert?" he asks quietly, not wanting to ruin Lindsay's fun.

She giggles. "Well, I have a few things in mind that might involve chocolate sauce and whipped cream, but you wouldn't be interested in hearing about that at work now would you?"

He grunts. "You're not playing fair at all."

"As a matter of fact, I'm not playing at all. I'm as serious as a judge. I love you. I have to go. See you at six o'clock, and don't you dare be late or my mood might change, and not for the better."

Before Steve can respond he hears a click on the other end and realizes she just hung-up on him. Steve looks at his phone, grinning, and thinks, *Nice talking to you, too.* Then he resumes his work.

When he looks at his watch again, he realizes it's time to finish up what he is working on and head to Lindsay's. His mind begins to replay their earlier conversation and his anticipation starts to build. The more he allows his mind to wander the more his excitement mounts. When he arrives at Lindsay's Euclid Street apartment and is buzzed into the building, he calms his nerves by telling himself he has probably blown this whole conversation out of proportion. He makes his way up the stairs and knocks on the door to her apartment.

"It's unlocked!" he hears her yell from inside. "Come in!"

He enters and wonders if her mood has shifted, since she didn't come to greet him, but that thought is immediately erased when he walks into the kitchen to find Lindsay in a black, see-through corset, thong, and high heels. She smiles at his approving stare.

"Dinner is almost ready, so why don't you take off your jacket and tie, grab a beer from the fridge, and put some dressing on the salad and toss it please."

As he puts the finishing touch on the mixed salad, he watches with delight as she bends over in front of him, giving him a magnificent view of her ass while she retrieves the cacciatore from the stove and moves it to the counter.

When all the food is officially ready, Lindsay picks up her glass of wine. "Here's to a wonderful dinner and an exciting evening."

"Now that is quite the toast."

"Shall we move everything to the dining room?"

"Are you really going to have me watch you eat in that?"

"Yes," she replies with a sly smile. "Why? Do you have a problem with my dinner attire?"

"Not at all. It's just quite distracting."

"It's to make sure you save enough room for dessert. That's all."

"You won't have to worry about my appetite. You know how I love dessert."

She presses her lips to his for a moment. "I'm counting on it," she says, then starts moving things to the dining room.

She dishes up dinner and, as they begin eating, she asks, "How was your day today?"

Steve explains. "It was business as usual. Just paperwork and nothing extraordinary. How was yours?"

"Well, I had a rather perplexing day today," Lindsay says, taking a casual bite of her chicken.

"Why is that?"

She pauses. "Remember I came up with a theory after having lunch with my mom and Kimberly Taylor a few weeks back? I've been doing some investigating on my own. Kimberly mentioned that the counselor she had during her divorce from Jack was Wendy Stevens. It turns out she is the same counselor for a couple of other friends of my mom's, and it seems that all of them have spouses who have died recently. Two committed suicide, like Jack, and one had a heart attack."

"Really. Go on?" he asks, putting down his fork.

She narrows her eyes. "You're awfully intrigued. What do you know that you're not telling me?"

"You know I can't talk about my work, babe," Steve chides.

"There is something here, then? I knew it."

He sighs. "I didn't say there is or isn't anything going on. I just wanted you to finish your story. That's all."

"Well, in that case, I was just saying I thought it was kind of a weird coincidence that this same counselor has had multiple former clients' spouses die recently. I wonder what kind of counseling practice she has."

"Domestic violence," Steve says before he can stop himself. He barely refrains from slapping himself on the forehead.

Lindsay gasps. "How do you know? Is she under FBI investigation?"

Steve thinks, *Shit, I was hoping she wouldn't catch that slip up. How do I handle this dilemma?*

He clears his throat and takes a sip of his beer while he thinks about how to divert her attention. "No," he says after a moment, "she isn't. I just know that because she's Mark Stevens' sister."

"You mean the billionaire that was murdered in Idaho?"

"Yep, that's the one."

"Wow. Did she inherit any of his money? Never mind, I know you can't answer that. Forget I even asked. Anyway, I sent FOIA requests to several police departments and her name came up in three other death investigations in southern California just in this past year, and that's besides the three I found out about from lunch with Mom. Isn't that a bit weird?"

"Not really, Lindsay. Her clientele doesn't have very stable partners or they wouldn't be in the situation where they need a domestic violence counselor's help to begin with."

"I see your point, but I don't know if I agree. There are lots of domestic violence counselors who don't have the spouses of their clients dying left and right," Lindsay says, sipping her wine.

"Then continue your investigation, and if you come up with something let's talk about what you find."

"What are you not telling me, Steve?" Lindsay asks, pouting a little.

"All I'm saying is that I'm interested in what you're doing, and I'm curious about what you find out. That's all," he replies carefully.

"So you think I should continue to probe?"

"Given your curious nature, I think you should research until that conspiracy theory of yours is either confirmed or satisfactorily put to rest."

She snorts. "Uh huh."

After they finish dinner, Lindsay decides to do the dishes. Steve makes a grunt of playful annoyance, and Lindsay enjoys teasing him in the way she bends over to load the dishwasher or put food away. She also hands him another beer from the bottom shelf of the refrigerator. By the time she's finished putting on her show under the guise of cleaning up, Steven can't take it any longer.

He sweeps her feet out from under her, leaving a stiletto behind, and carries her into the bedroom. Laying her on the bed, he begins passionately kissing her neck and mouth. He pulls the corset down, exposing her breasts, and attacks them with his mouth and tongue. Lindsay squirms under his relentless assault. Panting, she tries to wiggle away from him and gain control of the situation, but he's having none of that because she has teased him for so long tonight. When she tries to sit up, Steve takes the opportunity to push her back on the mattress and drive his head between her legs. With one swift tug, Lindsay feels and hears the thong rip, and the garment comes away from her.

She jerks as she feels his tongue on her body, and the pleasure it produces is too much for her to resist, so she submits and moved her hips in time with his mouth. As her breathing becomes shallow and rapid, Steve instinctively knows she's nearing her release. He quickly inserts his middle finger, finds her g-spot, and strokes rapidly as his tongue flicks her clitoris. Lindsay feels the first warm wave of her release and lets go. She cries out, repeating Steve's name over and over, then suddenly her legs begin quivering as she reaches the pinnacle of her orgasm. Finally, she can take no more. She pushes his head away from her and squirms away from his magnificent tongue, curling into the fetal position and demanding he give her a second to recover.

As her sense of awareness returns and her panting subsides, she takes control again.

"Go get me your handcuffs," she orders, and when he returns with them, she cuffs both of his wrists in front of his body. She double locks them to prevent them from tightening, then pushes him onto his back on the bed.

"Now it's my turn to drive you crazy," she says, grabbing the belt from her terry cloth bathrobe and tying Steve's hands above his head, securing them to the headboard. Next, she straightens the corset and refastens the snaps. She begins a slow strip tease, exposing one breast, then covering it, and doing the same with the other. She continues to dance seductively, then she climbs onto the bed and straddles Steve, facing away from him and allowing her vagina to come within inches of his face but not close enough for him to touch her.

Then, leaning forward, she takes him into her mouth, bobbing her head rapidly up and down. She continues her onslaught until she senses Steve is getting close to his release, and then stops.

Steve groans, begging her for release, but Lindsay gets off the bed and slowly removes her clothing, exposing her naked body to his view. She climbs on top of him, straddling his hips, and slides his penis along the outside of her labia.

Seeing the tortured look on his face, she says, "What do you know about Wendy Stevens that you're not telling me?"

Groaning, Steve shakes his head and begins pleading with her.

Lindsay smiles and slides the entire length of him into her, then rocks forward and back.

Steve's breathing intensifies, and she raises her hips and allows him to slide out of her.

"Please, Lindsay, don't stop," Steve gasps, looking up at her.

"All you have to do is tell me what you're hiding, or else I'll leave you here to cool off."

"And if I tell you?"

She smiles seductively. "I will make your every dream come true. The choice is yours."

He groans. "Fine. She had dinner at the Bistro with the guy who died of botulism. We checked everything out and it was all just a terrible tragedy, apparently. That's all I've got, but you can't write anything about that or my career is ruined."

Lindsay slides him into her again and begins rocking back and forth with tremendous fervor. As she senses Steve reaching his release, she explodes into an orgasm in conjunction with his. She falls forward onto his chest and they relax into the spasms of their passionate lovemaking.

After their breathing returns to normal and the spasms cease, Lindsay unties Steve and they both lay in each other's arms, drifting off into sublime slumber until the alarm goes off the next morning.

Steve, concerned about what he revealed last night, snuggles close to Lindsay.

"Baby, you know the information you so expertly extracted from me in the throes of passion is confidential and it needs to remain that way, right?" he asks quietly.

She gives him a sly smile, cocks her head to the side, and assures him. "I would never, ever reveal my source or the circumstances under which that information was revealed."

He isn't amused, and sighs. "Please, promise me you won't use that information in any reporting that you do concerning Wendy. You know they'd trace it back to me."

"Babe, don't worry. Now that I know what I'm looking for, I'll verify it with other sources. If I can't, I promise to keep it confidential. I love you, and I would never compromise your career to advance mine."

"Thank you. Now I've got to run to my place, take a quick shower, and change my clothes. See you later?"

She simply nods. He kisses her goodbye and rushes off to start his day, assured his lack of will power will remain between the two of them.

***

Several weeks pass before the police reports arrive. Lindsay devotes significant time reading and analyzing the interviews, then proceeds to request the files devoted to the autopsy reports for Harder Gould, Arnold Davis, Gayle Baxter, Zach Rawlins, and Kenneth Quan, with the San Diego Medical Examiner's office.

She receives the redacted reports several weeks later, and as she analyzes each report carefully, she is perplexed that nothing in any report identifies anything suspicious. The overdose of Harder Gould falls in line with other fentanyl-laced-heroin overdoses in San Diego County. Arnold Davis' findings, based on blood spatter analysis of his hands and body, are consistent with a self-inflicted wound. There are no defensive wounds or indications of any type of struggle in Gayle Baxter's hanging, and the ligature marks and fiber analysis indicate they were produced by the rope she herself had to have placed around her neck.

Lindsay sighs, becoming more frustrated and convinced that something is wrong as she continues through them.

Zach Rawlins' death results clearly indicates high levels of cocaine and a moderate amount of alcohol from toxicology, along with significant damage to his heart indicating the cause of death to be substance induced heart attack with nothing else abnormal. Kenneth Quan's cause of death was drowning. The water in his lungs matched the water in the pool, and there were no indications of any type of struggle or altercation found on his body.

Lindsay considers for a moment that she may just be wrong and, while all these deaths are tragic, there is no correlation to Wendy Stevens other than her counseling connection.

She shakes her head, the same thought running through it that has from the beginning. *What kind of domestic violence counselor experiences so much death in less than a year's time frame?*

She decides to do research on other domestic violence counselors' track records and interview some about their reactions to a hypothetical situation based upon her recent findings.

Lindsay quickly learns that research on offender suicide rates in a domestic violence relationship is virtually non-existent. The general industry perception is that approximately half of all deaths associated with a domestic violence situation are homicides.

However, since most threats of suicide from offenders are considered to be a form of aggression with the purpose to manipulate the victims, little research has been conducted, and as such bars any evidence to the contrary.

Lacking decent statistics, Lindsay is disturbed by the generalization that fifty percent of deaths within domestic violence relationships are homicides.

What role, if any, did the victims or their counselor play in the deaths of their partners? she wonders and dives deeper.

Lindsay finds that each of the victims in the cases she is concerned with had strong alibis, clearing them from any involvement in their partner's death. Tina Gould was at work; Nancy Davis was in the hospital; Jim Baxter was travelling between San

Diego and Los Angeles; Jill Rawlins was staying in a hotel; and Mike Prichard was in Los Angeles. The only disturbing connections are through Wendy Stevens, who had dinner with Ricardo Montes before he contracted botulism, found Gayle Baxter's body, was the last known person to see Harder Gould alive, and paid for Jill Rawlins' hotel room. Hardly evidence strong enough to have her arrested.

Lindsay decides she is going to try and interview Wendy, and see if she can make Wendy reveal anything suspicious. She locates and dials Wendy's office number. When Mona answers Lindsay identifies herself.

"Hello, Mona. My name is Lindsay Parker. I was hoping to make an appointment with Wendy Stevens sometime in the near future," Lindsay says pleasantly.

"Okay, Ms. Parker. What is the reason for the appointment?"

Lindsay represses a sigh. "I'm a reporter and I was hoping to get some information from her about the excess of deaths we've had in the area," she says, thinking, *Shit. I blew that I should have just called as an individual and paid for her time.*

Mona is silent, wondering how to handle this, and Lindsay recovers. "I'm investigating the connection between Wendy and the deaths of several of her client's spouses."

Mona makes a strangled sound. "Excuse me, Ms. Parker, while I speak with Ms. Stevens for a moment."

Mona walks briskly into Wendy's office, explains the gist of the conversation with Lindsay, and asks what to do.

Wendy smiles. "Just tell her she'll need to purchase my time for an interview. It's payable in advance and I charge two hundred and fifty dollars an hour. Otherwise, perhaps her time would be better spent speaking with the detectives who investigated each case. Thank you, Mona."

Mona chuckles and returns to the phone to relay the message to Lindsay.

It catches her off guard. "That's fine. I just need to get authorization for the expenditure before I can set the appointment."

"Of course. I understand. I'll wait to hear back from you. Have a nice day," Mona replies, and sets the phone back in its cradle.

***

When Lindsay approaches her production manager for authorization to spend two hundred and fifty dollars to interview Wendy Stevens, she is laughed at and the request is denied.

"We don't pay to interview people," he scoffs, "find another way to get the information you're hoping to dig up. Lindsay, you need a lot more than a hunch to get me to authorize money for an interview, and what you have doesn't amount to anything, especially with the results of the law enforcement investigations already conducted."

Lindsay frowns. "There's something here, though. I know it. If I could just interview her once—"

"I like your spunk, kid, but I'm not paying that kind of money for a single interview when it's not based on cold, hard facts. End of discussion."

Irritated, Lindsay begins to doubt her reporter's nose again. She heads home to do some more research and see if she can find anything more promising to try to get the money for the interview.

CHAPTER 12

MOUNTING TENSIONS

Bonnie telephones Wendy's cell phone and she answers, "Bonnie, what a pleasant surprise. Are you coming to San Diego?"

"No, but you're coming to Marin County this weekend."

Wendy pauses, surprised. "I don't think I have a trip planned up north for this weekend."

"That's probably true, but I need to call a special board meeting. There are some mounting tensions between SERF and Mother Earth Cooperative, and everyone needs to be informed of certain events. I'll have the company jet pick you up tomorrow morning. What time works best for you?"

Wendy snorts. "What if I had a date or something? This is really short notice."

"Oh please, dear, I know better than that," Bonnie scoffs, then stops. "Wait, do you really have a date?"

"No," Wendy replies, half-embarrassed, "but what if I did?"

"Well, since you don't, this discussion is irrelevant. What time can you be at the airport tomorrow? We'll have a quick board meeting Sunday morning and you can return to San Diego the same day."

"Jeez, woman on a mission today. Fine. Let's say eleven o'clock, and I have a client in San Francisco that I'll try and schedule an appointment with while I'm there, so if I could fly back around nine Sunday evening that would great."

"Done. My pilot will be in San Diego at eleven, and I'll meet at the airport when you get here."

Wendy represses a sigh. "Terrific. I guess I'll need to borrow your car for my appointment Sunday."

"Of course."

As soon as they hang up, Wendy telephones Jim and is pleased to hear his voice on the line.

"Well, this is a pleasant surprise," he answers smoothly.

"I'm going to be in Sausalito Saturday and Sunday, and I thought it would be nice if I offered to buy you a late lunch Sunday, if you're interested."

"Absolutely I am. When and where do you want me to pick you up?"

"I don't. I'm staying with Bonnie because there's a board meeting Sunday morning. I told her I needed to borrow her car to visit a client Sunday afternoon before flying out at nine o'clock that evening. But I also didn't want to miss an opportunity to return the favor of a meal."

"I'm glad you thought of me. But since it's such a short timeframe, why don't you let me make you lunch or dinner at my place? As long as you don't mind the fact I'm still unpacking."

She doesn't answer for a few moments and he adds, "I'm an awesome chef."

She sighs. "Well, in that case, I'll look forward to that treat. I'll see you around three then if that works?"

"I'll make it work."

Wendy gets his address and they hang up. She does a little fist pump and starts to get an overnight bag put together. As she's packing, she decides to take some nice business clothes under the guise of meeting her client, but secretly knows she hopes to please Jim with her appearance. She knows she'll travel in jeans and a t-shirt, like she always does, but packs a black linen pantsuit from Beauty Boutique Clothing and a purple silk blouse. She also selects a lacey, purple, matching bra and panty set, just in case things go well with Jim on Sunday.

At the last minute she remembers her curling iron and make up bag. She shakes her head, thinking, *Trips were so much easier when I wasn't concerned about my appearance. Now I have to pack all this crap in order to try and make a favorable impression on some guy.* She bites her lip. *Well… a really, really hot guy. But still. Ridiculous.*

She arrives at the airport, meets the pilot at eleven, and has a pleasant trip to San Francisco.

When Bonnie sees her, she just snickers, having known Wendy would be wearing jeans and looking like she was late for an early morning college class.

Wendy notices Bonnie's disapproving once over. "Don't even start with me. You're lucky I made it on such short notice."

"Yeah, because you had so many other pressing dates!"

"You can be such a judgmental bitch," Wendy says, laughing and giving Bonnie a huge hug.

"I love you, too. It's so good to see you, even if it's a short trip."

"You know I'd be here for you, even if I had to move heaven and earth just to get here."

Bonnie smiles and they link arms to walk to the car. "Do you want to stop for lunch or just head to the house?"

"Let's head to the house. I'm not really hungry and a snack and wine by the pool seems like a winner for me today."

"Sounds like a great idea. I've been so busy lately I haven't taken time out for myself."

"Well, then as your counselor I insist you take a mental health day today."

"I guess I have to because the doctor ordered it!" Bonnie says and they giggle.

After they arrive at Bonnie's home and get situated by the pool with their wine, Bonnie gets a call from Skip Duran. Wendy watches Bonnie's expression go from relaxed and upbeat to stern and cold.

It is a look reminiscent of the one she saw on Mark's face that horrible night so long ago, and it sends shivers down her spine, making the tiny hairs on the back of her neck stand on end. The tone of Bonnie's voice is void of emotion and somber, and Wendy knows what she is being told isn't pleasant. After a few moments of conversation, Wendy sees a single tear drip down Bonnie's cheek and fall to the patio.

As soon as Bonnie hangs up the phone, Wendy asks, "What in the hell just happened?"

"Skip called to tell me he just received a very disturbing call from Hector Sosa. He received an anonymous call at his office, on his cell phone, from an unidentified number, and the caller demanded that SERF quit stealing MEC's large donor base or individuals on our board would wind up like Mark Stevens. Then the caller hung up. Hector has his staff tightening security for him and suggests each of us do the same, especially given the board meeting he is missing but calling in to tomorrow. I knew tensions were mounting because Jim has done an incredible job and has already secured over twenty-two million dollars in donations in the first ninety days of working for SERF. I didn't expect things to get this bad this quickly though."

"Yes, it's very extreme. Are you serious about the twenty-two million?"

"I most certainly am! Jim has been all over our top fifty targeted donors like a rat on a Cheeto and has secured all the checks for at least that much."

"So what you're telling me is that Jim has earned a bonus of one million dollars in the first ninety days of his employment with SERF?"

"Actually, he's earned more, but all the checks haven't cleared the bank, so he won't get paid his full bonus until the funds are verified and received," Bonnie says, watching Wendy carefully as she reacts to the news.

"Holy crap! That's a hell of a bonus. Maybe we should take a closer look at his contract."

"Absolutely not! I want him earning those kinds of bonuses, because look at the financial strength he has brought to SERF in the first quarter. I'll gladly pay him a million-dollar bonus for every twenty million he puts into SERF's bank accounts. I'm telling you, he is an absolute stud when it comes to raising money."

Wendy ponders Bonnie's statement. *I hope he is as much of a stud in other areas of his life as well,* she thinks, then says, "Alright. Good point."

"But now I'm concerned about everyone's safety, especially Jim's."

"Does this mean MEC has admitted some culpability in Mark's death?" Wendy asks, realization dawning on her.

"It's seems that way to me," Bonnie replies quietly. "Skip did call the FBI here in San Francisco regarding this threat, and I believe they are having one of their agents in Brazil see if they can get better information from Hector."

"What type of precautions should we take?"

"I don't know. Skip is seeing if he can get any guidance from David Hill here in San Francisco so we'll have some information to go on tomorrow."

Wendy sighs. "Well, I guess we should have some concern, but also treat it as just a single isolated threat at this point. I know I'm not going to let one crazy phone call change my lifestyle, and you shouldn't either unless there is something more substantial and tangible to work with."

Bonnie shrugs. "I suppose you're right."

They decide to not let Skip's call ruin their day. Wendy asks for an update on Sean and Jessica and is pleased to hear they are doing extremely well, not only as a couple, but also because Beauty Boutique Clothing is exceeding all expectations both nationally and internationally due to the expansion and increased production in Brazil.

"So how are things in your world, Wendy?" Bonnie asks, sipping her fourth glass of wine.

"I've been really busy and, frankly, getting a little tired of all the drama. It seems my clients are experiencing much more violent behaviors, and spouses seem to be more manipulative these days. I'm not sure if this is truly the case or if I'm getting close to burnt out, but lately I've been considering retiring and taking some time to travel and just enjoy life. Maybe I'll set up a counseling foundation and let others do the heavy lifting. All I know is I'm way too young to feel this ancient, and I believe it's time to let my hair down and enjoy life and my new found wealth."

Bonnie gives her a look. "That all sounds terrific on the surface, but can you really stop counseling and focus on yourself without losing your mind?"

"Well, I'd hope so."

"What about dating? When was the last time you actually went out on a date?"

"Funny you should ask. I actually had a date last week," Wendy replies, sitting up straighter in her lounge chair.

"Really? Do tell. Who is this mystery date?"

"It was nothing serious, just dinner. I'm not really sure we'll continue dating, but if we do you'll be the first person I tell about it. I'm just not ready to say anything more at this time."

Bonnie grunts. "You know I hate it when you're so vague about things."

"I know, but we've only had dinner once. I don't know if it will progress any farther. If it does, I'll share all the details you want to know."

Temporarily placated, Bonnie moves on to other topics, and the two women enjoy a relaxing evening.

The next morning, Bonnie is stunned to see Wendy dressed up with make-up on and her hair done.

"You look absolutely stunning today, and I love what you did with your eyes! Very alluring. Are you sure you're meeting with a client? Because it looks to me like you're going on a date."

Wendy smiles. "Please, I'm meeting a fairly new client and I want to make a good impression."

"Well, looking like that I'm sure you will," Bonnie says as they get into the car.

They arrive at the SERF offices before the others. The caterers bring in brunch and champagne for mimosas. Skip Duran is the next to arrive followed shortly by Sean and Jessica, and David Hill.

When everyone had been fed and has settled into the board room, Hector is reached via telephone and placed on speaker phone. After greetings, Bonnie turns the meeting over to SAC Hill.

David begins. "As courtesy and perhaps extra security, I suggest we also bring SAC Dominic Hughes, and agents Jay Mather and Steve Davis from my office, as well as SAC Bob Grinstead, from the San Diego FBI field office, and Jim Bush onto the line."

Everyone agrees, and the connections are made. Once everyone is on the line, David begins summarizing the threat Hector received.

"Apparently, the call was made from a pay phone in Sao Paulo and no further information can be retrieved at this point. Given the circumstances of not knowing who the caller is, and their very specific reference to Mark's murder, we believe some steps must be taken to insure your personal safety—"

Wendy interjects. "Specifically, what type of steps is the FBI considering?"

"We would like to place phone and wire taps on all of your phones for the next couple of months, including cell, home, and office," replies David Hill.

Wendy shakes her head. "I'm sorry, but absolutely not! I cannot have confidential conversations with clients recorded. I have no issue with the phone taps being place on all phones, so in the event I get a threat we can isolate the number, but I will not agree to a wire-tap. It's unethical, at least at my office."

Sean, Hector, Jessica, Bonnie, and Jim all reject the idea of voluntary wire taps as well, feeling it is too much of an intrusion into their lives and business affairs.

David Hill responds to their concerns. "We all can appreciate your particular predicaments given the confidentiality issues involved. This was merely a suggestion, and a dramatic one, at that."

"Thank you all for your understanding," Bonnie says, addressing all the FBI men.

"Of course," Hill answers for them. "We also suggest that each of your homes and office locations be analyzed by an FBI agent from a security perspective, in order to ensure maximum security with minimal interruptions to your daily lives."

Jim asks, "So am I to assume the FBI is considering this threat to have merit and it in some way has been deemed to be credible?"

"Mr. Bush, given how specific the threat was, the training Jesus Rodriguez, who came forward admitting to being Mark's killer, had and his connection to MEC, and this organization's systematic dismantling of the established donor base of MEC, I think we would all be foolish to not consider the threat to have validity."

"Agent Hill, there is a limited pool of donors for what we do, so of course we're all playing in the same pool. I, for one, am not going to apologize or be intimidated because my track record is better than the others," replies Jim.

"Please don't take my comment as a judgment or even a criticism of your operations in any manner whatsoever. It's just a reality that SERF has upset those associated with MEC and, given Mark's murder, until we determine who is really behind this threat, caution on all our parts is strongly advised. Let me explain how the FBI would like to proceed. Hector, agents from our field office in Brazil have already been in contact with you, and on Monday they will get your phone traps established and your personal premises inspected for the possible need of additional security procedures. Here in San Francisco, Agent Steve Davis will check on SMG, Beauty Boutique Clothing, and the SERF offices, and then will inspect each of your homes, which we believe should include Skip's and Jim's. Phone traps will be established with your permission, and if anyone receives a threatening call they must notify my office within 24 hours of receiving it, so we a can trap the call and begin investigating its source. Wendy, SAC Bob Grinstead in San Diego will arrange with you to inspect your office Monday, and then make the appropriate recommendations for your office and home. Any questions?"

He looks around the room, giving everyone plenty of time to digest and consider the implications of what now has to happen.

"Okay. Since there are no additional concerns, we'll leave you to conclude your board meeting. Thank you all for allowing us the time to address you with these concerns, and thank you in advance for your continued cooperation."

After all the FBI agents hang up and SAC Hill leaves the building, Bonnie has Jim hang up as well. She then turns the first item of business over to Skip Duran.

"Well, the main thing we have to talk about today is Jim's first quarter bonus," Skip begins, and after a brief presentation of the funds received, Skip points out that any bonus exceeding a quarter of a million dollars needs board approval.

"Very well," Bonnie says, "I make a motion to approve the payment to Jim. All those in favor?"

Sean seconds the motion to approve, followed by a unanimous vote and Skip's release from the meeting.

"Our next order of business is the donor problem we seem to be having. Given the threat received, I'd like to take a vote on whether or not to continue pursuing the MEC top fifty donors, as it seems to put us all at risk," Bonnie begins.

After a fairly lengthy discussion, it is decided that SERF will continue its current strategy and reevaluate if any further threats are received. With that, the board meeting is concluded.

CHAPTER 13

THE SEDUCTION

Wendy arrives at Jim's promptly at three. When he sees her walking down the walkway, he calls out the kitchen window, "The door is unlocked, just come on in!"

Wendy finds him busy in the gourmet kitchen of the guest cottage he's rented on a magnificent estate in Sausalito.

The smells emanating from his endeavors are mesmerizing, a combination of garlic, spices, and his amazing cologne.

Briefly, he turns from his labors and hands Wendy his glass of Hanzell Vineyards Chardonnay for her to taste.

Wendy takes a sip and is amazed. "This is fantastic. Where is it from?" she asks.

Jim explains. "It's a small Sonoma County vineyard known for award winning chardonnays and pinot noirs."

Next, Jim places a plate of shrimp and avocado stuffed portabella mushrooms, broiled and encrusted with imported Romano cheese, in front of Wendy for her tasting pleasure.

She selects one, takes a bite, and says, "If this is a foretaste of what's to come, this dining experience will be absolutely orgasmic."

Jim smiles. "I'm glad you enjoy the food, and that's an interesting choice of words." He pours another glass of wine, allowing her to keep the one he handed her when she came in.

"Well, you didn't mislead me. You're a fantastic cook."

He grins at her and returns to the stove. Wendy gets up from the barstool she is sitting on and walks around the counter into the kitchen. When Jim turns away from what he is preparing, Wendy puts both arms around his neck and kisses him, slowly and sensually at first, then intensifies her kiss until they are standing in the middle of his kitchen locked in a passionate exchange.

Finally, Jim breaks away, his breathing heavy. "Remind me to cook for you more often!"

"Only if you agree to continue wearing that sexy cologne of yours."

"Consider it done. Now get out of my kitchen and behave, so I can finish our meal. After dinner I'd be delighted to resume where we just left off."

"Oh, you would? Perhaps this was just fleeting moment and you blew it," Wendy teases him, returning to her barstool and wine.

"I certainly hope that's not the case. But I promised you a great meal and that's what I intend to deliver."

Wendy watches him for a while, moving surely around his kitchen. "Do you excel at everything you do?" she asks.

"What do you mean?"

"You just received a million-dollar bonus in the first ninety days of employment, you are a terrific cook, you're charming, you're a wonderful kisser… What don't you do well?"

He chuckles. "Well, I don't dance, but other than that, if I'm not good at something I'll work at it until I become good at it. Unless, of course, it's something I don't really care about. Why?"

"I was just wondering, that's all."

Jim gives her a look, then checks on his dinner and finishes the salad preparations. He looks at Wendy over his shoulder. "Do you like anchovies on your Caesar salad or not?"

"Not particularly."

"Good, because I hate them and I was hoping you'd say that."

She smiles. "Well, if you hate them, why did you ask instead of making it the way you like it?"

"Because if you like them I would have made the salad with them and suffered through it for you," he replies with a grin.

"That's ridiculous. Don't ever do something you hate just to satisfy my desires. I can compromise, and if it's something I won't compromise on then we both will have to discuss the issue and make our own decisions."

Puzzled about how anchovies could be taken so seriously, he tosses the salad. "Fair enough," he says finally, "I'll remember that. Tell me why you keep everyone at a distance."

"Wow. This just escalated quickly," Wendy says, avoiding and drinking more wine.

"Hey, you started it with the anchovy thing," Jim replies.

He pulls some type of fish out of the oven and places it on a plate with risotto and fresh Caesar salad, then tops off Wendy's glass of wine.

They both move to sit at the dining table, and Jim says, "I hope you like it. It's crab stuffed halibut with fresh morel mushrooms."

Wendy takes a bite and moans, letting Jim know he was successful. They enjoy some light dinner conversation before Jim hits her with the same question she coyly avoided earlier.

"So why do you keep everyone at a distance?"

Wendy adjusts herself uncomfortably in her seat and tries to skirt the subject, but Jim isn't having it.

Cutting her off in the middle of an excuse, he says, "I'm serious, Wendy. I really want to get to know you, but I'm not going to play this game with you of having to figure you out all the time. Either you and I are going to begin trusting each other or we can agree right now to be just business associates. After that kiss in the kitchen I certainly hope you'll trust me enough to give me a little glimpse of who the real Wendy Stevens is. Let's start by you telling me your hopes, fears, and desires."

He takes another bite of his dinner and watches her as she watches him.

Finally, she sighs. "You're not going to let this go are you?"

"Nope."

"Then I guess I need to give you some insight on me. I had a wonderful childhood until eighteen when my brother, Mark, stole my dad's company through a hostile take-over and kicked him completely out of the company he built. Dad committed suicide a year later and Mark became the provider for my mom and me. At age nineteen, Mark and I had an incredible falling out and I never spoke to him again."

"What was the falling out all about?"

"That's something I'm not ready to share with you yet," Wendy replies flatly.

He gauges her reaction, then nods. "Fair enough. Please continue."

She shakes her head. "I don't know how I feel about this, Jim. I haven't had a man insist I open up to them emotionally in ages, so it's been easy to keep them at a distance. I'm extremely attracted to you intellectually and physically. But your insistence that I need to be vulnerable with you scares the shit out of me."

"I can appreciate that, but how else am I going to get to know you?"

"Oh, I understand your reasons. It just scares me because when you open up to someone you also give them the ammunition to hurt you. I have been successful in avoiding that land mine for a long time."

"Is that what you think? That I'm going to use the information you share with me to hurt you?" he asks, almost incredulous.

"No, of course not. At least, not intentionally. It's just that, when you really know someone well, you know the buttons to push to get a reaction from them."

"True, but they also know how to support you when you are scared, threatened, or even weary. They can help you deal with certain situations and can provide the encouragement necessary to keep going. Is this why you never married and have avoided serious relationships? Fear of being hurt by someone you care about or even love?"

She gazes at him for a long moment. "I need you to ask me a different question."

He represses a laugh. "Okay. How is dinner?"

"Thank you for not pushing," she says quietly. "It's absolutely fantastic."

"You're welcome. For dessert, I've prepared a fresh berry tart with some French vanilla bean ice cream and coffee."

"I am truly impressed with your culinary skills."

"Don't be," he says with a chuckle as he clears their dinner plates. "I bought the tart at a local bakery earlier today."

"You know, you could have claimed you prepared it and I would have believed you after this dinner."

"Perhaps, but that would have been dishonest of me, and if nothing else can be expected of me, total honesty can be."

"That's good to know."

"Let's have dessert on the back deck with our coffee shall we?"

"Let me help you clean up first," Wendy says, heading for the sink.

"No, leave it. I'll get it later. For now, I just want to enjoy the time we have getting to know each other better."

Wendy concedes, and they make their way to the deck. Once they're seated, she asks, "So what do you love besides making millions in quarterly bonuses?"

"That is certainly a highlight for me and this quarter has been outrageous for my career, as well as for Stevens Environmental Restoration Fund. I didn't expect we would achieve such success in this short a time frame, but I suspect things will slow down. My job is to keep a steady stream of donors coming into SERF."

Wendy gets up. "I'm sorry, it's just too bright out here, and I would like some more coffee."

He nods and rises with her, heading back into the living room. Jim gets them both a fresh cup of coffee and they settle on the couch. He hands her coffee and begins to answer her earlier question.

"I love cooking, old rock classics, fine wine, and impressionist abstract art. What about you?"

"I really don't know how to answer that. For so many years my life has been tied up in my work and clients, so my ability to pursue any real passions had been controlled by my budget and I never really developed any of them. I love the sun, water, and the beach. I read a lot and, now that I can, I intend to travel. In fact, recently I've been toying with the idea of scaling back my practice and taking more time for myself. I guess I'm feeling a little burned out recently, which is something I never expected I'd ever be saying because I love what I do and how I help others survive devastating circumstances. Watching them grow and thrive is truly a joy."

"Well, I have to tell you how much I admire what you do. It's certainly something I could never do without wanting to kill some of the people your clients have to get away from."

Wendy chuckles. "I have to admit there are days when that would be much easier."

They both laugh for a moment, then Wendy looks at Jim with a piercing stare that unnerves him a bit but quickly dismisses it when she leans into him and kisses him with an intensity that excites him immediately. He returns the kiss with just as much eagerness, then pauses and looks at his watch.

Wendy quirks her head at him, "What the hell is that all about?"

"I'm sorry, but I needed to make sure if we were going to kiss like that we wouldn't lose track of the time. You still have a plane to catch at nine, right?"

"Yes, but it's only six now."

"I understand. I just didn't want to be the cause of you missing your flight, and if you kiss me like that again, I'm going to lose all track of time and get lost in your embrace."

"Why don't you let me worry about the time and kiss me. Please?"

As he kisses her, she slides into his embrace on the couch and runs her hand through his hair. As their passion for each other's embrace increases, they both decide to lose their inhibitions.

Wendy's hand slips down Jim's chest, over his muscled stomach, and down the front of his slacks. She cups him in her hand and gently begins to massage him. He responds immediately to her gentle touch and begins to unbutton her blouse. As his kisses move from her mouth to her neck, she moans softly and responds by removing her hand from his groin and holding onto his neck. Placing her other hand on the back of his head, she softly applies pressure directing his head to her breasts. Instantly he kisses her chest and, slipping her lacey bra aside, flicks her nipple with his tongue, causing her to cry out with pleasure.

Pulling away, Jim stands and takes her by the hand, leading her into his bedroom. He removes her blouse and takes a moment to admire her tan upper body, enhanced by the purple bra. Wendy removes his shirt, kissing him passionately, then runs her tongue from his neck, over his chest, and down his rippled abs. On her knees, she stops at his pant line and unfastens his belt, pants and zipper. With one fluid movement, she pushes his pants and boxers to the floor as she stands, then kisses him again, exploring his eager mouth with her tongue.

He quickly spins her around and brings his hand up to her breast while simultaneously allowing his other hand to find the button of her pants. He unbuttons them and she hears the zipper slide down.

As his hot breath along her neck ignites a shameless desire that must be quenched within her, she feels her pants slide down her legs. Instinctively, she pushes her hips back against his firm body and as his hand finds her, he slides a finger into her and her legs weaken instantly. She uses his body to support herself as he removes her bra and panties.

Reaching back, she places his penis between her legs, twists an arm around his neck, and pulls his mouth to hers. He slides his penis back and forth between her legs, and the friction on the outside of her labia is almost too much for her, so she turns to face him. He begins to lift her and she helps him. As he catches her, she wraps her legs around his waist, but doesn't have long to wait. Jim's passion has been enflamed and with a single swift thrust he penetrates her, sliding himself completely into her body. Wendy groans with intense pleasure as Jim slowly lays her on the bed without leaving her body or missing a thrust.

As he continues to push into her, Wendy becomes lost in the intense pleasure he is bringing her and thrashes her head from side to side. They both become lost in the moment when suddenly they erupt, reaching the pinnacle of their lovemaking.

Laying there, catching their breath in the afterglow, Wendy decides there is more pleasure to be reached. She rolls Jim onto his back while he is still inside her and begins to rock forward and backward. Within moments, both sense their passion and pleasure mounting once again, and he begins to meet her rocking motions with upward thrusts. Suddenly, he grabs her hips, rocking her in back and forth while applying downward pressure onto himself. This increased friction is more than she can stand and she explodes in another intense orgasm. He quickly rolls her onto her stomach and penetrates her again, this time with his constant and forceful thrusting. Wendy's breathing intensifies again and they each reach another shattering orgasm. He collapses onto her back, and they lay there struggling to catch their breath, gasping through the shockwaves of the aftermath of their lovemaking.

As they each return to themselves, Jim rolls to his side and holds Wendy tenderly in his arms. She snuggles into his chest and, overwhelmed with the emotion of allowing herself to be intimate with him, teardrops fall from her eyes, unobserved by Jim.

After a while her tears dry and they begin to talk. They decide to take a shower together and find more passion under the hot water.

Afterwards, Wendy thanks him. "This was a wonderful evening. Thank you for a wonderful dinner, conversation, and evening entertainment."

He smiles, "The pleasure was all mine."

"No, it certainly wasn't. I found it to be quite pleasurable myself!"

"I think I'll be in San Diego soon. Not this week, but next. Can I call you?" he asks, cupping her cheek.

"I'd be extremely disappointed if you didn't. How long will you be in town?"

"I'll probably come into town Wednesday and leave Friday night."

Wendy looks at her calendar on her phone and realizes she will be at a conference Thursday and was planning on spending the night.

"You should just stay at my place instead of a hotel," she says, handing him her key. "Here, take this. I can use the one I have at the front desk. I'll see you Wednesday, but I have to leave early Thursday. I'll be back around midnight. If you can arrange your schedule to return to San Francisco later Friday evening we'll be able to spend time together Wednesday evening and Friday after your meetings."

Jim kisses her gently. "I'll rearrange my schedule so my meetings will all take place on Wednesday and Thursday to maximize our time together."

With their plans set, Wendy kisses him goodbye. "I'm sorry I didn't help you clean up," she says, and he hushes her and kisses her again.

After a long goodbye, Wendy drives back to Bonnie's.

Bonnie greets her. "How did your appointment go?"

Wendy smiles. "It was an incredible appointment, even better than expected, and very enlightening."

"That's terrific. Have a glass of wine with me in the limousine on the way to the airport. We have plenty of time to get you to the pilot and home by ten."

"I'd like that. I've missed you, and it is so good to see SERF is doing so well. You picked some incredible people to launch this project and it has definitely paid off."

"I know. It's fantastic. How are things going in San Diego after the difficult past few months?" Bonnie asks, pouring the wine.

"You know, it has all just made me think about what I really want in life and accept the fact that I will eventually get burned out. I may need to reevaluate my priorities."

"Well, dear, the things you deal with daily are enough to cause one to burn out. So tell me where are you thinking of travelling?" Bonnie replies, accepting that Wendy could be serious about this.

"I'd like to see Paris, London, Italy, Spain, and, of course, spend some time on the beach in Mexico."

"Paris is beautiful in the spring. Italy is kind of gross and dirty. At least, it was when I was there. Spain is wonderful, but I haven't spent much time in Mexico, so you would have to tell me about it."

"I haven't made any firm decisions at this point, but I think I need a break. It seems my clients are experiencing much more violence then I remember, and the courts seem to be much less help than they have been in the past. It's probably just me, and I suspect I'm just tired of it all. If that is truly the case, I won't be much help to my clients."

"Then why don't you take a short vacation trip? Go to Mexico and see how you feel. Can you get away for two or three weeks?"

"Probably. I'd have to do a little planning to free some time, but that's a pretty good idea. We don't have any more unexpected board meetings coming up do we?" she asks with a smirk.

"Not that I can imagine, but the FBI needs to check everywhere you spend your time for security purposes."

"You know, I'm not too worried about the penthouse, and I'm not sure what I can do with the office and still keep it warm and friendly."

"Listen, sweetheart, I want you to be safe, and if that means inconveniencing a few clients so be it. Your safety is more important! It looks like we're here, and the pilot is ready for you."

"Thanks for the limousine ride, and I'll let you know when I get back to the condo tonight. Thanks for the use of your jet as well."

"Don't be ridiculous. Just call me when you get in and don't forget or I'll call you."

"I got it, Mom."

"I love you, too."

"I'll call you in about two hours. Have a safe ride home."

They give each other a hug, and Wendy boards the jet for the quick flight back to San Diego. When she arrives at her place she gives Bonnie a quick call to let her know she is home safely and she will be in touch after the FBI makes their recommendations tomorrow.

Next, Wendy calls Jim to thank him again for a wonderful evening and confirms his trip to San Diego.

"I'll arrive a week from this Wednesday, and I should be done with my meeting by four o'clock," he says.

Wendy smiles. "In that case, why don't you let me make you dinner Wednesday night? It probably won't be as nice as yours, but I'll do the best I can."

"I would be delighted to have you make me dinner. In fact, I'll spend the next week looking forward to it."

"Well, reserve that delight until after you've consumed my cooking," Wendy says sarcastically.

He chuckles. "I'm sure it will be delicious, and if not I'm sure we can figure out things to keep our minds off of food."

Wendy giggles, playing with her pen like a teenager in love before she realizes what she's doing and stops herself. "I'm sure we can. I'll see you next week."

"I can't wait," Jim replies, and Wendy simply grins as they say good-bye and hangs up.

CHAPTER 14

BURN OUT

Wendy arrives at the office earlier than normal, and Mona is surprised to see her so early after a late flight from San Francisco last night. Wendy explains to Mona about the threats and the pending FBI inspection this morning.

Mona asks, "Are these valid threats or are they more of the same old crap and is the FBI overreacting?"

"I'm not sure how to answer that question at this point. It sounds like the same old stuff, but this time the caller referenced Mark's death and that has everyone a bit on edge," Wendy replies, leafing through messages left for her over the weekend.

"Yeah, but why worry about this office?"

"Probably because I'm on the board of SERF, and we are wooing away MEC's largest donors. Also, I'm Bonnie's sister-in-law so there's more of a connection to her for me."

"But you're just a board member not an employee. And why would they come after Mark's sister?"

"I know. I have the same doubts. I think we're probably in more danger from a spouse of one of our clients than whoever made the threat to Hector Sosa."

"So what are we going to do with the FBI agents today?"

Wendy smiles. "We're going to listen politely and then continue doing whatever the hell we want."

Mona chuckles. "I thought so."

Wendy leaves Mona to get a cup of coffee and head into her office. She begins reviewing the mail from Friday, checks her emails, and listens to her voicemails. As she is finishing responding to her messages, two FBI agents stroll into the front office and present their cards to Mona.

"Hello, gentleman. We've been expecting you. Just a moment." Mona picks up the phone and tells Wendy the G-Men are in the reception area.

Wendy comes out to meet the agents and they introduce themselves as Agent Jack Wessman and Nick Zakarian. She's surprised both agents are in their mid to late thirties, physically fit, nicely tanned, and neither is wearing a wedding ring. She sits with them in the reception area and includes Mona in the conversation.

While neither of the agents appears overly concerned, they quickly point out weaknesses in the office layout from a security perspective.

Wendy nods, acknowledging their point. "But agents, this isn't a government facility. It's a counseling office meant to be welcoming and not a fortress."

Both agents nod in understanding then make their recommendations, which include separating the office and work spaces from the reception area via a wall and bullet proof glass. They suggest a panic button linked to the San Diego Police Department, an intercom at the front door, and the ability to buzz clients into the reception area from a locked door.

Both Wendy and Mona listen politely and then Mona asks, "How much do you anticipate it will cost to make this facility as secure as you suggest it should be?"

Agent Zakarian hesitates. "Well, we're not sure exactly. An estimate would need to be received, but thirty thousand dollars wouldn't be out of the realm of possibilities given the size of the office."

Mona chokes on her coffee and Wendy gives them a small smile. "Well, I appreciate your concern, but I absolutely refuse to live behind bullet proof glass and locked doors. Besides, if someone really wants to kill me after all the security measures are put into place, all they would have to do is wait for me in the parking lot and shoot me or even plant a bomb in the car."

Agent Wessman replies this time. "You are probably right. They could find other ways, and would if they were motivated enough.

However, there is no sense in making it easy or being a sitting duck, like Mark."

With that, Wendy stands. "Gentlemen, my brother was a first class asshole that had no respect for others. He was ruthless. He used individuals for all they were worth then discarded them like garbage when he was done with them. I am not my brother. I'm compassionate and willing to help others however I can. I suspect if anyone has anything to worry about with this threat, it would be Sean Green, who devised and executed many of the plans my brother used. Thank you for your time and expertise, but I'm not changing anything about this office, and if someone walks in and kills me so be it."

The agents stand with her, and Agent Zakarian says, "We don't agree with your decision, but it's yours to make. We would like to inspect your penthouse also."

"Again, thank you for your time, but that won't be necessary because I refuse to live in the manner you'll recommend. So you can go tell SAC Grinstead I appreciate his efforts but I think the FBI is full of shit in their approach to my life."

Wessman presses his lips together. "We'll definitely deliver your message, but perhaps we will be a bit more diplomatic about it."

"Oh, no. I want my message delivered in the same manner I delivered it to you, and if SAC Grinstead has a problem with it he can call me himself. Is that clear enough for you?"

"Very clear. If you insist, we will deliver the precise message you gave us."

"I insist."

"Very well."

"Good day, gentlemen, and thank you for your suggestions and concerns. I'm going back to work now. Is there anything you need to do with the phone traps?"

"No, that's all taken care of at the phone company, but here are the instructions you'll need to follow if you receive a threatening call."

"Thank you again."

As they leave Wendy's office, Wessman turns to Zakarian and asks, "How do you think Grinstead's gonna react to that one?"

"I got the distinct impression Ms. Stevens doesn't care much for the bureau or our suggestions. I think Bob will just let her make her own decisions, but he is going to want everything documented to cover all of our asses."

Mona answers the telephone to discover Lindsay Parker on the other end, wishing to schedule an hour appointment with Wendy this coming Friday at four o'clock. Mona puts her on hold and relays the information to Wendy.

"Of course she does. I wonder what type of conspiracy theory she's dreamt up this time. Tell her absolutely, but I won't speak with her beyond an hour and she needs to pay in advance."

"Okay, but are you sure you want to do this interview? Reporters are all scum, and you know that. Besides they write whatever they want anyway."

"It'll be fine Mona, just book the appointment."

Mona sets the appointment, which surprises Lindsay, because she was expecting Wendy to refuse to meet with her even if she was willing to pay for her time.

"Terrific. Please thank Ms. Stevens for agreeing to meet with me. I look forward to speaking with her Friday."

As soon as Mona hangs up, the telephone rings again. This time it isn't a client, but her eleven-year-old daughter, Melissa, who is crying.

"Mom, this is stupid. I don't want to spend the next two weeks here, and Justin agrees with me," she sobs into the phone.

Mona is able to calm Melissa down, then asks to speak with her nine-year-old son, Justin. Neither of the children is happy to be in Auburn with their dad, and both feel that he is too busy working and not really spending any time with them.

Mona asks to speak with their father.

Tyler comes on the line sounding somewhat annoyed. "Mona, I'm busy, what do you want now?"

"Look Tyler, the kids called me at work wanting to come home because they say you're too busy working and not making any time for them. I just wanted you to know they called me, that's all."

"For Christ's sake, they just got here yesterday. I have a few more shoots scheduled tomorrow and after that I've cleared the entire time so we can do some things. They just need to be patient for the rest of today and tomorrow. Can you help me with this? I'll spend countless hours with them, I promise. I just need a day. I have to get back to work. Melissa, your mom wants to talk with you again."

Mona hears Tyler tell Melissa, "You shouldn't bother your mom at work."

When Melissa comes back on the line Mona calms her down again and asks that she and Justin just give their dad one more day to finish his work.

Melissa begins to protest and Mona interrupts, "Sweetheart, please. He promised he will do a lot of fun stuff with you guys after tomorrow."

Melissa sniffles. "Daddy's got all these creepy pictures around here of kids in clown outfits and stuff. We don't like it."

"Well, honey, your dad is a photographer, and a good one at that. He takes lots of kid's pictures for their families. If their mommy and daddy want them in creepy outfits, your dad has to take their picture. That's how he makes money to live."

"I know that, but these pictures are really weird."

"Why don't you ask your dad about his pictures and have him explain them to you? Maybe if you talk to him about it they won't seem so bad anymore."

"Okay," Melissa sighs. "We'll let him work and ask him about the pictures. If it doesn't get better, can I call you?"

"Honey, you and Justin can call me anytime. You know that. I just want you to have some fun with your dad. He only gets to see you for two weeks in the summer and he is trying to get all his work done so he can spend all his time with you guys. It will get better, I promise."

"Okay. We miss you, Mommy."

"I miss you guys, too, and I love you very much. Have some fun with your dad, because he loves you, too. Call me anytime, okay?"

"Okay, bye."

When Mona hangs up, she puts her head down on the desk. Wendy glances out into the reception area and sees something isn't right. Coming out of her office, she sits in the chair across from Mona and just waits. When Mona lifts her head up it's apparent she has been crying.

"Mona, what's wrong?" Wendy asks, hurrying to get Mona some tissues.

"The usual. Melissa and Justin called. They aren't happy being at their Dad's and they want to come home. I can't do anything about it because of his visitation rights. I just hate hearing them when they are so sad. I know I'm just being overly emotional. God, I hate this shit," she says, blowing her nose.

"Quit being so hard on yourself. Divorce sucks, and yours is still really new. Everyone will adjust with the passage of time. It will all get better, I promise you."

Mona gives a bitter chuckle. "That's the exact advice I just gave my kids."

"See? Great minds think alike. In a day or two everyone will have adjusted. Everything will be fine, you'll see. Why don't you take the rest of the day off and go get some sun on the beach with a good book?"

"No, I'll be fine."

"Let me see the calendar."

Mona shows Wendy the calendar which they kept very light, given she was flying back from San Francisco last night. Jim Baxter is the only appointment left for the day. Wendy grabs the phone, calls him, and reschedules for later in the week, telling him something has come up.

Once off the phone, she looks at Mona. "Get your stuff. We're closing the office, picking up bikinis, and going to the beach bar. Let's get drunk and lay in the sun. After that, I'm going to buy you a great dinner then take you home. I'm paying you for today, we're calling it a mental health day, and then I'll tell you all about my weekend."

"You don't have to do this just because I got a little emotional at my desk."

"I know I don't. But I'm going to because I want to, and frankly I'd rather be drunk on the beach than working in this stuffy office listening to other peoples' problems right now. It's time to let our hair down and have some fun! Now let's go, you're burning daylight."

After grabbing their beach stuff and dinner clothes, they head to the beach and immediately begin enjoying Mai Tai's.

Wendy explains in detail about the threat Hector received and the board meeting.

Mona asks, "Did you get to have dinner with the smoking hot guy that came in the office the other week?" Wendy blushes and Mona laughs. "Oh, boy, there is a story here. Out with it."

Wendy turns her attention to her drink. "We had dinner. That's all."

Mona is emboldened by the alcohol. "Bullshit! I know you too well to be lied to like that. You have never blushed with any casual date before. Oh, my God! You slept with him this weekend, didn't you?"

Wendy sighs, then giggles. "Okay. What I'm going to tell you now must remain absolutely confidential. Not even Jim can know you know about this, promise?"

"I promise."

"I didn't sleep with him," Wendy says, "but we did have incredible sex Sunday evening just before I flew home."

"Wait. Why did you come home if the two of you just had incredible sex? Why didn't you just call me and have me rearrange your schedule so you could spend the night?"

"Well, it's complicated. Neither of us wants anyone at SERF to know we're interested in each other, and even more so now that we are intimate. You're not supposed to know either."

"Why the hell not? You are both adults, and it's not like you're his boss."

"True. I just want it to be on the down low to see how things work out first."

"Did he enjoy the sex as much as you did?"

"I believe so."

"Sounds to me like things are working out pretty well. Neither of you even have kids. There's nothing in the way. What's the big deal?"

"I just want to keep it quiet. If it works out for a while I'll let everyone else know about the fact that we are dating."

"Wait, are you telling me Bonnie doesn't know either?"

"No, she doesn't."

Mona giggles. "Oh, she is going to be so pissed you didn't confide in her, especially after the way the two of you set Jessica and Sean up."

"I know, but I want to have more than two dinner dates before we let the cat out of this burlap sack."

"Well, sweetheart, I hate to say it, but it was more than just two dinner dates, now wasn't it?"

"Perhaps," Wendy replies, shooting Mona a look, "but things are still very new and time has a way of exposing flaws one or both can't live with. So I just want some time to pass to make sure this is a relationship both of us want to stick. Besides, you of all people know I'm not very open with men, and Jim scares me because he is forcing me to open up. That's when people really get hurt."

"Well, you can't go through life expecting every man to be out to hurt you. If you continue that way, you're sabotaging every potential relationship before it begins."

"I know, but I have been devastated by people I loved and it's hard to let myself really trust anyone now. Especially men."

"Believe me, I know men can be a real pain in the ass, but they can be equally supportive, encouraging, exciting, and fun. Just take it one step at a time and don't be afraid to open up to Jim. He seems like a neat guy."

"I think he is awesome. That's what scares me so much about him. I haven't felt this way about any man since I was nineteen. He's smart, extremely successful, good looking, he can cook, and he's great in bed. All the characteristics leading to a broken heart if he gets too close and it doesn't work out. Or maybe he's not who he appears to be on the surface."

"Everything you say about getting hurt could be true, and if it comes to be you'll survive. But what if it isn't true? What if he really is a terrific guy who is crazy about you? If you never let him close enough to hurt you, you'll push him away because you can't or won't trust him enough to become vulnerable with him. I, personally, think that would be the bigger tragedy; losing someone because of not letting him in as opposed to losing someone because they hurt you. Being hurt is the easy part. You get angry, depressed, and then heal. Losing someone and never knowing if they were worth your trust will haunt you the rest of your life. But hey, you're the professional counselor so who am I to give you advice?"

Wendy is quiet for a few moments. "You are a very trusted friend, whom I have let close to me without any second thoughts. You're a very wise woman. Why haven't you gone on to get your counseling degrees? You are really perceptive and you should finish your education and start counseling rather than continue to be an outstanding office manager."

Mona shrugs. "I can't afford to go back to school. I have two kids to care for, clothe, and feed."

"But now is the perfect time. You could be taking classes while they're in school and be home for them when they get out of school," Wendy protests.

"That's all fine and dandy, but there is the issue of the cost of school and books while I still have rent, food, and other child necessities to provide."

"If you had the money would you go back to school and get your Ph.D.?"

"Yes. I would love to."

"Then it's settled. I want you to enroll in classes next semester and I'll pay for everything. I'll maintain your current salary and I'll pay for all your expenses. Now, let's go get ready for dinner. I'm starving." Wendy tosses back the rest of her Mai Tai and starts to stand.

"Wait one frickin' minute! You can't do that."

"Why not? I'm rich."

"Who is going to run your office?"

"That's another issue we need to talk about, actually," Wendy replies, and explains about feeling burnt out. "I need a break. The biggest struggle for me was how to provide for my best employee, and today I figured out how to do just that, so after you get accepted into the University of California San Diego we can start scaling back on our clients. I won't be accepting any new ones, and I'll work on transitioning the current clientele to other counselors. After you get your master's degree we can reopen the office under both of our names, as long as you agree to continue on and finish your doctorate as well."

Mona sits silently, mouth gaping. "Wendy, that means you'll be paying my salary and benefits for almost three years before we reopen the doors again. I can't let you do that. It's a lot of money for nothing."

"First of all, it's not for nothing. It's to properly compensate you for being such an incredible employee, as well as help you get a break so you can provide a better life for your kids. Reopening is because we are good friends, and I'd love to have a partner who is also a great friend. I also need some time away and wanted to make sure I had you taken care of first, so it's also for a good cause. I'm not taking no for an answer. It's settled. Tomorrow I want you to see what you need to do to get enrolled as soon as possible. I'm going to look at places I want to travel in the meantime. Please don't protest, it's a win-win situation for both of us so let's make it happen."

Mona sputters a moment, then starts crying and Wendy just holds her for a while. Finally, when her tears subside, she hugs Wendy fiercely.

"I can't thank you enough. What an awesome gift."

"You deserve it, and you'll need to work hard to get your counseling degrees. Now, can we please get ready for dinner? I know this place has fantastic fresh caught lobster. Tonight is a celebration!"

They get ready and enjoy the rest of the evening dining on lobster and strategizing on the things that need to get accomplished over the next six months. With their plans firmly in place, Wendy takes Mona home and then heads to her penthouse. She decides to call Jim. She tells him about her decision to close her practice for few years and travel a little. Jim seems disappointed at first, thinking Wendy is running away from him, but by the time they end the conversation he recognizes she needs to do this. They make plans to see each other constantly, partly through her visiting and partly through him joining her in some of the travel.

"Thank you for being understanding," Wendy says with a relieved sigh. "This feels really good, and perfect, and just... *right*. I can't wait to see where all of this goes."

"Me either, love. Thanks for including me in your plans. I'll talk to you later," Jim replies, and they say goodnight.

Wendy goes to bed feeling relaxed and refreshed and enjoys the best night's sleep she has had in years.

CHAPTER 15

WATER UNDER THE BRIDGE

Over the next few days, Mona and Wendy are amazed by the way key elements of their plan keep falling into place. Several times, Wendy has pointed out to Mona that this was meant to be.

The two are working out the details of Mona's continued salary and Wendy says, "Well, just keep the corporate operating account open and I'll keep a year's worth of salary, benefits, and school expenses in it for you to write yourself paychecks and incidentals as needed."

They go back and forth about how much the amount should be for a few minutes, and before either of them realize the time of day, Lindsay Parker walks into the office for her four o'clock with Wendy. Mona collects the two hundred and fifty dollars required by Wendy and escorts her to Wendy's office. As the two them are introduced, Wendy motions for Lindsay to have a seat on the couch.

Wendy asks, "Would you like a coke, water, beer, or perhaps something a little stronger?"

"I'd actually love a beer, if that's okay," Lindsay replies, settling onto the couch.

"Did you drive down from San Francisco, or did you fly?" Wendy asks as she's retrieving the beer.

"Oh, I drove. This trip is on my dime. The station wouldn't authorize the expenditure."

"And yet you still came and paid my fee. Why would you do that?"

"I just really wanted to interview you, that's all."

"That's very obvious. But why? What are you hoping to find that would be the least bit news worthy?"

"I'm not sure. I just want to get to know you."

"Okay. Let me remind you that you have one hour, so let's just cut through all the bullshit and get to your questions and whatever theory you're trying to prove before you run out of time."

Lindsay smiles, a little bit surprised at Wendy's directness. "Very well then. I find it odd that so many of your clients' spouses have committed suicide or died for accidental reasons recently. Can you explain this phenomenon?"

"No. It's not all that unusual, actually."

"Well, don't you think it is statistically weird that there have been so many recently?" Lindsay presses.

"I don't know. You have obviously done the research. What do the statistics reveal from that?"

"They don't really reveal anything because there hasn't been adequate research into offender suicide rates. Everything I've found indicates suicides by offenders are viewed as an aggressive act on the part of the offender towards the victim."

Wendy nods. "So did you want my professional opinion on offender suicides? Or are you trying to link the deaths of my client's spouses to a conspiracy or malpractice accusation?"

"Neither, really. I'm trying to figure out why there is such prevalence toward suicide with your clients' spouses as opposed to other counselors in the same field."

"Is there prevalence? I thought you just said the research you've conducted isn't adequate to justify such a conclusion?"

"Well, umm, I did. That's why I wanted to interview you."

"So it sounds like what you're really interested in finding out, then, is whether or not I have any responsibility or culpability in their deaths. Or, more specifically, did I cause their deaths. Is that it? Why don't you ask the question you're dying to ask me? Or don't you have the guts?"

Lindsay shifts uncomfortably on the couch. "You're very blunt, aren't you?"

"I'm simply waiting for you to ask the question as I'm watching your time slip away."

"Very well then. Are you in any way responsible for the deaths of your clients' spouses?"

"I don't know the answer to that question. What do you think?"

"What do you mean?"

"I thought it was very clear. Do you think I'm somehow responsible for their deaths?"

"Are you?"

"Like I said, I don't know how to answer that question. Perhaps I could be."

"Really. How so?"

"Well, I give advice to my clients about how their spouses use power, control, and manipulation in both the physical and emotional realm. In essence, I teach them how to avoid being further victimized. If that creates frustration in the offenders, causing them to commit suicide, then I guess one could broadly attribute causation to me in some perverse way."

Lindsay makes a face. "I see. Is there any other way in which you could be responsible?"

"I haven't a clue. Individuals who commit such heinous acts on those they claim to love are very obviously not right in the head. I have absolutely no way of knowing what goes on in their warped minds. So how the hell do I know if I'm somehow responsible for their delusions?"

"Is it normal for a counselor to be the last person to see a spouse of one of their clients alive?" Lindsay fires at her.

"That's a pretty broad question. Can you be a bit more specific for me?"

"I'm specifically referring to Gayle Baxter and Harder Gould."

"Have you read the police reports on either of those deaths or spoken to the detective investigating their deaths?"

"Yes, I've done both."

"Then can you give me your definition of 'normal' so I can answer your question intelligently?"

"What do you mean?"

Wendy smirks. "For example, I define normal as standard, ordinary, customary, even conventional."

"Works for me. So is it normal, Wendy?"

"Your question is a complex one, so let me see if I can break it down a little. First, there are no ordinary, customary, or even conventional ways of dealing with a domestic violence offender because there are no ordinary, customary, or conventional ways they act in a given circumstance. There are some standard protocols, but even they differ given any set of circumstances. To answer your question in a literal sense, no it isn't 'normal.' However, if you have read the police reports, you should have noted I went to both residences at the request of my clients. Therefore, from a standard protocol, yes, it would be 'normal.' Finally, your question is both misleading and factually incorrect."

"How so?"

"I wasn't the last person to see Gayle Baxter and Harder Gould alive."

"Really?" Lindsay starts flipping through the police reports.

"Let me save you some time, since you are almost out of it. I don't know who the last person was to see Gayle alive; presumably it was Jim. Since I found her hanging by a rafter, obviously dead, it wasn't me. With regards to Harder, it's suspected I was the last to see him alive, but I left him in the middle of the afternoon and Tina found him in the early evening after she returned home from work. Can you tell me definitively no other person saw either of them? If so, how do you know that to be true?"

"Of course I can't," Lindsay replies, her frustration growing, "it's just presumed by law enforcement."

"This is why I believe your question is factually incorrect. I believe the police reports would say I was the last *known* person to see them alive. Or at least it should, which leaves the possibility open for someone other than me to have been the last person to see either alive."

"You're splitting hairs now, aren't you?"

"No, I don't believe so. I have worked in the courts for so many years and have had to deal with asshole cops, attorneys, and reporters who like to play fast and loose with the facts. I have learned, through experience, to be extremely precise when dealing with any of the three. Good day, Ms. Parker, your time is up."

Lindsay bites back a snide remark. "Thank you for your time and courtesy, Ms. Stevens."

As Lindsay leaves the office, Mona is waiting impatiently to hear how the interview went. Wendy explains to her it was a typical young reporter trying desperately to find something that doesn't exist to make a name for herself, and become the next Bob Woodward.

After explaining, Wendy says, "Well, that's it for the day. It's time to go home."

Mona shrugs. "For what?"

"That's right! Your kiddos are with their dad. Why don't you have a date on a Friday night?"

"Please, don't you even try to go there."

"Hey, I have a great idea! How do you feel about having dinner with me in Santa Monica tonight? It's a two-hour drive but it's worth it."

"I'd be up for it," Mona replies.

"Great. Have you ever eaten at the Estate Restaurant and Bar?"

"No. Like I'd drive two hours one way to have dinner by myself."

Wendy rolls her eyes. "Well, you're going to love this place. It's on Wilshire Boulevard, and it's a true farm to table dining experience. They have ribeye medallions in a cabernet-Szechuan sauce that is to die for. But if that's too hot, then their New Zealand lamb chops in a vadouvan sauce is the ticket," Wendy says as they gather their things and head out the door.

"What the hell is a vadouvan sauce?"

"It's a type of French curry with some Chinese spices. Oh, and after dinner we'll go upstairs to the Guest Room and enjoy the speak easy style 1920's music. They have a drink there called the 'Ethel Waters' that's incredible. It's tequila with a floral twist. They use hibiscus and rosewater cordials with splashes of lime and pomegranate. It's very smooth. We can call and make reservations in the car. We'll get there around seven and if we leave by eleven thirty, I can have you back here by two o'clock so you'll be home by two thirty. This is going to be a blast, Mona, I'm so glad you said yes!"

"It's not like I had anything else to do," Mona replies, starting to get excited because of Wendy's happiness.

"Well, that just makes me sound like a shitty choice. Am I a last resort?"

Mona smacks her arm gently. "You know what I mean."

They laugh and get in the car. Mona is able to get reservations for seven thirty. It's a beautiful drive, and they are surprised the two hours go by so quickly. Dinner is incredible and the entertainment is fun and relaxing. They each get home around three in the morning.

Mona calls Wendy around five the next evening and thanks her again for a great time.

Wendy laughs, "It was a great evening, but I'm exhausted. I haven't stayed out that late in forever, and I think I'll need the rest of today and all day tomorrow to recover."

"That's why you should date more! Maybe you should take Jim there and spend the night in Santa Monica."

"What a great idea. I think I'll probably make that happen."

They chat a little bit more and then Wendy apologetically ends the call, claiming exhaustion.

The next week flies by at the office for both Mona and Wendy. It isn't until Jim calls Wendy at three to tell her he has one more appointment before heading to her place that she realizes what time it is.

On her way out of the office, she tells Mona, "I'm heading home for the day, and I'll be back Friday morning, because of the conference in Los Angeles."

"Okay, dear, see you then," Mona says, barely looking up from her research on her school.

Wendy arrives home before Jim gets there and begins preparations on the seafood polenta. When he walks through the front door, she meets him with a nicely chilled glass of sauvignon blanc. She gives Jim a soft, sensual kiss and points him to the bedroom.

"You can put your stuff in there and get comfortable, when you come back I should be ready to sit with you, and we'll go out to the patio."

Picking up his stuff, he says, "Actually, it would be wonderful to take a quick shower. I've been sweating all day. Then I'll come relax with you."

"Okay, go right ahead," Wendy replies, returning to her dinner preparations.

Wendy hears the shower running and decides she has enough time to join him before finishing dinner. Jim is startled and yet very pleased when Wendy steps into the shower with him. He pulls her body toward him and he locks onto her mouth with a passionate kiss that sends her head reeling.

As she struggles to catch her breath she feels Jim's hand exploring her body and gasps when his finger slips into her. She pulls away from him momentarily, and murmurs, "I don't have much time. I have to get back to dinner so it doesn't get ruined. But I want you, right now."

She turns away from him, reaches between her legs, and guides him into her eager body. Instinctively he starts thrusting, and as their pleasure begins to mount, Wendy leans forward and braces herself against the wall. Jim grabs her hips and continues his assault on her senses, and before either of them expect, they erupt into an amazing orgasm. Jim braces himself against the wall with his hands and Wendy decides to sit down on the shower bench until her legs regain their strength and stop trembling.

Looking up at him from her seat, Wendy says, "I've missed you more than I realized and I truly needed that, but now I've got to finish dinner. Take your time. I'll be the woman in the kitchen in shorts and a tank top, just in case you forget why you decided to stay here, rather than a hotel."

He grins at her. "That must be why! It's the entertainment before dinner of course."

He gets out of the shower with her and watches as she slips into a pair of running shorts and a tank top, thinking, *I'm so lucky to have found this woman. She is comfortable enough with herself to slip into the shower for a quick romp then not worry about her hair, make-up, or even putting on a bra.*

Wendy blows Jim a quick kiss as she heads to the kitchen to continue making dinner.

When the preparations are through, they enjoy their meal at a little table on the patio, overlooking the ocean.

Jim is thrilled by the polenta. "This is fantastic. You can cook for me any time," satisfied with the way the night is turning out.

They enjoy the rest of the evening catching up on current events in each of their lives. After a little while, Wendy tells Jim, "I probably need to go to bed and get some sleep. I have to leave very early in the morning for my drive to Los Angeles."

"And you'll be back when," finishing his glass of wine.

"Around midnight. You don't need to wait up for me. I'll kiss you gently when I come to bed, and we'll have all day Friday to enjoy each other's company."

"I'm looking forward to it."

"So am I, Jim."

Wendy is distracted all day during the conference so she decides to leave early and surprise Jim at home. She becomes increasingly more excited the closer she gets to La Jolla, anticipating what their lovemaking is going to be like this evening. She smiles, amazed at how much she is enjoying letting Jim into her inner sanctuary a little more each time they are together. She makes good time and arrives just before six thirty. Wendy quietly opens the front door of the condo and hears music coming from the bedroom.

Hoping she can catch him by surprise, she steps into the bedroom doorway sneakily. Stunned, she inhales sharply then begins to pant, trying desperately to regain control of her breathing at the sight of Jim's naked body intertwined with another man. Jim bolts up into a seated position and stares at Wendy in disbelief. He watches as the dam breaks and tears stream from her eyes, falling silently to the carpet below.

Wendy takes a deep breath, then calmly tells them both, "I'm going to leave for two hours, and when I come back both of you had better be gone. Jim, you need to grab your shit and leave the key on the dining room table, and anything left behind by either of you will be immediately thrown away."

She turns and starts walking toward the front door. Jim jumps out of bed and chases after her yelling, "Wait! We need to talk about this."

Wendy whirls around with ice in her eyes. "There is *nothing* that needs to be discussed. If you both aren't gone by the time I get back, I'm calling the police, and I'll have you arrested. Now get the fuck out of my house, you worthless bastard."

With that, she rushes out the door and hurries to her car, refusing to let Jim see how much he has hurt her. She drives on autopilot and finds herself in her office parking lot. She weeps uncontrollably for quite some time, then decides to call Mona at home.

Mona answers the phone somewhat surprised to see it's Wendy calling. The second she hears Wendy try to speak she knows something is terribly wrong.

"What happened? Where are you?"

"I'm in the office parking lot," Wendy rasps, then clears her throat. "Can I come over?"

"Absolutely. Are you okay to drive?"

"Yes, I am now. I just really need someone to talk to."

"I'm here sweetheart, in my PJ's and all my fabulous glory."

Wendy chuckles but it's half-hearted. "That's perfect. At least you're dressed. I'll fill you in when I get there."

Mona grabs a bottle of cabernet from the pantry and pours two large glasses. When the doorbell rings she rushes to open it, placing both glasses on the entryway bench. Wendy steps in and Mona wraps her in a giant hug and just holds her while the emotions come pouring out.

After several minutes, Wendy settles down a little bit and Mona hands her a glass of wine. The two take a seat on the sofa in the living room. Mona just sits quietly and waits for Wendy to explain. When she begins, everything comes pouring out, including a new flood of tears. As she explains, Mona begins to tear up as well, feeling the pain that Wendy is feeling.

"Oh, sweetheart, I'm so sorry. What a fucking asshole. I hope he contracts HIV!" she exclaims, then makes a face. "I'm sorry, maybe that was a little over the top."

Wendy just shrugs her shoulders, absolutely devastated. When she finally does speak again, it's filled with more anger towards herself than Jim. "This is why I never want people close to me, because they always hurt me deeply. And... shit! It felt really good to be with him!"

Mona puts down her wine glass and takes Wendy's free hand. "This is not your fault. It has nothing to do with you, and everything to do with the fact that Jim's an asshole."

"But I know better. I should have been able to read the warning signs."

"What warning signs?" Mona asks, confused.

"I don't know. The one's I obviously missed," Wendy replies bitterly.

"Wendy, you didn't 'miss' anything! The two of you weren't together long enough for you to pick up on any signs. You just seemed so happy, and I don't ever remember seeing you giddy until recently."

"Well, that side of me is gone forever now," Wendy says dramatically, downing the rest of her wine in one gulp.

"No, it's not. I won't let it be. Besides, there are plenty of other men who would love to get to know you."

"Yeah, how well did that work for me the last time?"

Mona sighs. "You just haven't found the right guy yet, that's all."

Mona's phone rings and Wendy motions for her to answer it.

After a moment, she can hear Mona's daughter crying in the background. As Mona calms her down, Wendy can no longer hear Melissa's voice, but from the look on Mona's face she knows trouble is brewing.

Suddenly, Mona blurts out, "He *what*?!" There's a pause as Melissa repeats what she said. "Do you still have your thumb drive from school in your backpack?" Mona asks, a hardness in her voice. Tears start streaming down Mona's face, and Wendy kicks into counselor mode.

"What is it?" she asks quietly, putting down her wine glass.

Mona cups her hand over the phone and replies, "Melissa just told me Tyler was taking pictures of her in a thong with no top on, and that he also photographed Justin with and without his underwear."

Before Wendy can say anything, Mona replies back into the phone, "Good, baby. Can you copy the photo file on your dad's computer without him knowing?"

There's silence as Melissa replies.

"Now, listen carefully to me baby, make sure your dad doesn't know you are copying it and when it's done call me right back, okay?"

Mona hangs up and comes back to the sofa, sitting down hard. "I don't know what the hell is going on there, but I have a really bad feeling. I think I'm going to be sick," Mona says, and Wendy eases Mona's head down between her legs.

"Just breathe," she says, "How long of a drive is it to Auburn?"

"Nine hours. Why?"

"Because we're going to drive part way there tonight, and the rest of the way in the morning, and we are getting your kids and bringing them back to La Jolla."

"What about his visitation rights?"

"Screw them. He lost them when he photographed your children inappropriately. Even if they aren't pornographic, I believe the judge will excuse your behavior as that of being a concerned parent for your child's safety, and I'll tell him I insisted you do this so it can't come back on you. Now go get packed, and then we'll go to my place so I can pick up a few things. We'll ride together in your car. I've had too much wine to drive at the moment."

"You've got enough stuff of your own to worry about," Mona begins to protest.

"Mona, stop! I'll have plenty of time to deal with my crap. I'm going with you, and we're leaving tonight. No further discussion, period."

Mona's phone rings again and Melissa tells her she copied as much as the thumb drive would hold. She got most of the file but not all of it.

"Melissa, you did a great job. Wendy and I are coming to get you and Justin, but we won't be there until tomorrow morning."

"Oh, good. Daddy has a shoot at eleven and will be busy for about an hour. Can you be here by then?"

"We will be there. Call me when your dad leaves to go to the shoot."

"He's not leaving. The shoot is in his studio here at the house."

Mona bites her lip and shakes her head. "Okay. That's okay. Just make sure both you and Justin are packed, and don't let your dad know. When we get there, you both need to get in the car right away so we can go, okay?"

"Okay, I'll take care of everything," Melissa replies in her best grown-up voice.

"Baby, I love you and Justin, and we will see you tomorrow."

"We love you, too. Hurry please."

"I'll be there as soon as I can."

After Mona is packed, they head over to Wendy's. They walk in the front door and it's obvious that Jim and his lover have left. The key is on the dining room table with a handwritten note under it, which Wendy throws away without reading. She grabs an overnight bag and packs a few things and they head to Auburn in Mona's SUV.

They both vent about what a horrible day it's been for each of them. They drive until they reach San Jose where they rent a hotel for maybe five hours of sleep, knowing they only have two hours left to go in the morning.

Before they know it, their wake up call comes in. They jump up, get dressed, and hit the road again. They arrive into Auburn at ten thirty, just in time for Melissa to call and tell Mona her dad's appointment arrived early and the session has begun. Mona verifies that Melissa and Justin are packed and ready and when she hears they are she tells them to watch for the car because she will be there in fifteen minutes.

"I want to avoid a scene, so please just come out and get in the car quickly so we can leave immediately," Mona reiterates to Melissa, and Melissa says she understands.

When they get there, the kids are waiting. Wendy jumps out of the car and loads the kids' luggage while they jump into the backseat and everyone is on their way in just a few minutes.

As they are on the road heading home and they enter onto the Foresthill Bridge, Wendy sees a vehicle approaching their SUV rapidly.

"Mona, we have company. I think it's Tyler. If he catches up, let me out, drive away, and call 911 to report the incident. We shouldn't put the kids in the middle of this mess."

Mona just nods, and suddenly Tyler whips his vehicle in front of Mona's SUV, screeching to an abrupt stop in the middle of the bridge. Wendy jumps out and distracts Tyler while Mona maneuvers her car around his vehicle and calls 911 leaving, Wendy alone on the bridge with Tyler.

As Tyler starts to yell and demand answers, Wendy calmly begins to explain. "Mona is taking the kids back to La Jolla because we have proof you were taking pornographic photos of them and presumably other children as well. Why in the hell would you do that to your own kids, much less anyone else's?"

"Money, you bitch! I get thousands of dollars a day from those photographs. There is a certain look that sells extremely well, and my kids have that look!"

"You're a pig, and you don't deserve to be a father!" Wendy exclaims.

Tyler hears the sirens of the police vehicles approaching from both directions, then glares at Wendy. "What have you done?"

"We called the police. So the way I see it is you have two choices. Be a man, do the right thing, and jump off this bridge, saving you and the kids all the embarrassment about to be unleashed when I turn over the thumb drive of your photo file to law enforcement. Or get arrested and become someone's cafeteria bitch in prison."

Tyler looks a bit confused by her comment, and she laughs.

"Oh, I see you don't understand the term. A cafeteria bitch is the term inmate's use for the guy they bend over the table and rape anally without mercy, while grabbing his hair net from behind." Wendy then smiles, "They are going to love your sweet little ass, Tyler! The choice is yours, but either way your life is over. You will never be able to visit your kids without supervision again, and your career is completely fucked, especially after you are charged with possession of child pornography, exploiting children for financial gain, and distributing child porn over the Internet."

He looks over her shoulder and sees a Placer County Deputy vehicle coming onto the bridge, anger turning to fear in his eyes.

"There's another one coming up behind you. Only one way out now, Tyler," Wendy says, just loud enough to be heard over the sirens.

He looks over his shoulder then turns back to her. "I hope you die an agonizing death, you fucking cunt!" Then bolts towards the edge of the bridge.

"No!" Wendy yells as he grabs the railing and flings himself over the side, falling to his death in the shallow waters of the north fork of the American River some five hundred feet below.

Wendy rushes to the side of the bridge as the deputies reach her side. Feeling the incredible rush of forcing someone to take their own life through psychological means, Wendy knows she needs to stifle these emotions and appear distraught for the deputies.

She drops to her knees and cries out, "Why?!" and begins sobbing, thinking about how Jim has hurt her in order to maintain the charade. When she reaches a fevered pitch of uncontrollable crying, paramedics place nasal tubing under her nose and over her ears, delivering a steady flow of oxygen so she can catch her breath.

As her breathing returns to normal, the deputies ask if she is up to answering a few questions back at the station. Wendy just nods.

"Is that your car, ma'am?" They ask. She shakes her head.

The deputies have her sit in the back seat of one of their patrol vehicles and transport her back to the station.

"Before this interview starts, I really need to call my friend, Mona," Wendy says, and the officers begin to protest. "I'm sorry, I have to. She's the ex-wife of the man who just jumped off the bridge. She and her children should probably also come to the station."

"Oh, well, yes, we're going to need to speak with them also. Go ahead and do that and just let us know when you're ready," the officer says, and the deputies leave her alone to make the call.

Mona answers her cell phone and Wendy's asks, "Are you driving?"

"No, I stopped at a fast food place for the kids and they are playing right now. Why?"

"Listen to me and try not to react so you don't disturb the kids, okay?" Wendy says carefully.

"Okay, but you're scaring me. What happened?"

Wendy sighs. "Tyler jumped off the bridge. I'm so sorry, I tried to stop him."

"Oh, my God!" Mona pauses and waits for a moment for the shock to dissipate. She's surprised when all she feels afterwards is relief. "Well, good. That's probably best for the kids, the sick bastard. Is he dead or did he fuck that up, too?"

Wendy struggles for a moment to stifle her pride for how far Mona has come, then cautions, "That's probably not the best way to express your emotions, right now for yourself or the kids' sakes."

Mona recognizes the subtle message in Wendy's voice then asks, "Are you at the police station right now and can they hear you?"

"Yes. I need you to bring the kids to the station with the thumb drive. The police will have counselors available for them when you get here, so don't tell them about their dad. The counselors will do that. Do you understand?"

"Perfectly. We'll be on our way as soon as they finish eating. I'll just tell them we are picking you up there and that's all."

"Great. I'm glad you understand."

"Well, I've worked with you long enough and I know the subtleties in your speech. I've received your messages loud and clear. Thank you for everything you have done for me."

"You're so very welcome. Thank you for being a true friend of mine."

Wendy thanks the Deputy for letting her call Mona.

"They should be here shortly," she says, and the deputy escorts her to an interview room.

"Okay, Ms. Stevens, this interview is being recorded by video. Do you understand?" the deputy says.

Wendy nods.

After collecting the basic personal information, he asks, "Why were you on the bridge, and how did you get there without a car?"

Wendy explains her background with Mona and the kids, the telephone calls Mona received from Melissa, and the emergency trip to Auburn to pick the kids up. She continues with Tyler speeding past them and coming to a screeching halt in front of them on the bridge.

"I told Mona to get the kids out of there and tried to reason with him. He demanded to know why we were taking the children, despite his visitation rights, and I told him what Melissa had relayed to Mona, then asked why he would do that to his kids much less anyone else's. That's when he told me he made thousands of dollars a day from those photographs and I was absolutely stunned. When he saw your vehicles approaching, he bolted for the railing and jumped before I could stop him. Did you see me try to stop him?"

"Yes, ma'am. It was all recorded on our dash cams. We didn't get any of your conversation, but we saw you yell to him and rush toward the railing. There was no way you could have prevented his suicide. Desperate men do desperate things, and this is in no way your fault."

Wendy lowers her head, allowing tears to cloud her vision once more. "I suppose you're correct."

Right then, Mona walks into the station, and Wendy gets up and gives her a huge hug. Before they break apart, Wendy whispers, "Tell them everything except the sense of delight you experienced when you heard about the suicide."

Mona gives her a squeeze of acknowledgement then turns towards the deputy and introduces herself. She is questioned in much the same manner as Wendy and, after reviewing the thumb drive from Mona, they ask if she is on the title to Tyler's house.

Mona shakes her head. "No, he moved up from La Jolla immediately after our divorce and bought the house. I don't know if anyone else is on the title or not."

The deputy nods. "Well, there are definitely pornographic photographs of children on the thumb drive, many of which are not your children. We're going to get a search warrant, and there is a good possibility the kids could be witnesses in later prosecutions."

Mona acknowledges the possibility. "If at all possible, I would really rather not get them any more involved than they already are. They need to heal from this whole ordeal."

After the kids are interviewed and statements are taken, the deputies express their condolences to everyone involved and Mona, Wendy, and the kids begin their long trip home.

CHAPTER 16

LIFE AFTER DEATH

After arriving back in La Jolla, Mona drops Wendy off at her house.

"I'm so sorry all of this happened," Wendy says. "Take Monday off and spend some time with the kids. If you need more time, just let me know and I'll take care of the office no problem."

Mona nods. "Thank you so much. I'll call you tomorrow afternoon and let you know if I'll be in Tuesday."

The kids are thrilled to be back with their mom, but struggle with knowing their dad committed suicide after such a horrible experience with him during this visitation. Continued counseling is scheduled for them and it gives Mona some time to get enrolled in her graduate courses.

Wendy arrives at the office bright and early Monday morning to a ton of telephone messages taken by the answering service, most of which are from Jim. She opens her emails and finds pretty much the same thing, and she deletes all of them without opening a single one. Wendy expected it. She had ignored all the calls to her personal cell phone over the weekend, and had deleted all text messages he sent without reading more than the first line of each.

She decides it is time to call Jim back in order to stop the constant calling, emails, and texting. Sighing, she dials his cell phone.

Jim answers immediately. "Thanks for finally returning my call."

"Look, there really isn't anything further we need to discuss, and I'd appreciate it if you would stop will all the messages. I respect you as a business associate, and I won't let anything that has happened between us affect our professional relationship. But as far as any type of continued personal relationship is concerned, there's no chance. It's over."

"I know I've hurt you, but I think we need to get together and talk about everything face to face, please," Jim says, an edge of desperation creeping into his voice.

"I don't think that is necessary or even possible. I trusted you enough to let you close to me, a place where very few men ever get the privilege of being, and it took you an extremely short time to violate that deep trust. I'm more than happy to deal with you on a professional level without any animosity. Let's just keep it that way."

"And on a personal level?"

"On a personal level, I think you're a worthless piece of shit and I'll never trust you again. End of story."

"Wendy, please, we really need to talk. I'm not the person you thought I was."

"We certainly agree on that point."

"So that's it? No further discussion with regards to any of this?"

"Wow, you're finally catching on. Congratulations. I'm sleeping in the guest room until the furniture company brings me my new bed. I just can't ever sleep in that bed again after the way you defiled it. Why did you have to do that in my bed? Why not a hotel room? I mean if he makes you happy that's fine, but you should have been honest with me from the start and told me you are at the very least bisexual. Instead, you're just a dishonest, inconsiderate jerk."

"I'm sorry, but there is so much more to everything that you need know, and I'd like an opportunity to at least explain everything from my perspective," Jim says.

"There really isn't anything to explain. Maybe sometime later on, but for now, I really have no desire to discuss any of this further. Please stop calling me. This is our last conversation regarding our brief personal life."

"Fine. I'll give you some time, but I really want to have a discussion in person and if, after that discussion, you still feel the same way about me as you do now, I promise I'll never bring any of this up again. I won't call you for a month. If you decide you want to talk sooner than that, just give me a call. I'm just telling you now, I'll continue to call you on a monthly basis until we have an in-person discussion."

Wendy rubs her temples. "Whatever. I don't want to hear from you again for a month, starting now. Deal?"

"Fair enough. I'll call your cell one month from today."

As she hangs up the phone, she wonders how long he'll continue to call to meet with her and, after a short analysis, she figures he'll schedule a follow-up telephone call every month until she finally agrees to meet with him. She shrugs, trying to disregard the feelings that realization brings up, and then begins to focus on a review of her current clients, where they are in their counseling plans, and who she will refer most of them to.

Ultimately, she decides to call Pegge Peterson, the counselor she is most interested in sending all her clientele to, and leaves a message with her secretary. Within an hour, she receives a return call.

After she explains her situation to Pegge, she says, "You're the only person and counselor I would trust my clients to. I hope you'll be willing to take them on as your clients, but if not I'll continue searching until I find someone I trust as much as you."

Pegge is stunned. "Well, thank you so much for that compliment. I'd be honored to accommodate your request, because I respect you immensely. When do you need to transfer them?"

Relieved, Wendy sets a time to meet with Pegge to deliver all her files, after copying them to a disc. "I'll be sure to keep tabs on all the clients who agree to meet with you, so I can brief you on their files and expectations before you meet with them for the first time. I'll make sure all of them know you have the best recommendation from me, and I think eighty to ninety percent of them will follow my recommendation. Thank you so much for even considering doing this. It's completely amazing of you, especially on such short notice."

Pegge can't help herself and asks, "What has prompted such a drastic change?"

"It's a couple of things actually. First, I've decided I need to take a sabbatical for a couple of years to prepare to reopen a counseling practice after my assistant, Mona, gets her counseling degree. I'm not sure I want to specialize in domestic violence any longer, as it has taken its toll on me psychologically. I've become very negative and sarcastic lately. Second, I was dating a guy whom I thought was fantastic and came home the other night to find him in my bed with another man. That didn't do much to help my negative outlook on life. I think I need to step back, find some joy, and learn to love life once again."

"Oh, no! I'm so sorry to hear that. Is there anything I can do? Do you want to talk about any of this?"

"Thank you for your concern and offer, but you taking over my clients is a huge load off my plate. With regards to the guy, I just need to process through the hurt and grief personally. So I decided the best way to do that is travelling, laying on the beach in the sunshine, and reading all the trashy novels I want to."

"You left out cocktails with umbrellas and fit, tanned cabana boys to wait on you hand and foot!" Pegge says.

"Yeah, that's what I'm looking for in life nowadays."

They laugh and promise to keep each other up to date as the transition unfolds. Wendy thanks her again and hangs up to meet with her next appointment.

Jim Baxter walks into her office and sits down. Wendy notices he has lost weight and looks much more confident and composed.

She welcomes him. "Hello, Jim. It's nice to see you. How are you doing now that things have settled down a little bit?"

"Things are starting to fall back into place, work is going well, I've been exercising regularly, and I've lost a few pounds," Jim replies proudly.

"Wow. That's absolutely wonderful. I noticed the weight loss. How much have you lost?"

"Thirty-two pounds, to be exact, but who's counting?" he replies with a grin.

She smiles back at him. "You are, of course. Isn't that what all accountants do?"

He nods in acquiesce, and Wendy proceeds to tell him that she is closing her practice. "I would never just leave you on your own though," and gives her recommendation of Pegge Peterson. "I trust her completely. Would you meet with her to see if you two can work together?"

He agrees. "She sounds like she has your full support, so I guess I trust her, too. Congratulations on your decision to enjoy life and take time for yourself. That's hard to do."

They chat a little bit about Jim's life currently, and then Wendy repeats the process throughout the day with much the same results.

Mona is in the office when Wendy arrives on Tuesday morning.

"Good morning, how are the kids doing?"

Mona lets out a sigh. "Surprisingly well. I think the photographs Tyler took of them bothered them so much they knew it was wrong of him to do so, and the fact that he committed suicide cements that his behavior was very wrong. I think they are actually relieved they won't ever have to go through that again, but they are also sad their father is dead, of course."

Wendy nods. "I'd keep them in counseling for a while, but I think they are going to be just fine. I started referring clients to Pegge Peterson yesterday. She agreed to accept all of my clientele until further notice."

"Wow, that's wonderful. You are really going to do this, aren't you? I thought maybe you were just drunk at the beach."

"Oh, I was definitely drunk at the beach, but that's beside the point. Yes, *we* are doing this. Have you filled out your application yet?"

"Yes, and it's been sent off. All there is to do from my stand point is wait, and we both know how much I love to wait for anything," Mona replies, making a face. "It's only that much worse when it's something I want as badly as I want this."

"Relax," Wendy says reassuringly. "Everything is going to fall into place perfectly, and then your real work will begin."

"Have you told Bonnie about this decision yet?"

"Not yet. I was going to call her after this conversation and let her know. I'll still be able to make all the board meetings through conference calls or flying back from wherever I am at the time. And for the board meetings already scheduled, I'll just arrange my travel schedule to be in San Francisco for each one."

"Call her now, before you forget and she gets really pissed at you."

Wendy chuckles and walks back into her office to call Bonnie.

When she answers, Wendy asks, "Do you have time to talk for a few minutes?" "I always have time for you, and if I don't, I'll make the time. You're my family," Bonnie replies easily.

"Okay. I wanted to tell you about a few decisions I have recently made, and I want you to hear me out before you react."

"Well, that sounds ominous. But okay, go ahead."

"Here it goes. I'm going to close my practice within the next six months. I'm sending Mona to graduate school and, when she graduates, we're going to open a new counseling practice, with both of us counseling. In the meantime, while she is busting her backside in school, I'm going to travel and just bum around."

Bonnie is quiet for a moment, "I think that's a wonderful idea, but what has brought on this sudden change in lifestyle? Besides a six-billion-dollar inheritance, I mean."

"Well, I'm kind of feeling burnt out. You were here the week two of my client's husbands died, and now I've got this pesky news reporter insinuating I'm somehow responsible for their deaths. While I know it's all garbage, it has made me realize just how tired I am of dealing with people like that, so I'm going to take some time for myself and do things I've always wanted to but never could afford."

"Do you think you're going to go back to dealing with domestic violence victims when you reopen your practice or do some different type of counseling?" Bonnie asks, curious.

"I'm not sure right now, but I suspect I'll do something different. I don't have to decide that right now. Why do you ask?"

"Well, my hope is that maybe I can get you to move up north and open your new practice in San Francisco."

Wendy smiles. "Probably not. I like the weather in La Jolla better than San Francisco and people know me here, so a new venture would be easier for me to get off the ground. Plus, Mona's kids are in school here. I want you to know I'll set my travel schedule so I can make the SERF board meetings. I don't want to put you out or inconvenience you in anyway. If you have to send your jet to get me, I'll pay for the expense."

"I'm not worried about the board meetings. We can use conference and video calls if we need to, so don't let that worry you too much. If an emergency arises and you have to get here, we'll figure out how to make it happen. Given the recent threats and your unwillingness to work with the FBI, it might just be the safest thing for you to do right now."

"You know as well as I do I would be a very unlikely target given my limited involvement. I'd be more concerned about Jessica, given her intimate relationship with Sean and her lifelong friendship with you. If it was up to me and I was looking to strike at the core of the SERF organization and board members, she would be the one I hit."

"What a scary thought. I never even considered her as a target," Bonnie says quietly.

"She's the perfect target. Her kidnapping or, God forbid, death would be equally devastating to you and Sean."

"You have a disturbed mind young lady. Where on earth do you come up with things like that?"

"I suppose it comes from years of working with deranged individuals," Wendy says matter-of-factly.

"I suppose."

"Did you get all your security issues worked out at the SERF offices and your home? What about SGM and Beauty Boutique Clothing?"

"Sean's office already has all the security features he needs, and his home is good to go as well. Jessica's place is fine and SERF has already put in surveillance cameras and some other special features at the Beauty Boutique Clothing production plant, so everything we can do is completed already. Why were you so difficult with the FBI agents in San Diego?"

"I wasn't difficult. I just don't want to run my practice or life like I am in a maximum security prison. Hey, I've got to go. I'm having a new bed delivered at my place, and they just called the office and said they would be at the condo in thirty minutes."

"Call me later. I want to know why you're buying a new bed. Is there a chance of someone sharing it with you soon?"

"God, no. I just want a better bed, that's all. Part of this new taking care of myself thing I'm doing. I love you, I've got to go."

"Okay, love you, too," Bonnie says, and they hang up.

Wendy rushes out the office door and arrives at the condo before the delivery people. She is excited to see the new bed set up in her room and the old one taken away. Next she has the locksmith change all the locks to the condo, scrubs the shower from top to bottom, and finally starts to feel like the place is just hers once again. She pours herself a glass of wine and basks in the moment on the patio, considering where she wants to travel to first.

CHAPTER 17

DISCREPANCIES

After a couple of months have passed, Mona gets her acceptance letter to the University of California San Diego, Graduate School of Psychology, and immediately strolls into Wendy's office.

She comes in nonchalantly. "Well, Jim has called again and is now beginning to intensify the number of calls requesting to meet with you. He even offered to buy an hour of your time, but I told him I would have to get your approval before I booked an appointment. He wasn't very pleased with me."

She then hands Wendy the letter from the university. Once Wendy recognizes it's an acceptance letter, she is excited for Mona, but their mini celebration is interrupted by an urgent call from Bonnie. Mona hands Wendy the telephone after placing Bonnie on hold and closes Wendy's office door as she leaves.

"Bonnie, is everything okay? Mona said this call is urgent."

"We have a developing situation at SERF that needs the board's immediate attention. Can you break away from your practice and be here tonight for what will probably be an all-day meeting tomorrow, and I can have you back in San Diego on Thursday?"

"Hang on let me check with Mona. I have transferred a lot of my clients to Pegge Peterson over the last two months, so I suspect we can make it work. Do you want to hold on or shall I call you back?"

"I'll hold if it won't be too long."

Wendy checks with Mona and explains she needs to head to San Francisco, probably tonight.

After reviewing her schedule, Mona nods. "We will need to rearrange the appointments scheduled for tomorrow and Wednesday, but I'll make it happen. Just tell Bonnie you'll be there."

Wendy gets back on the telephone with Bonnie. "Mona is awesome. She said she'll rearrange multiple appointments, which means I'll be able to just work this weekend. I would only do this for you, you know. What is this all about?"

"It's a financial issue with SERF. I'll tell you all about it when you get here tonight. Can you meet my pilot at the airport at five o'clock?"

"Can we make it six? My last appointment today is at four and will finish by five. I'll need about an hour to get through traffic to the airport."

"Six it is then," Bonnie says and huffs out a breath. "Thanks for dropping everything. I've got to go, and I love you."

Before Wendy can say anything else she hears Bonnie hang up the telephone. She stares and her phone in disbelief, wondering what could be so urgent Bonnie would hang up so abruptly.

Checking her schedule once again with Mona, she sees she has about a forty-five-minute window to go pack her bags and be back at the office over her lunch time.

"Okay, I'm going to go pack," Wendy tells Mona. "Please go ahead and move some of this week's appointments to either Saturday or Sunday. Whatever day works for the clients. Congratulations on your acceptance! I promise we'll celebrate next week."

Mona smiles. "I'll hold you to it."

The day passes quickly and before either of them can imagine, Wendy's last appointment arrives.

As she's guiding the client back to her office, Mona says, "Make sure you grab the rest of the week's calendar for review, as well as your scheduled appointments on Saturday."

"Are you going to be gone before this appointment is finished?" Wendy asks, confused.

"No, I just don't want you darting out of here before you get it and I don't want to forget to give it to you. This is just my way of making it both our faults if you fail to get it before you leave."

Wendy rolls her eyes. "Oh, I see how it's going to be now that you're a grad student, blame shifting and all. Besides, the calendar is updated and I can access it via my cell right?"

"Yes, you can, but you know you prefer a hard copy," Mona replies, going back to her work.

Wendy disappears into her office with her client and emerges forty-five minutes later. She grabs her revised calendar from Mona and heads to the airport.

Bonnie greets Wendy in San Francisco. During the limousine ride back to the house, Bonnie explains to her that the emergency is to discuss some financial shenanigans Jim Bush has been perpetrating on SERF.

Wendy asks, "Have Sean and Jessica been informed about this? And how did you find out?"

"Yes, they are aware. Skip received a telephone call from one of our large donors explaining she received a receipt for her million-dollar donation to SERF, but didn't get a receipt for her ten-thousand-dollar donation to the SERF1 account. Skip, being smart enough to cover his confusion, told our donor he was sure it was an oversight error by his new staff and would get it out to her by early next week. Knowing we have no such account, he decided to do a little investigation on his own to determine what is going on. He called every large donor asking if they had received their receipt for their SERF1 donations because he feared it was a clerical oversight on the part of his staff. He received the same answer from every one of them. After verifying a few dollar amounts, he quickly realized each of them made two separate donations, and the SERF1 donation was always one percent of their original donation. One donor said he thought the one percent administration fee was a brilliant idea to insure the entirety of the donation dollars were being utilized on restoration projects. Skip traced the Limited Liability Company funds to Caiman Islands Bank. At this point, we don't know for certain that the LLC is Jim's, but he is the only one soliciting money on behalf of SERF and, since we don't have a SERF1 bank account, we know those funds aren't coming into our coffers."

Wendy allows this to settle in for a moment then asks, incredulous, "So what you're telling me is Jim receives a base salary of three hundred and seventy five thousand dollars, he was paid a first quarter bonus of one million dollars, and now he's skimming another two hundred and something thousand dollars from SERF into an offshore bank account for himself?"

"Only if the LLC belongs to him. But, yes."

Wendy rolls her eyes. "Who else would it belong to? None of us are seeking donations at Jim's rate. What are you planning on doing?"

"Well, that's the topic of discussion for the board members tomorrow. Do we fire him? Do we make him transfer the funds to SERF? Do we seek criminal charges against him? Each possibility has pro's and con's to them."

"My vote would be get the damn funds back from him, then fire his ass quietly so there is no negative press and issue receipts to our donors," Wendy says, a little more savagely than she intends to.

"That seems like the best solution, and we will issue receipts to our donors regardless of what we decide tomorrow. But the bigger questions are, do we really want to fire someone who has raised so much money in such a short time? And if we don't press charges, what liability might we have if we let him move to another company?"

"Ugh. This is making my head hurt, and I know we will cover it all tomorrow, but seeking charges is going to put SERF in the media spotlight and I don't think any of us want this to happen so early in the organizational life span."

Bonnie sighs. "No, we don't, but something has to be done and what if Jim isn't the one who is responsible?"

"Come on, you can't really believe he isn't. Besides, didn't Skip say a donor mentioned it and Jim was the one who was in contact with the donor? Who else could reasonably be responsible?"

"It's not that I don't think Jim is the culprit. It has to do more with what can I prove."

Wendy nods and they sit in silence for a few moments before she says, "Bonnie, I need to share some information with you, because I'm not sure what I should do from here, but before you say anything please hear the entire story. Deal?"

"Deal."

"Remember during our last telephone conversation when you asked me to come to San Francisco and I told you I had casually dated someone but it wasn't anything serious?"

"Yes. Is it more serious now?"

Wendy represses a sigh. "Substantially, but let me explain. The person I was seeing was Jim. He stopped by my office and took me to lunch. When I told you I needed to see a client in San Francisco, I actually went to Jim's place in Sausalito. He made me dinner and we had some terrific sex, then he came back down to San Diego and again we had a fantastic time. I had to be up early the next morning for a conference and was supposed to be back very late. Instead, I wound up thinking about him all day and skipped out on the conference, arriving home much sooner than expected. Long story short, I found him in my bed with another man, I told them to get out, and I have only had one conversation with Jim since then, telling him we were nothing more than business associates. He keeps calling my office and cell phone wanting to speak with me face to face at least one more time. So two questions. Should I meet with him and see what I can find out, and should I disclose all of this to the other board members and abstain from voting on anything that pertains to Jim this meeting?"

"Wow. That's a lot to absorb. First of all, why didn't you trust me enough to tell me it was Jim you were seeing?"

"At the time we talked, we had only had lunch and agreed we would have dinner and see where it went. It wasn't until we had dinner at his place anything developed. Then I was scared, because of how I was feeling about him. He hurt me. I had let him close to me and not seen the true man whore he is. Men are off the table for me for a while."

"I'm so sorry it turned out that way, but you can't judge all men by what he did."

"Sure, I can."

"No, you can't. Anyway, let me answer your concerns. I think to avoid any potential conflict of interest we should disclose you and Jim dated very briefly but aren't any longer. Because of that, you will voice your concerns but will abstain from any vote that may be taken. With regard to any meeting you may or may not have with Jim in the future, the board will advise you will not discuss any matter pertaining to SERF. That way there is no need to discuss the sordid details of what you just endured with anyone else. Now that the business crap is taken care of, how are you doing?"

Wendy smiles bleakly. "I'm crushed. He insisted I open up to him emotionally, and I did, only to have him destroy that trust I placed in him after two dates. I really liked him. We got along incredibly well; he's sarcastic, intelligent, witty, monetarily stable, emotionally supportive, and perceptive. I was falling hard for the man, and then I came home and got hit right between the eyes."

"Do you think he's gay? Or was he just experimenting?"

"I really don't know, nor do I care. It's not about any real or perceived orientation for me. It's all about violating my trust in him. I don't trust him any longer and I never will."

"Wendy," Bonnie scolds softly, "people make mistakes. People overcome infidelity all the time, and believe me, I know. You should at least speak with him in person and if you still feel as you do now, fine. But I think you need to find out how you truly feel after you meet with him and hear what he has to say. I bet you haven't even spoken to him about your feelings since then, have you?"

"No, not really, and I don't care what his reasoning is at this point. If he had told me he was dating other people, I might have been able to deal with this better. I know I could have if it was another woman, but it never should have been in my home and my bed. I'm still not sure about how I'd feel competing with another man. And if he's been embezzling, that proves trusting him is a bad idea!"

"Meet with him and either close this chapter of your life or determine where the two of you could go from here. Promise me you will at least speak with him about all this in an adult fashion."

Wendy pouts for a moment. "Fine. Next time he calls to tell me he's in San Diego I'll get together with him for dinner."

"You promise?"

"I promise. Thanks for listening, even though I don't like your advice."

"Sweetheart, I hope you know I'm here for you no matter what and I'll support you even if I disagree with you. We're family, and that's what family does. We love each other all the time, even if we don't like one another sometimes. That's a non-negotiable!"

"I know. I'm just really embarrassed. I should have been able to see this coming and I didn't. It has even shaken my confidence in my perceptive instincts and abilities as a counselor."

"Is that why you want to take such a long break?" Bonnie asks, prepared to reassure her.

"No, not really. I'm truly just burned out, but I'd be lying if I said this didn't have some impact on my decision. It was probably the pivotal point in making up my mind. Well, this and Mona's ex-husband's suicide."

"You are an incredible counselor. Look at all the people you have helped in very trying times! Hell, without you, I doubt Sean and Jessica would be together and they are so happy and madly in love with each other."

"Well, good. At least it's working out for someone."

"Oh, dear, it's going to work out for you, too, one day, if you remain open to the possibility."

"I'm not sure I want it to. I like being by myself. It's easier."

"That it is, but it's also very lonely at times. Think about how you felt when everything was going well with you and Jim, and remember that feeling regardless of what happens between the two of you. It can happen again, and it is possible for it to remain. It did for Mark and me. As long as you're open to it, it will for you as well."

"If you say so, Bonnie."

"You'll just have to trust me on this one."

The limousine pulls into the estate and, after a light snack and a couple glasses of wine, they both call it an evening and head to bed.

The next morning, Bonnie has her staff prepare poached eggs and fresh fruit for breakfast, then she and Wendy head to the SERF offices. Skip Duren is the first to arrive, followed shortly by Jessica and Sean. Both Hugo and Hector are brought into the board meeting via video teleconferencing. The meeting is called to order and Bonnie explains the purpose then turns it over to Skip. Skip carefully details every donation and each subsequent deposit suspected to have been transferred into that SERF1 account, based upon donor acknowledgements.

"While I can't verify the deposits into the off shore bank account, I have no reason to doubt the donors' truthfulness, especially given every declared donation into SERF1 is exactly one percent of their larger donation."

Hector asks, "Is Mr. Bush aware he is being investigated at this moment?"

"No," Skip answers. "The only people aware of this investigation are those currently present."

Hugo interjects and offers, "My opinion is that it is fairly clear. Jim is the one responsible for the diversion of funds into the Caiman Island bank. Someone on the board must confront Jim with the information they have, and insist he return the funds to SERF."

Everyone is quiet for a moment, then Sean asks the questions everyone is thinking about. "What if he refuses to return the funds? What's our next step? And if he returns the funds do we fire him, seek criminal charges, or allow him to quietly disappear?"

After a very lively discussion sparked by Sean's question, it is decided Bonnie will confront Jim with the information they have, and see how he reacts, with the goal of retrieving the funds for SERF. The board decides not to pursue any criminal charges due to the potential of devastating negative press, but they are split on firing or retaining Jim, because he is truly a talented fund raiser with many more significant contacts.

Wendy, not being able to remain silent any longer, says, "We can always simply withhold the skimmed amount from any more of Jim's bonuses. Then, if he continues his practice, we simply fire him and let the chips fall where they may."

Everyone makes some sort of approval of this plan, and Bonnie says, "Well, we can play this tricky game. Let's not say anything to Jim until after he has finished calling on his entire significant donor list. When he is done, which should be by the end of next quarter, we withhold all the funds from his bonuses, like Wendy said. This way, SERF gets the benefit of all his skills and contacts, and we can fire him once his initial usefulness is achieved in firmly establishing SERF's cash flow for the next ten years. At that point, SERF can hire someone not as dynamic and with less significant contacts who can maintain the donors and develop others over time."

Hugo makes a motion to accept Bonnie's proposal and is seconded by Jessica. There are four affirmative votes and one abstention. The motion is carried and the meeting is concluded. Skip is told to closely monitor Jim's situation and report back to the board with any significant changes.

CHAPTER 18

EXCUSES

Upon returning to San Diego Thursday morning, Mona gives Wendy several messages from Jim. When she laughs, Mona tells her, "You have got to return his calls. The man is driving me crazy."

Wendy, still chuckling, says, "Well, get him on the line while I get a cup of coffee and I'll speak with him."

"Finally. Thank God for small favors."

Wendy gets her fresh cup of coffee and by the time she reaches her desk Mona has already transferred Jim to her.

"Good morning, Jim."

"Thank you for finally taking my call. I'm going to be in San Diego next Tuesday. Can we have dinner Tuesday evening?"

Wendy sighs. "Where do you want meet?"

"How about the restaurant we went to for lunch the first time I was in San Diego?"

"That will be fine. Six o'clock? Or would seven be better for you?"

"Six o'clock will be perfect," Jim says, slightly confused at this new acceptance.

"I'll see you there," she says and hangs up. She walks out to Mona and explains she is having dinner with Jim, so he won't be bugging her for a little bit.

"Fantastic. How do you feel about having dinner with him?"

"It unnerves me a bit. I'm not sure if I should be angry, curious, or empathetic."

"Are you interested in continuing to date him?"

"No, I can't imagine anything he could say that would alter how I feel, but Bonnie insisted that I hear him out for my sake more than his, and I think she has a valid point. Even if I could get over the infidelity and dishonesty, I'm not sure I can get over the fact it was with another man. It's really strange, but I now have a greater empathy for men who find their wife is seducing or being seduced by another woman. How does one realistically compete?"

"Well, I can't say I have ever really thought about this type of dilemma before," Mona says, genuinely puzzled.

"I've counseled men when their wives were having affairs with other women, but I have to admit, until now, I have never really understood the hurt, shame, or helplessness associated with that type of infidelity."

"None of this is your fault or anything to be ashamed of. It's a choice that Jim made. Personally, I think he is an idiot. You're an amazing woman, smart, beautiful, and caring. He's the one that screwed up, not you!"

Wendy smiles and shakes her head. "I love you, too."

When Wendy walks into the restaurant, Jim is sitting in a booth and stands to greet her. She orders a glass of wine and senses indignation rising within her being. Before Jim can say a word, she asks, "So how are you doing?"

"I'm fine, but I'm really concerned about you."

"I'm a big girl, and I'm okay. But I need to know, why in my bed? Why would you do that in *my* space?"

"I'm sorry. Things were not supposed to happen the way they did, and you weren't supposed to be home until midnight."

"That's not an answer."

"It's the best one I've got."

"Well shit, that makes me feel so much better about you and myself."

"This isn't about you at all," Jim says pleadingly.

"The hell it isn't! I come home, excited to be with my lover, who has gotten me to open up and trust him – something no one has been able to get me to do for a very long time, mind you – only to find him in *my* bed with another man. From my perspective, it's all about me," Wendy replies, indignant.

"You don't understand."

"Then enlighten me, please. And this had better be a better answer than the last one."

"It was all business. He was attracted to me and the idea of introducing me to my first male experience. Because of it, SERF received a two-million-dollar donation."

"Oh, well in that case, I completely understand."

"Really, you do?"

"Yes, I do. Not only are you completely without morals, a player, and dishonest, you're also a whore who feels no shame in prostituting himself for a five percent bonus. Shit, if that's all it takes to get you to leave me alone I'll gladly write you a check for whatever sum necessary. That would come with one condition. Leave SERF and crawl back under whatever rock it was from which you came."

When Jim tries to respond, Wendy raises her hand, stopping his speech. She stands up from the table and drops a twenty-dollar bill on it.

"That should cover my wine," she says bitterly, then walks away and out of the restaurant. She drives home with tears streaming down her face, unsure if they are because of how much Jim hurt her, or the sheer rage that he was so flippant about his reasoning. She throws her keys onto the kitchen counter and pours herself espresso vodka on the rocks, then calls Bonnie.

"Hi, Wendy. What a pleasant surprise."

"Pleasant indeed," Wendy says, her voice thick with emotion.

"Oh, no, baby girl, what's wrong?" Bonnie asks immediately.

"I just met with Jim. He is a complete pompous ass."

"Okay, slow down and start at the beginning."

"I followed your suggestion, thinking it would be good closure for both of us. I asked him a few questions, and his answers were flippant, self-serving, and totally without any remorse for his actions."

"Well, I guess you know how you feel about him and you can close that chapter of your life. But what are we going to do to stop you from hating or distrusting all men?"

"At this point in my life, I don't hate or distrust all men. I'm just not sure I want to be involved with one."

"That's what I'm talking about. You can't just close yourself off from any type of emotional experience."

"Sure I can. I'm actually very good at it."

"That may be true but it's not healthy for you, and you of all people should know that."

"I just need some time to recover, that's all."

"Well, that I understand. If it's just time to take a vacation, you're welcome to come up north and lay around the pool."

"Actually I think I'm going to travel for a week or two, and maybe go somewhere different and be pampered. I have a few days I promised to work at the local animal shelter first though. Mona has basically transferred all my clients and she is getting ready to begin school, so now would be a good time for me to start my travels. Anything new with the SERF situation?"

"Nothing since our last board meeting."

"Okay. Thanks for listening. I think I'm going to relax, finish my vodka, and then head off to bed. Let's touch base later in the week okay?"

"Okay. Just call if you need anything."

"I will. Goodnight, Bonnie."

Wendy spends the rest of the evening researching all-inclusive vacation spots and decides Cancun looks good. She marks the Hyatt Zilara in her favorites then heads off to bed.

She arrives at the office a bit later than normal and looking a bit rough. Mona gets her a fresh cup of coffee.

"I suspect your meeting with Jim didn't go well last night?" Mona asks.

"I wouldn't say that. I got all the answers I needed, then I went home and got drunk. All in all, I'd say it was a successful evening," Wendy replies sarcastically.

"And?"

"He's a complete ass who only cares about himself."

"Okay then. I'm so sorry. He called this morning and wants you to call him back."

"Screw him. If he calls again tell him I'm not interested in any more of his excuses and, unless he has a business item he wishes to discuss with me, I'm done talking with him."

"I can do that."

"Oh, if we don't have any pressing appointments at the beginning of June please don't book anything. I'm going to go to Cancun for two weeks, lie on the beach, do some site seeing, and relax while you begin your studies."

"I've pretty much cleared your calendar, so you are free to travel your little fanny off. All the SERF board meetings are on your schedule for the next year and unless there is some type of emergency everything is up to date."

"Terrific. I deposited a year's salary, benefits, and office rent in the business account along with the estimated amount for your books. To be sure, I put in an extra ten thousand dollars, in case I'm out of the country and you need extra funds unexpectedly."

Mona shakes her head, tears welling. "I can't thank you enough."

"Sure you can. Pass all your classes and get your degree so we both can get back to work as soon as possible."

"You got it."

***

Over the next few weeks, as all Wendy's business affairs are winding down, Mona helps get her vacation plans in order for the trip to Mexico. Shortly after she leaves for Cancun, Jim calls again to try and speak with Wendy, and Mona delivers the message Wendy left for him loud and clear.

"Very well. But can you please put her on the telephone?"

"Nope, I can't. She's in Cancun and won't be back in San Diego for another ten days."

"Don't worry about it. I'll call her cell phone."

"You can if you'd like, but she left it on her desk, so she won't answer that for at least ten days as well."

"I don't suppose you'll give me the name of the hotel she's staying at in Cancun will you?"

"Sure I will. As soon as hell freezes over."

"That's pretty rude don't you think?"

"Yeah, I suppose you're right, but I don't think it's as rude as fucking some other guy in her bed," Mona replies sweetly. "I'll let her know you called, and if she's interested in talking to you, which I don't anticipate her being, she'll get back to you. Is there anything else I can help you with today?"

"No, thank you, you've done enough. Just let her know I called again."

"Good day, then."

Meanwhile, Wendy sits in a cabana on the beach in Cancun and watches the sunrise as she listens to the surf crashing on the shore. She is lulled into the melodious ebb and flow of the ocean as she studies the purple hues of the emerging sunrise. The warm breeze accentuates the previous calm of each passing moment as she contemplates how the world is beginning to come back to life. She is somewhat saddened by the realization of the oncoming hustle and bustle, recognizing the absolute peace she has just experienced will yield to the commotion of vacation life, even in the manufactured serenity of the all-inclusive Hyatt Zilara resort. In this moment, Wendy decides that although she isn't a morning person, the peace she has experienced watching the sun greet her will require her to revisit this spot tomorrow morning. She likes the feel of quiet contemplation and for the first time in a very long time she is content to do absolutely nothing.

CHAPTER 19

VENGEANCE IS WHOSE?

Wendy returns to San Francisco from Mexico reluctantly. The next day, she walks into SERF's monthly board meeting and senses things have begun to escalate with Jim.

According to Mona, he has been trying to reach her, but to her surprise Bonnie has been the more persistent and urgent recently. Bonnie is vehement as she discusses the emerging revelations about Jim and MEC. As the board listens intently to her about the recent discoveries Skip has made, a sense of an inevitable impending conflict between Jim and the board becomes an insidious undercurrent in all the various conversations.

Hector Sosa interrupts with an interesting twist to everything. "I received a telephone call from a friend who was asked to sit on the board of MEC as my replacement. When I suggested to him it probably wouldn't be a good decision for him given the financial ruin they are struggling to stave off, he began specifically inquiring about Jim Bush. When asked why he was inquiring about Jim, I was told that since Jim has done so much damage to MEC by wooing most of their largest donors to SERF, MEC administration recognized its operations have almost been destroyed. Massive layoffs have occurred and the organization hasn't been able to stop the hemorrhaging. The administrative staff has been cut to below minimum standards, and international operations are suffering so badly many of MEC's affiliates are considering closing their doors.

But here is the really interesting part for us. While we have been extremely brutal and effective in minimizing MEC's political influence internationally, they have decided to use a page from our playbook, that being they have offered Jim a job at the same base salary as ours, but have sweetened the pie by offering him a ten percent bonus of all the dollars he brings in *and* a 15 percent bonus for every donor dollar he gets back from SERF. It appears he is in final contract negotiations with the MEC board, and SERF is going to lose him whether we fire him or not, especially since we deducted the three hundred and forty thousand dollars he skimmed from his bonus this quarter."

Sean begins to laugh and when everyone turns and focuses upon him he acknowledges, "It's a brilliant move on the part of MEC. A little desperate but, none the less, brilliant."

"So how do we stop it?" Bonnie asks.

"We don't. We all have good working relationships with each of these donors and we simply continue to build upon these relationships. I think our best strategy now is to fire Jim and let rumors leak out to our donors and others about his Caiman Islands account," Sean replies.

Jessica interrupts, "Won't this hurt some relationships with our donor base because of the time it took to discover the skimming?"

"Perhaps with some of them, but the facts that Skip covered the issue so well and that we honored their donations by covering the theft internally only speaks well for this organization."

Hector says, "If I may offer an alternative, why not allow Jim to leave without firing him and then leak the story of his theft after he is employed by MEC?"

"What would be your reasoning for that?" Bonnie asks.

"I believe it would demonstrate a lack of due diligence in vetting Jim's background thoroughly, further putting MEC's organizational structure at risk. From my perspective, it could actually be the crowning blow to the organization, and what better way to destroy Jim's career?"

Everyone in the room turns to Sean for his reaction. There is a long, awkward silence as Sean takes the time to ponder all the possible ramifications before speaking. "I agree with Hector's assessment. The only better scenario I could imagine is Jim dying after beginning work at MEC because that way nothing would need to be leaked."

"Sean, don't say such a thing," scolds Bonnie.

"I'm not serious, and I'm sorry that was a bit crass of me," Sean says with an apologetic smile.

"I should say so," Jessica chimes in.

Wendy makes a motion. "Let the board choose not to pay Jim the remaining two hundred and sixty thousand dollars in bonuses for this quarter and tell him we've decided to do this in lieu of turning his skimming matter over to the proper authorities. If he threatens to take us to court, we can always pay it later, but let's see if he will call our bluff."

The motion is seconded by Hugo and passes unanimously. The rest of the meeting deals with updates on the Diablo Mining restoration project and consideration of a second proposal in Brazil which Hector is championing. The board grants approval of this project, pending an audited financial statement of the parent mining company and authorizes Hector and Hugo to deliver the news next week. Several other restoration projects are discussed and prioritized according to relevance for the most significant environmental impact and success within SERF's mission statement.

After concluding the board meeting, Bonnie catches Sean and Jessica on their way out. "Why don't you two join Wendy and me for dinner? She's going to spend a day or two more at my place before she heads back to San Diego."

Sean looks at Jessica who turns to Bonnie and says, "We would be delighted to join the two of you for dinner."

"Wonderful. How does everyone feel about Moroccan food tonight? I know of this great place in the city where you sit on the floor on these terrific pillows and everyone eats with their hands. It's kind of funky, and I thought it would be right up Wendy's alley. Since we are all in jeans already anyway it's the perfect place for tonight."

"Sounds great," Sean says, and Jessica agrees.

Bonnie looks at Wendy and says, "You can sit on the floor and eat without utensils. You should he as happy as a pig in mud."

Wendy rolls her eyes. "Pretty much! It actually sounds quite interesting."

"Jess and I will follow you to the place," Sean tells Bonnie, and they all get in their cars.

During the ride, Wendy says, "Sean and Jessica appear to be very much in love."

Bonnie agrees. "I believe they are indeed, and I wouldn't be surprised if they eventually get married."

"Really. Do you think that might happen any time soon?"

"No, not soon. I think Jessica wants to get Beauty Boutique Clothing firmly established internationally before she will allow herself to get that distracted. However, Sean is probably more ready than he thinks."

"That's wonderful. I just really like the way they look at each other, and hopefully one day someone will look at me the way Sean looks at Jessica."

"Oh, sweetheart, I'm so sorry things went so poorly the last time."

"It's for the better, given all we know about him now. It just shows how truly selfish a man he is, and karma has a way of dealing with people like that."

"Isn't that the truth. But tonight we are going to have fun and not worry about anything other than the food."

"Sounds perfect to me."

"One more thing though, and then I promise to change the subject. You mentioned you needed some time for reflection. Can I ask what that's all about?"

"Well, when I was in Cancun, I started getting up before everyone else, walking down to the beach, and sitting in a cabana reserved for my room to watch the sunrise. I found that to be the most pleasant part of the day, and somehow the sunrise felt cleansing as it started a new day off fresh and new. It was very peaceful and cathartic for me as I pondered many aspects of my life, like the things I am proud of and the things I'm not, but in those moments I found peace in my life, and regardless of all the things I have done I was able to forgive myself and others. So if I'm up early sitting by the pool don't be concerned."

"I never figured you for a morning person, but what you're describing sounds almost spiritual."

"Well, it kind of was for me but not in a theological type of way. More like for the first time in my life I realized the world still maintains a perfect balance regardless of what yesterday held, and we all get a fresh new start every day we are alive. Since all we can count on is today, we need to live it to the limit and accomplish good things for mankind."

Bonnie smiles at this revelation. "You're going to be just fine, and I think taking time off and travelling might just be a great way for you to reevaluate things that are important to you."

"I suspect you're right, and I'm really looking forward to travelling now that I can afford to. There are just a few things I'll need to wrap up before I take off."

Bonnie nods. "Oh, I almost forgot to tell you how proud of you I am for the way you're taking care of Mona. She is truly lucky to have you in her life."

"Thank you, but I feel the same way about her."

"Then your eventual partnership should be very fulfilling for you both."

"Unless of course I decide to travel for the rest of my life."

"Trust me, even travelling can get old after a while."

Bonnie pulls into the parking lot and gets out of the car as Sean pulls in behind her and parks his BMW.

As they enter the restaurant, they are stunned by the contrast of the dark lighting making it very hard to focus for a moment. They regain their vision and are seated and told which courses are planned for the evening. They order two bottles of wine and spend the rest of the evening enjoying a wonderful meal with terrific conversation.

The next morning, Wendy gets up early and sits by the pool watching the sunrise, but quickly recognizes it isn't as spectacular as it was in Cancun. She fixes herself some coffee and smiles to herself, deciding she doesn't need to do this again until she is somewhere she can watch the sun rise out of the ocean.

Shortly after, Bonnie joins her by the pool with coffee of her own, and they talk for about an hour before Bonnie needs to get ready and head to the office. Wendy chuckles at the thought of her punching a time clock, then realizes it has been good for Bonnie to have something she loves to focus on. Honoring Mark is very important to Bonnie, and Wendy vaguely wishes for something that important in her own life. While Bonnie is getting ready, Wendy decides to spend the day bumming around San Francisco doing the tourist thing, riding the cable cars and walking on the wharf.

Around mid-afternoon, she calls Bonnie and asks, "Can I bring you anything from the city?"

"Oh, God, yes. Can you bring a half a dozen cannoli back from Stella's Pastry on Columbus Avenue?"

"Consider it done. I'm on Broadway now anyway."

"Oh, I love you so much. You have no idea how badly I've been craving their cannoli today."

"Ask and ye shall receive," Wendy says, laughing. "I'll be heading back in about an hour. When will you be home?"

"I'll be there before you get home with my cannoli."

Wendy laughs again and heads toward Stella's Pastry. She picks up the required cannoli and then heads for Bonnie's.

When she walks into the house, Bonnie says, "I asked my staff to serve a carbonara for dinner tonight, which should be ready within an hour now that you're home."

"Terrific. That sounds amazing, especially with the cannoli. I'm going to take a quick shower before dinner, okay? The city always makes me feel dirty."

"Okay," Bonnie says. "Hey, wait, how long are you planning on staying?"

Wendy considers for a moment. "I'll probably leave the day after tomorrow."

Bonnie says, "Okay. I'll have the pilot ready to take you home whenever you want."

"Thanks. Ten o'clock would be perfect. I'm just planning on laying by the pool tomorrow. Can you take the day off and spend it with me?"

Bonnie grins. "I can do whatever I want. I control a billion-dollar company. Besides, I can take the calls I need to from home and the dreaded paperwork can wait for another day."

"Thank you for doing this. I have really missed just hanging out with you."

"Well, now that you're not working as much, maybe we can do more of it," Bonnie suggests.

"Yes, but now you are working as much as I was," Wendy says with a laugh. "I would really like that though."

"So would I. Let's just make it happen, starting tomorrow."

They spend the next day lounging by the pool and catching up on each other's lives. Wendy spends an enormous amount of time talking to Bonnie about Jim, the hopes she had about their relationship when it first started, and how terribly hurt she was to find he didn't feel the same way she did about their relationship. Bonnie recognizes how significant Jim's betrayal is to Wendy and encourages her to not close herself off to another man coming into her life.

"I know, not all men are like him. I'm still open to the possibility but I'll probably be much more careful about opening up so quickly in the future. Any man worth it will understand and allow the relationship to evolve slowly, over time," Wendy says, sipping a mimosa.

Bonnie agrees. "Sometimes, in spite our better judgment, things progress faster than we expect them to, and even though we often get hurt it's worth the risk to experience the intimacy, passion, and thrill of a new exciting relationship. Love truly sucks when you both don't feel the same about each other, but when you do love each other intensely there is nothing in this world that compares."

Wendy thinks about what Bonnie has just said, then admits, "I know you're right. When I remember how Jessica and Sean look at each other it keeps me hopeful. There is so much admiration and devotion in their eyes and actions towards each other, and I just think I'm ready to have that in my life now. In fact, if I were to be completely honest, I kind of crave it. Does that make me desperate?"

"No, of course it doesn't. It makes you human."

Wendy nods. "Thank you for that."

"There is a man out in the world somewhere who will adore you completely, and for whom you will long to be with most of the time. You'll feel empty when you are apart from one another, and you'll have the utmost respect for one another. Your responsibility is to remain open to the possibility of meeting this man. Who knows, maybe it's even someone you have already met."

"Well, if I've met him that means I've ignored him. Why would he still be interested in pursuing any type of relationship with me?"

"Because you are a beautiful woman both inside and out, and I suspect if a man can ignite the passion within you, you'll rock his world like it's never been rocked before."

Wendy blushes. "Again, thank you, and I suspect you see way more in me than I do in myself."

"That's the way it works my dear, unless you're an ego maniac."

Wendy's cell phone rings and she answers it without looking at it. She instantaneously regrets her lack of judgment, cringing when she hears Jim's voice on the line.

Covering her disgust, she says, "Jim, how are you?"

"I'm fine. I hear you're in town, can we get together?"

"I'm spending the day with Bonnie and flying back to San Diego in the morning, so I really don't have any time for you. Maybe next time."

"I figured you would try to put me off, but I have some business matters I need to speak with you about soon, per your rules according to Mona. I'm going to be in San Diego next Monday can we have dinner then?"

"Fine," she grinds out between her teeth. "Call me Monday morning and we will arrange a time for dinner. There's a new restaurant that I want to try that supposedly has great sea bass. Will that work for you?"

"Perfect. I love a great sea bass filet. Thanks for agreeing to meet with me, and I promise after this meeting, if you don't ever want to speak with me, I'll honor your request and never bother you again. Fair enough?"

She rolls her eyes, realizing that this promise is probably empty. "Sure. I'll give you the address of the restaurant Monday. I can't remember the name of it right now. Buh-bye, now." After they hang up Wendy turns to Bonnie, asking, "What business does he have to discuss with me?"

"Probably none. He just wants to try one last time."

"Yeah, it would be just like him to pull that kind of low life trick."

Bonnie shrugs. "That's enough about that douche bag. Dinner's ready."

They spend the rest of the evening talking, and Wendy takes the time to tell Bonnie how much she loves her and would do anything to protect her. She expresses how much she truly appreciates her insights and advice on relationships.

After dinner, they enjoy the cannoli and coffee spiked with brandy before saying good night and heading off to bed. It's the first time in a really long time Bonnie sleeps peacefully throughout the night and wakes up truly refreshed.

She makes a light breakfast of epic proportion with bagels, cream cheese, smoked salmon, and red onion for Wendy.

Wendy walks out into the kitchen and is surprised to see all the preparations Bonnie has made.

"This is why I always hate leaving, it seems you go out of your way to make it difficult for me to say good-bye," Wendy says, accepting a cup of coffee from Bonnie.

"I rarely get the chance to do this, so allow me this one little indulgence. Besides, I used to love getting up and making Mark a special breakfast before he went out of town. I guess it's my way of showing you that you have something special to come back to."

"Honey, you don't have to make me breakfast for me to know that, but thank you. It is truly very special to me that you would go to such an effort."

"I do it because I love you, and you're welcome."

Wendy simply hugs her, enjoys the breakfast, and promises to call Bonnie after she has dinner with Jim to let her know what they discuss. Bonnie drives her to the airport and wishes her a great weekend then heads off to the office.

CHAPTER 20

BASS ATTACK

Jim calls Wendy's cell phone on Monday morning and gets the location of the restaurant. When Wendy arrives, she finds Jim has reserved a booth towards the back of the restaurant and away from most of the clatter. Wendy gives him a quick kiss on the cheek and hugs him. He is somewhat surprised by her display of affection and seems puzzled.

Wendy shoots him a look. "Is something bothering you?"

"Well, the hug and kiss for one. I thought you hated me."

"I don't hate you, I hate what you did," she replies matter-of-factly.

"Then I have to ask, is there a chance we can get passed that and start dating again?"

She sighs. "Let's just take things slowly. What you did has destroyed my self-confidence."

"I never intended for that to happen, and I'm sorry."

The server comes to the table then. "What can I get you two to drink? Is this a special occasion, because that's the vibe I'm getting from you," she says with a smile.

Wendy chuckles and explains. "Well, we were dating, but we broke up. Now we're hoping we can work out our differences and start fresh."

Jim's expression is one of total shock, not expecting anything as wonderful as that. He orders a gin and tonic, and Wendy orders a bottle of Chardonnay. When the server returns, Jim proposes a toast to fresh starts and Wendy leans in a gives him a soft kiss.

"So what did you want to talk with me about?" she asks after a moment.

"Well, I have been approached and offered a job at MEC. It's a great offer. The salary is the same, but I'd also be getting a ten percent bonus for the dollars raised and fifteen percent for any money I recruit away from SERF."

"Interesting. What are you going to do?"

"I don't know, now that there may be a chance we can get back together."

"Why would our relationship, or lack thereof, have anything to do with your business decision?"

The server arrives to take their order, and Wendy orders the sea bass filet. Jim follows her lead, but asks for additional vegetables rather than rice pilaf.

"Anyway, I just figured I could make a lot more money winning the dollars back to MEC that I raised for SERF. If SERF doesn't want to lose the exceptional work I did for them, they should raise my bonus percentage to fifteen percent."

"Well, regardless of what happens between us in the future, you need to know that as a board member I will never agree to raise your percentage to fifteen percent."

"Why is that?" he asks, bemused.

"Because what you are doing, in my estimation, is really sleazy, and trying to extort additional dollars from the people I love is just wrong. So if you want more money, my suggestion would be to go to MEC and do your best."

"You know, none of this is personal."

"I know, I know. It's all about business and the money."

"Exactly!"

"Then you've got to do what's best for you, and SERF has got to decide what's best for us. You must believe me when I say, it really is nothing personal." Then, Wendy offers a toast raising her glass to Jim, and leans in and kisses him. "To new beginnings and focusing on what's best for us, without regrets."

"Perfect toast. I'm so glad you understand me, Wendy."

They chat for a few minutes until their food arrives.

She smiles and takes a bite of her meal. "Wow! This fish is awesome."

Jim follows her lead and takes several bites. After a moment, he clears his throat, takes a sip of gin, and looks concerned.

Wendy watches him without emotion. "Everything okay?" she asks.

Jim reaches up to his throat, clawing at it and making the universal sign for someone choking.

Wendy slides over next to him, reaches into her jacket pocket, retrieves a syringe, and injects the contents into his hip. He gives her a panicked look as he becomes fully conscious of the fact that he is now unable to move or breathe, while still being aware of his surroundings.

Wendy leans into him and whispers in his ear, "It's Succinylcholine, a strong paralytic that will release histamines which will exasperate your bronchoconstriction caused by the bass. The paralysis you're feeling is because it's also a mild anesthesia. Poor Jim. You forgot to ask about the bass. It was pan-seared in peanut oil. Soon, all of this together will lead to cardiac arrest."

She pauses as Jim lays his head on her shoulder and she feels him begin to spasm. Then she continues to whisper. "I swore after my father committed suicide I would never let anyone hurt or steal from the people I love. Not even the man I made love to and trusted. Good-bye, Jim."

She allows him to slide off of her as she sees the server heading in their direction. Quickly, she grabs the Epi-pen from Jim's left jacket pocket and slams it into the seat cushion underneath him, discharging its contents, then yells for someone to help her.

The server rushes over now, and Wendy tells her to call 911 while another customer helps Wendy pull Jim onto the floor. After making sure everyone sees he is not breathing, Wendy begins mouth to mouth while the customer tells her he has a pulse. Wendy watches as each breath delivers the customary rise and fall of the patient's chest as air reaches the lungs but she knows, with each breath, life is losing its grip.

By the time paramedics arrive four minutes later, Jim's face is ashen and there is a slight bluish tint to his lips. Checking for a pulse, they find none and have Wendy move back while they administer the AED shocks, to no avail. They intubate him and begin quickly loading him onto a gurney in order to rush him to the hospital. One paramedic pulls himself away to ask Wendy several questions in quick succession.

"He just started choking, and he told me if that ever happened I should get his Epi-pen. So I did, and stuck it in his hip, but it didn't seem to help. After that, we got him on the floor and I began mouth to mouth, and for a while he had a pulse. What happened?"

The paramedic considers for a moment. "He had an Epi-pen. What is he allergic to?"

"He said he was allergic to peanuts. But we were eating fish! I'm so confused," Wendy says, allowing a little hysteria to creep into her voice.

As the paramedics are rushing Jim out the door, one of them says, "Could you please stay and give his basic information to the police? They'll be here in a moment."

"Yes, of course. After that I'll meet you at the hospital," Wendy replies, then turns to the crowd of customers that have gathered at the scene. "Excuse me. I need to go throw-up," she says and rushes toward the bathroom.

Once there, she moves quickly into a stall, and a woman follows her into the bathroom. Wendy closes the stall door, drops the syringe into the toilet, sticks her fingers down her throat, and vomits several times. She flushes and watches as the syringe disappears, then waits a few more seconds and flushes the toilet again.

As she walks out of the stall and over to the sink to rinse her mouth and wash her face, the woman who followed her introduces herself.

"Hi, my name's Sarah. Can I help in any way?"

Wendy gives her a shaky shrug and leaves the restroom. Sarah walks with Wendy back out into the restaurant and into a ring of police officers.

Wendy introduces herself to the patrol officer and answers each of his questions.

The server, hearing that Jim was allergic to peanuts, asks Wendy, "Did Jim read the menu? It clearly identifies in the small print that we fry our fish in peanut oil."

Wendy plasters a horrified look on her face. "Neither of us looked closely at the menu. Our focus was just on enjoying our date."

The officers interject again, and as soon as she has answered all of their questions, she rushes to the hospital. Upon arrival, she is ushered into a private office. Within seconds the doctor arrives and informs her Jim has died.

"I'm sorry, ma'am. We did everything we could to save him. Why didn't you use the second Epi-pen?"

"What second Epi-pen? Jim only carried one, and it was always in his left pocket. I used the only Epi-pen he had with him."

"Individuals with this type of sensitivity know they should always carry two Epi-pens with them at all times."

Wendy shakes her head morosely. "Jim has never carried two of them with him for as long as I have known him."

"That's unfortunate. If he had followed the instructions I'm sure he received, it might have made a difference in the outcome today."

Wendy begins to cry as the doctor leaves, and a nurse comes in to determine Jim's next of kin. She gives the nurse Jim's parents' names and phone numbers, asking, "What is going to happen with Jim's body? I'll take care of any costs not covered by the insurance."

The nurse explains, "Since this was a physician attended death, the hospital will conduct an autopsy tomorrow to determine the actual cause of death. After that his body will be released."

The two of them make arrangements for his body to be delivered to a local funeral home after the autopsy so his parents can decide on the next steps. The nurse calls Jim's parents and tells them about his death and introduces them to Wendy via telephone.

Wendy expresses her condolences. "What would you like done with Jim's body?"

His mother tells Wendy Jim wanted to be cremated.

"Okay, Mrs. Bush, I can have him cremated in San Diego, and then the funeral home can ship his remains directly to you."

Jim's dad asks, "How much is something like that going to cost?"

Wendy hears the tentative nature of the question and replies, "Don't even worry about it. I have it covered."

After a few moments of protest that Wendy will not succumb to, they both express their gratitude. "We can't thank you enough for doing something like this for our boy," Jim's father says, and Wendy can hear his mother crying in the background.

Wendy makes the arrangements that once the hospital has completed the autopsy they can call the funeral home to pick up his body. Wendy then instructs the funeral home to cremate Jim as soon as they pick him up and send his ashes to his parents so they can hold a service for their only child.

After all arrangements are made and paperwork is signed, Wendy returns home. She makes herself a couple of Snakebites and drinks them before calling Bonnie to give her the news about Jim's death.

After explaining what happened and how she tried to stop the allergic reaction, she reveals to Bonnie that Jim had decided to ask for a fifteen percent bonus from SERF to not accept MEC's job offer.

"Jesus, what a sleazebag!" Bonnie exclaims, then cringes. "Sorry, I shouldn't speak ill of the dead. What did you say?"

"That it was nothing personal, but SERF would do what was best for itself and I couldn't have much to do with it anyway," Wendy replies.

"Never mind about all the business crap. How are you doing? This whole incident has to be devastating to you."

"Well, of course it is! And especially disappointing," Wendy says, tears clouding her voice.

"What do you mean?"

"When I first met Jim for dinner, I had decided if things went well and I liked his answers, I would try and overcome the infidelity and begin dating him again. But our conversation was interrupted by his allergic reaction and all we were really able to discuss was the business matter he brought up. He seemed okay with going to MEC, which I told him I thought was a sleazy move on his part but I didn't want to focus on business." She pauses, sniffling. "I wanted to see if we could work out our differences, and if there was any possibility of continuing a personal relationship, but we never got that far into our discussion because the egotistical ass died!"

"Well, I don't think Jim planned on dying to avoid this conversation with you," Bonnie says, only partly sarcastically.

"Probably not, but you know what I mean. Once again there is no real closure for me, and it pisses me off that I'll never get answers to any of my questions."

"Maybe it's better this way."

"How can that be?"

"This way, Jim will always be the asshole who cheated on you in your bed. In the long run, there will be fewer regrets about what might have been or what could have been."

"Hmmm, I hadn't thought of it in those terms. Perhaps, you're right and thank you for pointing that out to me."

"You're very welcome, and I'm glad I was able to help in some small way."

"You always have the right words at the right time."

Bonnie sighs. "Hopefully that will help me in the coming days. I need to notify everyone about Jim's death and will call you tomorrow after you receive the autopsy results verifying the actual cause. Sean will hold a press conference about this tragedy. I'm sure you're going to be inundated with media calls on Wednesday after the press conference, so you better let Mona know so she's prepared to handle the shit that's going to hit the proverbial fan in La Jolla."

"Oh, man, you're right. Thanks. I hadn't thought of any of that. I'll call Mona right now, and we can talk later."

After they hang up, both go to work making the necessary notifications. Sean gets to work contacting the press and setting up the necessary press conference for eleven o'clock Wednesday morning in his office, Bonnie notifies every employee at SERF, and when Mona hears Wendy's story she offers to bring the kids over and be with her.

Wendy declines politely. "There's no need to disturb the kids. Besides, I've been drinking since I got home and I don't want your kids to have to see me this drunk."

"All right, then we're going to talk this through on the phone until I'm satisfied you're okay to be alone tonight."

"Mona, I'm fine."

"Did you get to talk about anything? What business item did he want to talk to you about? Or was that just a ruse to get you to have dinner with him?"

"He wanted to talk to me about a job offer he received from MEC and to see if I would support his attempt to extort a raise from SERF. We didn't get to talk about anything else before he died."

"Well, I know it's not good to speak ill of the dead, but what a complete douche bag. Really, he was trying to get you to support him? I hope you told him not only no, but hell no, and you were surprised he asked."

"Funny, that's almost exactly what Bonnie said. I didn't tell him that in those terms, but I did tell him some other stuff that shouldn't be said now that he's passed. I stuck by SERF because that's my job."

"So you didn't get to ask any personal questions about your relationship with him?"

"No, we hadn't gotten that far in our conversation."

"Well, that's too bad."

"Perhaps. But Bonnie pointed out that it's probably for the better because now there won't be any regrets about what could have been with him."

"There shouldn't have been any anyway. He was an asshole, and he's lucky you didn't cut his penis off in front of his boyfriend. I know I would have been tempted to do so."

"Mona! He wasn't worth the effort or the risk. Besides, it wasn't personal just business."

"Bullshit. It was very personal for you, but you're better off without him. You need someone in your life that will cherish you."

"Besides you?" Wendy asks with a smile.

"Well if I had a penis, you would be in trouble and loving it. But since I don't, yes, someone besides me!"

"I'm coming to the conclusion I'm better off alone. There are less hassles and concerns that way."

"True, but there also isn't any romance, passion, or great sex either, and we both know how good great sex is. You wouldn't want to miss that forever."

"Perhaps you need to follow your own advice."

"Oh, I intend to. I'm going back to college and it's a target rich environment so I'm going to find someone to have great sex with even if I have to become Mrs. Robinson to do it."

Wendy laughs. "Now that's a disturbing image for me to have in my mind about you. You always seem so prudish and practical."

"From my perspective, I'm being both. There are plenty of young, firm studs wanting to sow their wild oats with a slightly older and more experienced woman. I get to enjoy their energy and enthusiasm and they get the benefit of my worldly experience. It's a win-win proposition."

"I see you've put a lot of thought into this. Now I feel like I need a shower."

Mona laughs. "Good night. I'm glad you're handling all this so well, but lay off the alcohol for the rest of the night and try to get some sleep, okay? I imagine the press will be calling to speak with you very soon. Especially Lindsay Parker. What do you want to do with her when she asks for another interview with you?"

"Just tell her we have covered it all, and I'm not going to grant another interview with her even if she pays for my time."

"Consider it done, and I'll see you in the office by nine. Don't forget your meeting with Connie Jackson."

"Thanks for reminding me. I had completely forgotten about her appointment. I'll see you tomorrow morning."

CHAPTER 21

NO PLACE TO HIDE

Wendy arrives about fifteen minutes early for her nine o'clock with Connie Jackson. She finds Mona has been busy communicating with SERF employees about the scheduled press conference in Sean's office on Wednesday, the structure of which depends on official autopsy results being released today. The script for the press release clearly identifies Jim Bush was having dinner with a SERF board member when he experienced an allergic reaction to peanut oil, and subsequently died from anaphylactic shock.

Mona quickly briefs Wendy about the tentative schedule of events surrounding the official cause of death being released and tomorrow's scheduled press conference. Just then, Connie Jackson walks into the office, and Wendy tells Mona she will follow-up with her on this matter after she finishes with Connie. The two head into Wendy's office and close the door.

Wendy begins their conversation with the same information she has been giving her other clients. "Because of this, I've selected a counselor that I know and trust to take on my clients. It would be beneficial if you would be interested in meeting with her before I actually close—"

Connie interrupts, "I don't have time to bring another counselor up to date right now. I need you to keep me at least until you actually close your doors. Things are beginning to spiral out of control with

Al. He has threatened to kill me if I see a counselor again, and I need *your* help, not someone I don't know or trust."

"Okay. I'll stick with you through this crisis, but then you'll need to follow-up with Pegge."

"Thank you, I will. What do I do now, though?"

The two of them discuss options and a safety plan for Connie with very specific instructions on how to alert the office after hours if she needs help.

After taking her through the process Wendy says, "Of course you can call anytime during office hours and someone will get back to you."

Connie nods. "I have other options, too. My neighbor across the street is in Europe for the next three months on business, and she told me if I ever need to get away from Al I can stay at her house."

"That's good. I'm glad you have other places to go as well," Wendy says. They finish their discussion and as Connie is leaving the office Wendy reminds her, "Don't forget about your neighbor's house. Don't tell Al that she's gone, because that can always serve as a safe house until the police arrive."

Wendy walks Connie out of her office, and Mona begins to brief Wendy as soon as Connie is gone.

"The hospital called," Mona says, "and the autopsy results confirmed the cause of death was acute anaphylactic shock. The funeral home has already been notified and should be picking up Jim's body for cremation this afternoon. The funeral home has been instructed to notify us when the cremation is completed, so you can notify Jim's parents when his remains have been shipped and when they can expect him to arrive home."

"And you've informed Sean's office about the official cause of death?" Wendy verifies.

"Yes, it's all taken care of and the funeral home anticipated shipping Jim's remains to his parents later today, and certainly no later than first thing tomorrow morning."

"You are so awesome. I'm going to miss having you as the office manager when we reopen our new office after you graduate from school."

"We'll just have to train someone new because we both know we're not going to find someone as awesome as I am at running this office."

"Probably not as humble either," Wendy retorts with a smile.

"Right?" Mona says, grinning back at her.

Wendy heads back into her office, and after several hours Mona walks in and tells her the funeral home just called, and Jim's remains have been shipped to Jim's parents in Illinois. Wendy thanks her for the update then calls Jim's parents to tell them they should be receiving Jim's ashes by Thursday.

Jim's mother fights back her tears. "Thank you so much for doing this for our son, Wendy. We're planning a small family memorial service in two weeks and would love it if you could attend."

Wendy hesitates at first but when his parents insist, she relents. "Okay, I will be there. Thank you for inviting me."

Jim's mother sniffs. "Good. We have a small pond nearby that Jim liked to swim and fish in as a child, and he told us when he went off to college that if he ever died before us he wanted his ashes spread in the pond, so that's where we're going to spread his ashes after the service."

"That's beautiful. Thank you again for including me in this precious moment. Your son was a good man, and you should be proud of everything he accomplished."

They thank her again. "We'll be pleased to finally meet you in a couple of weeks."

After they hang up, Wendy puts her face in her hands and desperately hopes that these two wonderful and loving parents never find out what a douche bag their only child had become.

At eleven o'clock Wednesday morning, Sean enters the largest conference room at his office accompanied by Bonnie and sees it filled with the local press and television reporters.

He sighs. "Alright, listen up. I have a very brief statement to make, and then Mrs. Stevens and I will be available for a short question and answer period. All of the employees at Stevens Environmental Restoration Fund are deeply saddened by the sudden and tragic loss of our Vice President of Business Development, Mr. James Bush, who died Monday evening of anaphylactic shock as a result of a severe food allergy while at a business dinner with a SERF board member in San Diego. On behalf of the Board of Directors, administration, and employees of Stevens Environmental Restoration Fund, we would like to express our condolences to Jim's family and friends. He was a great asset to the SERF organization and had made a tremendous impact on the organization in his short time with us. The loss of his expertise and presence will be felt deeply for many years to come. The CEO of SERF and I are now open to any questions you may have."

The first question comes from Lindsay Parker. "First of all, I would like to express my condolences to Mr. Bush's family and everyone at SERF. Can you please tell us who the board member was Jim was having dinner with in San Diego, and why?"

Bonnie takes the question. "Yes. It was Wendy Stevens, and they were having dinner at my request to discuss several issues that came up during the last board meeting regarding Jim's fund raising in San Diego on behalf of SERF."

Lindsay follows up. "Can you please elaborate on the specific issues they were discussing?"

Bonnie smirks. "I can, Ms. Parker, but I won't due to the confidential nature of our fundraising. I will say it was in regard to specific strategies being employed successfully and their limitations or expansion possibilities."

"One more question, then I'll yield to the others here. Was this a normal business meeting or were other factors involved?"

"I'm not sure what you're asking. Can you please clarify?"

"I'm sorry, that was a poorly worded question and I'll withdraw it. That's all, actually. Thank you, Mrs. Stevens."

Sean and Bonnie handle several questions regarding Jim's position at SERF and whether or not they intend to replace him, and then conclude the press conference.

As they recap in Sean's office, Bonnie asks, "What did you think about Lindsay Parker's question?"

"Well, isn't she the investigative reporter who did the critical special of the press because of the way they handled that restaurant owner who committed suicide? Maybe she wants to look closer at Jim's death and try to come up with some type of story about poor practices of restaurant management that results in a death of one of their customers. I wouldn't give it too much concern."

Bonnie shakes her head. "But there was something about her questioning that bothered me, and let's not forget that Wendy also had dinner with Ricardo just before he died."

Sean raises his eyebrows. "Do you think she is trying to tie Wendy in with their deaths? That's crazy. Each case has been looked at by the proper authorities and ruled to be nothing but a terrible accident."

"Just trust me on this one. Call it a woman's intuition if nothing else, but that girl was fishing for something. I don't know what, but she is up to something."

"If you're that concerned, let's just get Wendy on the line and talk to her about this situation and see if she has any insight. The inner workings of the human brain are her realm of expertise not yours or mine."

Bonnie nods and Sean calls Wendy's office. When Mona answers he identifies himself, then says, "Bonnie is with me and we really need to speak with Wendy."

"Absolutely, just a minute," Mona says and puts him right through to Wendy.

"Sean, Bonnie, what a surprise. How did the press conference go today?"

"It went well, but Bonnie is concerned by a reporter named Lindsay Parker. What do you know about her, if anything?"

"I know she is a good reporter and a pain in my ass. Why?"

"What do you mean?" Sean asks.

"Well, a couple of months ago she called my office and wanted to interview me about a couple of my clients' spouses who have died recently. I refused the interview, and then she booked an hour long appointment with me and paid for the time out of her own pocket. She was specifically asking about statistical suicide rates of offenders. There haven't been any valid studies in that area, so I couldn't help her very much, so I just handled her questions and sent her on her way."

Bonnie groans. "You should have told me about that before the press conference. I probably piqued her investigative curiosity because we told the press Jim was having dinner with a board member and she immediately asked which board member and we said it was you."

"Well, so what? What is your concern?"

Sean sighs. "Well Bonnie thinks she is going to try and tie you to both Ricardo's and Jim's deaths, but now it appears she's looking at more deaths than just those."

"Okay, both of you are sounding ridiculous and are worrying about nothing. Each death remotely associated with my counseling practice has been thoroughly investigated by multiple different law enforcement departments and all have been ruled either an accident or suicide. Can you honestly tell me that if I were somehow responsible for multiple deaths one of those agencies wouldn't have come up with some type of proof or suspicion? Hell, even the FBI questioned me after Ricardo's death and found nothing."

"Well, I have to concede to your point on that one."

"I just think you should be aware of her doing some type of investigative reporting on you," Bonnie says, still worried.

"Let her have her fun. She's wasting her time, and I'll be travelling soon so she'll lose interest after she keeps coming up empty handed. I've dealt with her type a lot during my counseling career. If she creates too much press around me, I'll simply resign from the SERF board and that way it won't reflect badly on SERF."

"We aren't suggesting anything like that, we just wanted to give you a heads up, that's all."

"I know, Bonnie. All I'm saying is, let me handle Ms. Parker and stop fretting, both of you. Now if that's all, I have work to do. I love you both and I'll call you if Ms. Parker attempts to contact me again."

Wendy hangs up and pages Mona. "Can you come in here please?"

"What is it?" Mona asks as she steps into the office.

Wendy rolls her eyes. "Lindsay is fishing for more information on me and if she calls the office again go ahead and schedule an appointment with her free of charge."

Mona makes a sound of disgust. "Now what is she looking for?"

"I don't really know, but since I was the person having dinner with Jim when he died and the last have to have dinner with Ricardo before he died, I suspect she is working on some type of conspiracy theory like she had with the Davis, Gould, and Baxter suicides."

"Oh, for the love of God," Mona says, rolling her eyes.

"I know, it's ridiculous, but I think perhaps I should humor her for an interview so that she sees I have nothing to hide," Wendy says. "It'll be fine."

CHAPTER 22

FOLLOW-UP

As soon as Lindsay returns to her office she immediately calls her boyfriend, Steve Davis, at the San Francisco FBI offices.

Steve answers his desk phone. "Lindsay, hi," he says, pleased to hear from her.

"Oh my God, Steve, I just attended a press conference at Sean Green Marketing on behalf of the Stevens Environmental Restoration Fund."

"Okay, how is that in the least bit exciting? There has got to be more from the exuberance I hear in your voice."

"Just wait and hear me out. SERF's Vice President of Business Development died in San Diego on Monday while having dinner with Wendy Stevens! He had a food allergy and died of anaphylactic shock and, and—"

"Okay, slow down. I think I know where you're heading but why would Wendy Stevens be having dinner with him?"

"She's on the board of SERF and they were supposedly discussing business strategies."

"Well, that sounds reasonable and normal," Steve says carefully.

"But how many people have you dealt with in the last year that died suddenly of strange circumstances or committed suicide?"

"Well, none, but I don't deal with as many mentally ill people as she does and the botulism has been thoroughly investigated by

SFPD, you, and the FBI. Two of the three have come to the exact same conclusion, so why are you still pushing this?"

"Just do me a favor and look into her again. And please come by my place tonight, I have some documents I want you to see before you blow me off as some wacko conspiracy theorist television reporter."

"But you are a conspiracy theorist television reporter."

She smiles and shakes her head at the jab. "Just come by my place at six and I'll make you dinner. Please."

Steve represses a sigh. "Okay, I'll be there. What's for dinner?"

"I don't know. I'll figure it out when I get home or we'll order out."

"Sounds good. I'll see you then."

They hang up, and Lindsay continues with her research and comes across an article in the Auburn Sentinel and Placer Herald about Tyler Crookshank, who jumped off the Auburn Bridge in front two Placer County Sheriff Deputies and one witness. Puzzled, Lindsay reads more about him and finds that the witness is Wendy Stevens.

"What the hell..." she mutters under her breath, and then quickly dials the Placer County Sheriff's Office records department.

"Hi, my name is Lindsay Parker. I'm an investigative journalist, and I was just hoping you could tell me whether or not the Tyler Crookshank death investigation is closed?" When she is told it is, in fact, a closed investigation she gives her specific identification and tells the clerk she is faxing a FOIA request and would appreciate it being expedited. Lindsay is told they will follow proper protocol and she should receive the report within two weeks. She copies the newspaper articles, then begins to calculate how many of these suicides or accidental deaths were somehow connected with Wendy Stevens. All told, she counts ten: Mark Stevens, Ricardo Montes, Jack Taylor, Arnold Davis, Gayle Baxter, Harder Gould, Zach Rawlins, Kenneth Quan, Tyler Crookshank, and Jim Bush to discuss with Steve over dinner. She grabs the police reports she has already received and copies of her FOIA requests which haven't been completed and rushes home.

Back at her place, she realizes she really doesn't have everything she needs to fix dinner for Steve so she just orders Chinese to be delivered and anticipates Steve and dinner will arrive about the same time. She double checks the frig and sees there is plenty of beer, so she opens one and tries to relax, waiting for Steve to arrive so she can reveal her findings to him.

As expected, he arrives slightly after the Chinese food and she ushers him into her living room where she has taped her flow chart to the wall.

Steve sees where this conversation is headed and interrupts, "If this is going to be a working dinner, babe, I need a beer and some food first."

"Well, the beer is in the frig and you can eat while I talk."

"Lindsay, please, just let me relax for a moment. Let's enjoy dinner first then I promise you'll have my undivided attention for as long as you need it."

"You're killing me with this lackadaisical attitude of yours," Lindsay says sharply.

"Sweetheart, I know you're excited to share what you found with me, but I haven't eaten all day. I need some food in order to concentrate on your discovery and it's apparent you have been quite busy laying out your evidence, so I want to appreciate it completely."

Lindsay gives in, and the two of them enjoy their dinner as much as possible with her being so anxious. Finally, Steve turns and says, "Now that I've eaten I feel better. Show me what you have discovered."

Lindsay gets up and walks to the wall where she has a picture of Wendy Stevens. Surrounding this picture are the names and photos of all the individuals connected to Wendy through her clients, and when and how their spouses died.

"Here's my theory," Lindsay says. "While all the individual law enforcement agencies have closed their investigations in each incident, I don't believe any of them have looked at all these deaths as a connected chain of events. The only agency capable of doing so correctly given all the jurisdictional issues would be the FBI." She continues to explain, listing reasons why the people she has taped to her wall are connected and how it could all tie back to Wendy.

Steve patiently listens to her then says, "Okay, I see your point, but couldn't all of these incidents just be an unfortunate string of events totally unrelated to Wendy Stevens?"

"I looked at that possibility. But honestly, how many people do you know of who have had ten people they are loosely associated die in the last year or so? What are the statistical chances of someone having such bad luck?"

"Interesting point. But, babe, Wendy Stevens is a domestic violence counselor and her clientele aren't involved in the most stable of personal relationships."

"I know that, too, and as hard as I have tried to do legitimate research, there aren't any really valid statistics on offender suicides or deaths in general. I even interviewed Wendy about it, and she was very educated and articulate on this issue, but even she couldn't really give me a viable excuse."

"Okay then, let's brainstorm a little. What would be the motive for Wendy being involved with orchestrating these deaths, given that most people murder for lust, greed, or revenge? There is absolutely no evidence she was in any type of sexual relationship with any of these people. She's a multi-billionaire, so greed probably isn't a factor. I can't even see revenge being any type of real motive here. Even if you want to claim she was killing people to get revenge for her clients it doesn't make sense, because Wendy would be losing money for everyone she killed because her clients wouldn't need her any longer would they?"

"Well looking at it that way you could reverse the logic. She's rich so she doesn't need the money from her clients. Why would she be concerned about it?"

"What would be her reason for revenge, then, since that appears to be the only viable motivation? I think it would have to be a huge stretch. Jay Mather actually questioned her after Ricardo's death and insinuated Wendy may have been somehow involved in it, but she ate from the same place. She just didn't eat the same foods, and that's why she didn't get sick. When we checked out all the possibilities, the only logical conclusion was poor restaurant management practices which allowed the botulism to develop. In that case, it seems like it could have just as easily been Wendy that died and not Ricardo."

"I can't accept that! Jack had been a very successful restaurant owner for over twenty-five years and never had any type of heath standard or food preparation violation."

"I know you don't like it, but that's exactly what happened. Perhaps one of his staff screwed up, who knows? But there is no doubt whatsoever that the botulism originated from his restaurant. We know for a fact she didn't kill her brother because we got a confession from the actual sniper, and nowhere in our investigation was Wendy even suspected as being involved, although his death is the one that would make the most sense for her to be involved in, given her inheritance. According to the attorney that read and arranged Mark's will, Wendy had absolutely no way of knowing her brother was leaving her any money. Jack Taylor killed himself, and that's clearly documented because of his financial problems. The only connection there is Kimberly, and Wendy hadn't been counseling her for almost two years."

"So are you saying she isn't involved in any way with any of these deaths?" Lindsay asks, frustrated.

"I'm not saying she isn't involved. But she isn't the cause, and it appears to be an awful chain of circumstances with her clients."

"Come on! You can't actually believe that ten people dying within a year that she is somehow associated with is explainable."

"Yes, I can, because you haven't offered any other viable possibility. Let's continue with all the other deaths," Steve says, getting up and going to the wall. "Okay, Arnold Davis. Other than counseling Nancy, we have no connection between Davis and Wendy. The only connection to Gayle Baxter is that Wendy was the person to find her and report it, and her story that Wendy went to the house at his insistence was confirmed by Gayle's husband. Zach Rawlins died of a cocaine induced heart attack, and again, Wendy was only counseling Jill with no indication she even knew Zach. All we know about Kenneth Quan is that he drowned in his own swimming pool, and he couldn't swim so that makes sense. Plus, there's no connection other than one telephone call to Wendy to try to set up a meeting, which she refused. The only cases that would raise any suspicion are Harder Gould, Tyler Crookshank, and Jim Bush, and only because she one of the last people to see them alive. But again, Harder was a junky who died of an overdose, and Wendy isn't associated with anything other than meeting with him at his wife's request. Finally, neither one of us has any information on the deaths of Tyler Crookshank or Jim Bush."

"You don't find it odd that so many people associated with her have died?" Lindsay presses.

"Yes, I find it odd. But I don't have any reason to question any of the investigations that have been conducted thus far, because each of these reports you have look very thorough and competent."

"Will you at least look into the Crookshank and Bush deaths before you determine I'm out of line here, please? I just know something isn't right."

He sighs and rubs a hand over his face. "Okay, I'll see what I can find out, but you know I can't share any of it with you."

"I know. Just tell me you have researched it, and if there is nothing there I'll never bother you with this again."

"I'll look into it and let you know if it's a closed discussion or if we are going to look further into the matter, but that's all you're going to get from me, period. And no seduction techniques like last time," Steven warns.

"Deal. Now, do you have to go home or can you spend the night tonight?" Lindsay asks, wrapping her arms around his neck.

"I thought you'd never ask. I'll spend the night but I'll have to leave fairly early."

"That's fine, but I wouldn't count on getting too much sleep tonight," she replies with a smile, and they go to bed.

CHAPTER 23

FBI PROBE

Agent Davis arrives at the office early the next morning and calls the Placer County Sheriff. After a fairly detailed discussion of the facts surrounding the case, Steve requests a copy of the Tyler Crookshank suicide report be emailed to him at his office in San Francisco.

Upon questioning by the Sheriff, Steve outlines his concerns about the ten individuals associated with Wendy Stevens, and that he just wants to take a more comprehensive look, since her name is also part of an ongoing FBI investigation.

The Sheriff says he'll forward everything to Agent Davis in a couple of hours, including all dash cam videos and recordings, adding that this is a very clear-cut suicide.

Steve thanks him for his cooperation and then calls the San Diego Hospital. He finds the emergency room attending physician on duty the night Jim Bush was brought in, and asks for a moment of his time. The physician is available and able to discuss the medical circumstances surrounding Jim's death.

"It was classic anaphylactic shock symptoms, which were later confirmed by the hospital's autopsy. There isn't anything suspicious here," the doctor tells Steve.

Next, Steve is transferred to the records department where he requests records be sent to him. The hospital tells him if he wants the records today, an agent would need to pick them up personally.

He sighs. "Alright, I understand. I'll have an agent drop by and pick them up in a bit," he says, then calls a fellow agent in the San Diego FBI office and asks if they could retrieve the records for him and send copies to him. The agent agrees and he has the files within two hours.

After he analyzes the records and all the police reports, he requests a meeting with David Hill. In this meeting, he outlines everything that Lindsay brought to his attention and shows him the records she compiled.

Steve explains. "My initial reaction to Lindsay's conspiracy theory was disbelief, but after receiving the two reports today, I found a few disturbing facts. Tyler Crookshank is Wendy's office manager's ex-husband, and Wendy had an estranged, intimate relationship with Jim Bush, according to the witnesses from the scene of his death. I think this could use some more investigation."

SAC Hill authorizes Agent Davis to continue investigating his concerns as long as Agent Mather works side by side with him. SAC Hill calls SAC Hughes in the Boise office, updates him on Agent Davis' follow-up investigation, and suggests Agent Davis assist Agent Mather, since he is the lead investigator on the case, and see where the facts take them.

SAC Hughes calls Jay Mather into his office and briefs him on the previous discussion, then tells both Davis and Mather to devise an investigation plan and keep SAC Hill and himself informed as to any progress.

After considering the files for a moment, he adds, "The key component you're going to have to establish is motive, and although it is highly unusual for someone to have ten people they know or are associated with die in a year or less, that alone doesn't prove culpability."

The agents agree to keep each other informed, and then Jay tells Steve he'll call Wendy Stevens and determine when and where they can get an interview with her.

"Also, if you would check with the San Diego Police Department's forensic lab to see if they were able to identify the unknown latent fingerprint found on the bathroom medicine cabinet in the Davis home that might be a good idea. I know the latent examiner was on vacation and then became ill, so if they haven't worked on it or made it a priority because this appeared to be a suicide it would be helpful if they could make it a priority now."

"Good idea. I'll call them as soon as we conclude here and get back to you," Steve replies, making a note to do so.

"Thanks. Somewhere along the line, if there is a break to be had, we'll need to get it."

"Amen to that sentiment."

Immediately after disconnecting with Steve, Jay telephones Wendy Stevens' office, identifies himself to Mona, and is immediately connected to Wendy.

"Agent Mather, to what do I owe this pleasant surprise?"

"Well, I was wondering if you were going to be in Boise anytime soon?"

"I can be, depending on if this call is for business or pleasure."

"While I appreciate the sentiment, it's a business call."

Wendy sighs. "In that case, I have to say I'm disappointed indeed. Why do you want to speak with me this time, and will your flunky be with you?"

"Agent Davis isn't my flunky, but yes, we both have some things we would like to discuss with you when you're available."

"What sort of things? That's a bit vague don't you think?"

"Yes, it is and it was meant to be. We can go into everything when we meet."

"Oh, very well. Jessica and Sean are heading to Boise to see about establishing a Beauty Boutique Clothing presence there next week. Let me see if I can get a ride with them, and I'll get back to you. It will probably require a late evening meeting, if you can handle that."

"If you can get to Boise, Agent Davis and I will accommodate your schedule."

"Let me make a few phone calls and I'll get back to you tomorrow, if that's okay?"

"That will be just fine. Thank you for your continued cooperation."

"Anytime. It's always a pleasure to see you. As soon as I have an answer you'll be the first to know."

Almost as soon as they discontinue their conversation, Jay receives a call from Steve, who tells him San Diego hadn't made the latent print a priority since the medical examiner's report didn't find anything inconsistent with a self-inflicted gunshot wound.

"I've ask they make it a priority and they said they would have the results by the end of the week," Steve says.

"Great. I just got off the phone with Wendy, and she thinks she might be able to be in Boise next week sometime but she'll get back to me tomorrow."

They agree to reconvene tomorrow after Jay has heard from Wendy.

Wendy telephones Jay the next day. "You're in luck. Sean and Jessica agreed to let me hop a ride to Boise with them next Friday, on the condition that I'm responsible for their dinner at the Parma Ridge Winery. We will land at three o'clock and drive to the winery for happy hour for Sean and Jessica's business meeting, which is expected to finish by six o'clock. So you and junior agent boy can join me in a separate meeting for happy hour, or I can have Sean drop me off at your office by seven thirty. Which would you prefer?"

"Why don't we all meet at my office? I'll need to pick Agent Davis up at the airport. And he isn't a junior agent, so let's extend him the courtesy he deserves as an agent of the Bureau."

"Oooh, I love it when you get that overprotective big brother tone. It's actually quite stimulating. Don't worry, I'd never say such a thing to his face, but really, what is he, maybe twenty-eight years old? If he has a graduate degree, he couldn't have been in the Bureau more than two years. I'll be respectful, but we both know he is terribly wet behind the ears. I'll tell you what, why don't we just keep this between you and me.? It can be our dirty little secret. By the way, you should probably check out Parma Ridge Winery. Their wine is tremendous and their food is fabulous."

"I will go to the winery soon, because you're not the first person to tell me it's fantastic, but not next Friday. I need to pick up junior agent boy at the airport, remember?"

"Agent Mather, you're such a naughty man," Wendy replies with a chuckle.

"You're a bad influence. I'll see you next Friday in my office at seven thirty."

"Yes you will, and it will be such fun I'm sure."

"Carrying on a conversation with you is always such a challenge, but next time can you try to infuse just a hint of sincerity."

"If that will make you happy Agent, then it will be my pleasure and sole desire."

"Good day, Ms. Stevens," Mather says with a smile.

"Ciao, baby," Wendy replies in a purr.

After Jay hangs up the telephone he laughs, wondering how he would react to her flirtatious ways if they had met under different circumstances. *Under different circumstance I would definitely pursue her vigorously,* he thinks, then stops himself, remembering this circumstance doesn't allow any room for such a fantasy.

He picks up the telephone and calls Steve. "We have an interview scheduled in the Boise office with Wendy Stevens at seven thirty next Friday evening. My staff has booked you a flight leaving San Francisco International at one fifty-eight and landing in Boise at four forty-two on United Airlines. We will have time to grab dinner and strategize before the interview in order to determine our best approach. We have got to handle this carefully. Otherwise, as smart as she is, we may not get another chance."

"I agree. Why don't we both give it some consideration before dinner Friday? Do I need to make hotel accommodations or do I have a late flight out of Boise the same evening?"

"Oh, I'm sorry, I forgot, we have a cheap hotel by the airport for you since we booked an early morning flight out. I didn't want to have to rush the interview in order to get you to the airport."

"Perfect. All I need is a bed to sleep in and a shuttle to the airport."

"Both have been arranged. I'll see you next Friday in Boise and I'll even buy you dinner."

"Works for me, Jay," and they end the call.

Steve calls Lindsay at her office and offers to buy her dinner. She readily accepts, and agrees to meet Steve at his apartment at six.

"So where are you taking me for dinner and what should I wear?" Lindsay asks.

"What you have on now should be fine, and I was thinking Italian in North Beach. Oh, and if you're going to stop by your place before you head over to mine, grab an overnight bag."

"I like the way this is sounding. What's the occasion?"

"You'll just have to wait and see," Steve taunts.

"Oh, you know how I hate it when you tease me like this!"

"As opposed to the way you tease me?" he fires back.

"Okay point taken. I'll see you at your place at six."

Steve makes dinner reservations for two at seven o'clock at a quaint Italian restaurant he recently read about on Columbus Avenue, then returns to more mundane matters like filling out a travel reimbursement and miscellaneous expense reports, and putting a complete case file together on Wendy Stevens. He makes sure to upload it to Jay Mather before heading home to meet Lindsay.

He gets home in time to lose his tie, gun, badge, extra magazine, and handcuffs before Lindsay rings his doorbell. He gives her a hug and kiss at the door as he's letting her into his apartment.

After she drops her things in the bedroom, Steve explains he wanted to take her to dinner tonight because he has to cancel their date for next Friday.

"Why? We have those comedy show tickets," Lindsay says, disappointed.

"I know, and I'm sorry. Maybe you can get a girlfriend from work to go with you."

"What's so important you have to bail on a show we both have been looking forward to seeing for months? You're even the one who bought the tickets."

"I hate missing it, but I have to go out of town for work on Friday."

She sighs. "Okay, I understand. Where are you going? Can you tell me that at least?"

"Yes, as a matter of fact, this time I can. I'm flying to Boise to meet with Jay Mather, and we have an interview scheduled for seven thirty Friday evening at his office."

"Who's the interview with and why so late?"

"Wendy Stevens, and it's the only time she had available."

Lindsay's eyes light up. "Really? You think I may be onto something with her? Wait, what did you discover that I don't know about yet?"

"Nothing definitive, but did you know the guy who jumped off the Auburn Bridge was Wendy's office assistant's ex-husband?"

"No I didn't. How did you find that out so quickly?"

"It's in the police report you'll be receiving in a couple of days as a result of your FOIA request from Placer County."

"What else is there?" she asks eagerly.

"Well, you'll also be receiving the police report from the San Diego Police Department on Jim Bush's death. Did you know Jim and Wendy had a brief intimate relationship that broke up, and the dinner they were having the night he died was to see if they wanted to try dating again?"

"Holy shit. I had no idea. So do you think revenge could be a motive for killing Tyler and Jim?"

"Whoa, slow down, that was a huge leap you just took from normal explainable deaths to murder. There is no concrete evidence that any of these deaths are anything except what they have been determined to be by very competent law enforcement agencies."

"If you really believe that, then why are you flying to Boise to speak with Wendy?"

"I think there is probably 'something rotten in Denmark,' as Shakespeare would say, but we don't have anything to stake a claim to that suspicion on, so Jay and I are going to try and rattle her cage and see what falls out."

"I think she's too smart to fall for something like that, so I hope you have more than you're telling me, or you're going to miss a great comedy show for a very frustrating, unproductive conversation with Wendy Stevens."

"We don't at this point, but don't forget it's unnerving for people to be questioned by the FBI even if they have nothing to hide. If they do have something to hide, most of the time they'll eventually slip up in their story."

"So you're just going on a fishing excursion hoping she'll make a mistake? Is that what you're really telling me?"

"Pretty much, but it's worth a try."

She rolls her eyes. "It didn't work for me, and people view the press in a similar way. While we can't arrest them and put them in jail, we can run a story with a lot less factual basis and wreak havoc in their lives. My word of caution is just to make sure you don't push so hard you piss her off, because if you do, I don't think she'll ever speak with you again voluntarily."

"I understand your concern. Jay and I are planning to be very careful," Steve assures her. "Now that we have covered everything we needed to with regard to that, can we go to dinner and have a nice relaxing and romantic dinner for two?"

"I'd like that very much."

As they head out to dinner, Lindsay takes Steve's hand.

"Thank you. I appreciate the fact that you actually listened to my theory and did a little investigating on your own. I promise if you tell me nothing is there after you interview her, that I'll stop bugging you about her and my instincts."

Steve gives her hand a squeeze while driving to the restaurant and says, "If you hadn't pulled all the reports together I doubt anyone else would have, so by doing that you'll at least get everything looked at as a whole and will be able to be confident in any outcome of this type of comprehensive investigative procedure. We're looking at it all at once this time."

When they arrive, Steve is lucky enough to find a parking space in front of the restaurant, and they spend the rest of the evening enjoying a quiet, romantic dinner for two, just like they wanted.

CHAPTER 24

PARMA RIDGE WINERY

Friday morning, Wendy gets a telephone call from Connie Jackson about the escalating circumstances at home.

"I'm sorry, Connie," Wendy explains, "I'm heading to the airport right now, but I can see you first thing Monday morning. Talk to Mona and schedule an appointment. If things get really bad over the weekend, go to your safe house, call the police, and alert Pegge Peterson. She has already agreed to help you."

"Okay, I'll try to hold out for the weekend," Connie says, and Wendy hurriedly transfers her to Mona and rushes out the door.

She meets Sean and Jessica at the airport and thanks them both for picking her up in San Diego before heading to Boise.

Once they're on board, Jessica asks, "Why are you making this urgent trip to Boise, anyway?"

"I have an interview with the FBI after buying your dinners at Parma Ridge," Wendy replies nonchalantly.

"Why on earth does the FBI want to interview you?" asks Jessica.

"Well, I don't really know. They were very vague about the purpose of this interview, but if I were a gambling woman, I would bet it has to do with how many of my clients' spouses have had unfortunate things happen over the past year. Perhaps they also want to talk about Mark and my inheritance. Who knows how many conclusions they have jumped to?"

"They know you didn't kill Mark because they know who did, and the United States Government granted him immunity for his testimony. How many of your clients' spouses are you talking about here?"

Wendy pauses for a moment, acting like she's trying to remember when really she knows the exact number by heart. "I think it's about ten. The suicides have all been closed, but it could probably be about Mona's husband, Tyler, jumping off the Auburn Bridge, and Jim's death, both of which I was present for. I'm sure it all looks terribly suspicious. This is why I need a vacation."

"Shouldn't you have an attorney present with you?" Sean asks carefully.

"Why? I've nothing to hide. As awful as all these deaths are, I'm not responsible for the choices the delusional spouses of my clients make, among other things. I also suspect Lindsay Parker may have something to do with getting this process started, since her boyfriend, Agent Davis, will be assisting Agent Mather during the interview."

Sean nods knowingly, and Wendy proceeds to explain to Jessica about Lindsay being on her ass about her clients' spouses.

They are all quiet for a moment as they ponder the fact that a personal relationship may be interfering with an FBI investigation.

Jessica finally says what they're all thinking. "It bothers me that the boyfriend of a reporter may have a prescribed agenda. It feels like you're walking into a trap. I think you should have an attorney present with you, and until you do, I'd cancel the interview."

"I appreciate your concern, I really do. But this is my realm of expertise, and if I show up with an attorney everyone becomes guarded. My experience is that if one has nothing to hide one should cooperate with the authorities. If I get any type of indication this is something more than an inquiry, I'll invoke my right to counsel immediately, but until then, it's best to cooperate."

"I know you're a very intelligent woman and you know what you're doing, but last time I talked to these people I felt more insulted and implicated then I have ever felt in my life," Sean says.

"I know, and so was Bonnie, but that's how the game is played. Things people do in marketing piss me off, and to you it's no big deal. It's just the way things work. That's how it works with investigations as well. I'm in my element, so let me handle things the way I deem best, okay?"

"I hope you know what you're doing, because I just don't trust those bastards," Sean says, and Jessica places her hand on his arm.

"Oh, believe me when I tell you I don't trust them either, but I do know what I'm doing. Now let's talk about something more pleasant, shall we? Jess, why are you looking at Idaho for expansion possibilities instead of other more metropolitan locations?"

"Well, it has the right demographics for my niche market and it's one of the fastest growing areas in the country. The only issue Sean and I have is the depth of the niche market and concern about whether or not it can sustain the demand in a manner worthy of the investment. There are really only two areas in Idaho for our consideration, those being Boise and Twin Falls. We have already made a trip to Twin Falls and Pocatello, and they offer some possibility, but there is a saying in Idaho: 'the way Ada County goes is the way Idaho goes' and that's the Boise area. Twin Falls has the most educated population because of the nuclear power laboratory, but isn't growing as quickly as Ada County, and Pocatello could be serviced through Salt Lake City if we were to expand into Utah."

"How serious are you about expanding into Idaho? Is this trip still a preliminary fact finding mission or…?"

Sean chimes in. "It's preliminary at this point, and we both feel it's probably too soon to expect the types of return on investment we want, but there is also something to be said for being the innovative market leader in new markets. If you're asking what the real possibility is that we will open a store in Idaho, it's probably even odds. This is going to be one of the tougher calls we've had to make in quite a while."

Jessica nods and asks, "What are your plans for tomorrow morning?"

"I was just going to relax until you guys are ready to fly back to San Diego. Why?"

"Sean wants to look at a couple of houses in the Idaho City area and if you want to join us you're certainly welcome to."

"Thank you, but house hunting isn't my cup of tea, so I'll just wait at the hotel or airport. Whatever is easier for you."

"We have a late check out at the hotel for all of us, so you can stay there until we come and get you. I'm guessing we'll pick you up by two o'clock," Sean says.

"Perfect. Maybe I'll catch up on some of the reading I've wanted to get to," Wendy replies, and then the flight attendant tells them to prepare to land.

They land in Boise, grab the rental car, and head to the Parma Ridge Winery for their meeting with the property management company and commercial realtor.

When they arrive at the winery everyone is taken aback slightly, expecting to see something equivalent to wineries in California. In comparison, this winery appears to be very small. The realtor and property manager find them in the driveway and they all walk together into the winery.

Despite the rustic appearance, when they are greeted by Stephanie they are amazed at the quality of the wines they sample and the charming service. Sean orders a bottle of the Private Reserve Merlot while Jessica and Wendy decide to share a bottle of the Winery's LaRea Dolce Sweet Reisling.

As they enjoy the wine and conversation, the smells emanating from the kitchen are alluring, and no one is disappointed when their food arrives at the table. Wendy's braised pulled pork sliders with black cherry barbeque sauce and garlic truffle fries are met with moans of satisfaction from her after her first bite.

Jessica is amazed at her grilled romaine salad presentation with blue cheese, bacon, Roma tomatoes, and candied pecans and is equally as pleased with the flavors.

Sean savors the aromas of his grilled flatbread with prosciutto, arugula, and a balsamic reduction. Both Wendy and Jessica enjoy the satisfaction on his face with each bite he takes.

Sean turns to the realtor and property manager and says, "I have to admit, I was quite skeptical when we arrived. I was concerned about what we'd gotten ourselves into here in Idaho, but obviously, first impressions can be deceiving. The food and wine here are fantastic. What an absolutely delightful find."

"We're glad you enjoy it. Do you ladies agree with Mr. Green?"

"Absolutely!" Jessica says.

Wendy simply nods her approval because she has just taken quite a large bite of her slider.

Everyone enjoys the weather, cuisine, and ambience, and is pleased with the friendly hospitality of the owners, Stephanie and Storm.

After they have concluded their feast and business discussions, Sean and Jessica drop Wendy off at the FBI office.

"Do you want us to stay until you're done?" Sean asks.

"Of course not. Go get settled at the hotel, and please just drop my bag off at my room. I'll call a taxi to get back to the hotel," Wendy says and waves them off.

Security notifies Agent Mather that Ms. Stevens is there.

"Perfect. I'm on my way down to the lobby to get her," he tells them.

When Jay arrives in the lobby he greets Wendy warmly, shakes her hand, and thanks her once again for her cooperation.

They make their way back upstairs in companionable silence. Once there, Jay walks her into an interview room, where Steve Davis is already seated.

Wendy asks for a bottle of water before they get started and raves about the dining experience she just enjoyed, telling both Agent Mather and Agent Davis they missed out by not joining her at the winery.

Agent Davis clears his throat and begins their conversation. "Ms. Stevens, do you understand that this is just an informal, fact finding interview and that you aren't being accused of anything?"

"Yes, I understand," Wendy replies.

"Okay. That being said, your cooperation is greatly appreciated here today. Let's get started, shall we?"

Wendy smiles. "Steve – can I call you by your first name? Aren't you Lindsay Parker's boyfriend?"

Surprised, he stutters, "Y-yes, you can call me by my first name. And, uh, yes I'm Lindsay's boyfriend. Why do you ask?"

"Because she paid for an hour of my time awhile back and started our conversation in much the same way you did just now, so I'm wondering how much of this conversation is designed to please her and satisfy several points she has obviously raised through pillow talk with you. Do you care to put my concerns to rest?"

Recovering from shock, Jay begins to jump into the conversation and is interrupted by Wendy, whose eyes never leave Steve's face. "Jay, please, let Steve answer my question. After all, it was directed to him."

Steve clears his throat, a small amount of sweat forming at his temples. "I have to admit, most of the reason we are looking into the issues that will be raised here is because Lindsay piqued my curiosity. I began to look at how many people you are associated with who have died or committed suicide in the last year. Do you know how many that is?"

"No, that's not a statistic I keep in mind, but I can think of three suicides."

"What about deaths?"

"Again, I couldn't say for sure, but two or three I suppose."

"In the last year, there have been ten people associated with you who have died or committed suicide," Steve says flatly.

"Well, now I know you're nuts. Name them, because that's a ridiculous number."

"Mark Stevens, Ricardo Montes, Jack Taylor, Arnold Davis, Harder Gould, Gayle Baxter, Zach Rawlins, Kenneth Quan, Tyler Crookshank, and Jim Bush."

Wendy bursts into laughter. "Are you serious? Hell, why don't you check all the death records for San Diego County? I'm sure there is someone out there I met at a grocery store who had a relative die at some point in the last year that you missed. I meet hundreds of people on an annual basis that I don't know on a personal level, and if you're saying anyone I meet during the year becomes associated with me then you need to get some counseling for your delusional fantasies."

"Are you denying you knew the people I mentioned above?"

"No, not at all. I knew of them, but I'm quite sure I had barely associated with most of them."

"Can you elaborate, please?"

She stares at him for a moment, incredulous. "Really? Okay, Mark Stevens was my brother, whom I hadn't spoken to in years, and you guys know who killed him so why is his name even on your list? Unless you're accusing me of somehow being involved in his murder? Don't answer that. Ricardo Montes I met once, and both of you have already questioned me about him. I did not know, nor was I associated with Jack Taylor, and I hadn't counseled his wife in almost two years since their divorce. I don't remember if I've ever met Arnold Davis. To my knowledge, I only knew of him through his wife, who was a client of mine. Harder Gould I spoke to once at the request of his wife, my client. I have never met Gayle Baxter because she was dead when I found her. Zach Rawlins and Kenneth Quan I never had the pleasure of meeting personally. I knew Tyler Crookshank because he's the ex-husband of my office manager, but I didn't know him well. Jim Bush and I were associated through SERF, and we dated briefly. So of all the individuals you mentioned, I knew Mark Stevens and Jim Bush on a very shallow level. Everyone else, at best, I only met briefly. Young man, at my age, I'm saddened to say two people that I know dying in one year is not out of the statistical norm."

"So you don't find any of this strange or unusual?" Steve asks.

Wendy rolls her eyes. "No, I don't. I have been counseling individuals for over ten years, and I've met or counseled hundreds, if not thousands, in my ten plus year career. Let me ask you, how many life insurance salespeople in San Diego County alone have ten or more people they've sold policies over a ten plus year period die in a twelve-month period? Does the FBI investigate each of them, as well?"

"I have no idea, but no. we don't investigate life insurance salespeople whose policy holders die."

"So then why is it seemingly so unusual for a domestic violence counselor to experience fewer deaths than a life insurance salesperson with similar career longevity? Shouldn't that require investigation by the FBI, since the life insurance salesperson certainly has a greater knowledge of his policyholders than I do of my client's spouses? Shouldn't they require the same scrutiny?"

"I see your point, Ms. Stevens, but please bear with me. Why hasn't this been the norm for your entire career, if it isn't so unusual?"

"Well, now I'm not sure it hasn't, given how loosely you've defined people associated with me. Do you have statistical data to indicate this year is an anomaly?"

"No—"

"Please don't tell me you had me fly all the way to Boise to question me on the hunches of your girlfriend to keep your position inside her panties and yourself in good standing with her," Wendy says, dripping disdain, and Steve's face loses all its color.

At this point, Jay can't let Steve continue to get beaten to a pulp, so he decides to jump in and start questioning Wendy about Tyler and Jim. "Wendy, let's shift gears here a little bit and focus on what happened with Tyler and Jim, please."

After a moment of prolonged eye contact with Steve, daring him to say something else, Wendy turns her attention to Jay and smiles sweetly. "What would you like to know about Tyler?"

"We were able to review the reports from the deputies and their dash cam videos, but we don't know what the gist of your conversation was with Tyler before he decided to jump off the bridge. Since you've been very clear that he wasn't your client, I suspect you'll have no confidentiality problem relaying your conversation for us."

"None whatsoever. Long story short, he was very upset," Wendy says, and proceeds to explains about removing the children from his custody, the photographs, and his admission to selling child pornography. "I told him we had a thumb drive, and we were going to turn it over to law enforcement. About this time, the police were arriving on the bridge and he looked around, then just… jumped." Wendy pauses, allowing mixed emotions to flash across her face. "I thought finding Gayle Baxter's body hanging was awful, but it's nothing compared to watching someone take their own life."

"I'm sure it was awful for you to witness. Did you or he say anything else?"

"Nothing that isn't in the police report."

"Alright. Let's talk about Jim Bush," Jay continues.

"What do you want to know?"

"Everything from how you two met to what kind of relationship you had with him to how it ended and why you were having dinner with him the night he died."

Wendy starts to tear up and allows several of the tears to run down her cheeks. Taking a few deep breaths, she gratefully accepts several tissues from Jay, so she can wipe her eyes.

After a few moments, she clears her throat and explains. "Jim and I met as a result of my being a board member of the Stevens Environmental Restoration Fund. Jim was at a dinner the board was holding for two positions and was being considered for the Vice President of Business Development. I remember thinking he was extremely attractive when I first saw him, and then when he sat next to me at the dinner table I became distracted by him again because of how good he smelled. Anyway, we hired him after an exhaustive interview process that weekend.

After Jim started working for SERF, he stopped by my office in San Diego and took me to lunch. We both admitted we were attracted to each other and decided we would keep our dating quiet until we were sure our relationship might progress beyond a few casual dates. Then a couple of weeks after our first date I had to be in San Francisco for an emergency SERF board meeting so I asked Jim to dinner, but since our timeframe was so short he decided to make dinner for me at his new place in Sausalito. The dinner was scrumptious and we wound up having incredible sex. In fact, I'd probably rate it the best sex of my life thus far. We decided to start dating more seriously after that, and I gave him a key to my penthouse.

He came to San Diego for a business trip and we had some terrific sex again, but I had to be in Los Angeles for a conference early the next day and didn't plan on getting back until late. I couldn't stop thinking about him so I skipped out on the conference and got home sooner than expected." She pauses, breathing deeply again. "I-I found him in my bed with another man. I was devastated. I kicked him out of my house and personal life, telling him I would only speak to him on a professional level from then on. He kept trying to get me to meet with him, and I finally couldn't say no anymore. The night we had dinner was the first time we had seen each other since I kicked him out of my place, and that pretty much sums up our entire relationship."

Steve and Jay sit in shock for a moment. "Um," Jay finally says, "Wow. Thank you for sharing all of that with us. Did you know Jim was allergic to peanuts?"

"Yes, I did. He told me on our first date. Oh, yes, I forgot to mention that. When he took me to lunch we went to a favorite restaurant of mine and he mentioned he was allergic to peanuts. That's when he told me he always carried an Epi-pen and that's how I knew where it was the night he... died. I tried to save him. The doctor said that, maybe, if he'd had a second Epi-pen it may have been enough."

"Who selected the restaurant for dinner?"

"I did, because I heard the food was good."

"But you didn't know about them pan searing the fish in peanut oil?"

"Not until someone mentioned it that night. It's not something I ever needed to be concerned about and quite frankly it never crossed my mind to check on it."

"Especially if you were angry with Jim for his infidelity," Steve interjects.

Wendy sucks in a breath. "Listen here, you asshole. I don't particularly like what you're implying. First of all, after you're weaned from your mother's breast and you've experienced a few heartbreaks, you'll come to learn that some people simply aren't worth the time and effort it takes to be with them. You don't plan to *kill* them; you just move on with life because you're better off without them."

"That may be true, but the server said you guys were looking to get back together because that's what you told her."

Wendy nods. "Yes. We had started to explore that possibility, but then he went into anaphylactic shock and we never got to a decision point, which doesn't help your girlfriend's theory. If we were getting back together, why would I want him dead? I've already told you, he was the best lover I have ever had in my life. I would have kept him around for the sex alone, and there was so much more for us than that."

Jay clears his throat, shooting Steve a look, and suggests they take about a fifteen-minute break so he and Steve can chat, and then come back and finish up.

"I promise we'll get you on your way soon, Wendy."

She sniffs. "Sounds fine to me. I could use a minute to myself."

The two agents leave her.

CHAPTER 25

CAT AND MOUSE

After fifteen minutes, Wendy is still sitting in the interview room, and Steve pops his head in.

"Are you okay to hang out for just another ten minutes or so? Jay just received an important phone call and he needs to finish it up before we can come back and conclude our interview."

Wendy looks at her watch, sees it's nearly ten o'clock, shrugs, and says, "I suppose so as long as it's not going to be too much longer tonight."

Steve promises he'll hurry Jay along and they'll finish up as soon as possible.

When Jay and Steve walk back into the interview room, Jay is carrying a yellow legal tablet with multiple pages of scribbled notes.

Wendy thinks, *what in the world is all of this about, and what angle is he intending on using now?*

Jay looks at Wendy and makes probably the most intense eye contact anyone has made with her in a decade. She finds it somewhat unnerving.

"Wendy, I'm going to shift topics now, and I ask that you please indulge me for a while because I need to get some information before I tell you about the conversation I just had with Detective Briggs of the San Diego Police Department."

"Okay, what information do you need?"

"Do you know Connie Jackson, and is she one of your current clients?"

Wendy's heart leaps into her mouth. "Yes, I know her, and yes, she is a current client, although I have also referred her to another counselor recently. Is she safe? Is she okay??"

"Yes, she is fine, but her husband is dead."

Wendy's mouth drops open. "Excuse me? What happened?"

"Before I answer that question, did you and Connie talk about a safety plan and will you please tell me what it was? This is very important."

"Okay, yes. Connie told me her neighbor across the street is out of town for several months and if there was a problem with Al, she could stay in the neighbor's house until the police arrived. I spoke with her right before I left today and told her to remember to go there if anything happened while I was gone this weekend. I don't know its location."

"Okay, thank you. Here is what we know so far. About an hour ago, Connie was upstairs getting ready for bed and Al was downstairs in the living room watching television. Connie heard glass break and thought Al was drunk again and probably dropped his glass on the tile and it shattered. She called downstairs to see if he was okay, and after about ten minutes she got concerned and went downstairs to check on him. She found him dead in his chair with his glass on the floor next to him, void of its contents. There was blood all down the front of him, and it's clear he was killed from a gunshot wound that entered through the back of his skull and exited through his face below his left eye."

"Oh, my God! Who shot him?"

"They don't know. They found the shot originated from the second floor of a neighbor's house, directly across the street. There was forced entry through the back door, and it appears the shooter used some type of homemade suppression device, because the forensic lab found a few fragments of plastic bottle and cotton. I'm sorry, but I have to ask. Do you own any firearms?"

"No and I never have. Can you seriously think I had something to do with Al's murder?"

"I'm just covering all the basics, that's all. You obviously couldn't have killed him. You've been sitting here with us. Do you know anyone who owns any firearms?"

"The only person I know with guns is Sean Green, and he's here in Idaho as well."

"Thank you. It appears the person who shot Al knew what they were doing. With the homemade suppressor, no shell casing found at the scene, and a .223 caliber weapon that's a favorite of the United States Military and law enforcement personal, it's obvious they know how to cover their tracks. No latent fingerprints or tool marks at the point of forced entry have been found," Jay says, looking puzzled and concerned.

"Who in the hell would do such a thing and why?" Wendy asks.

"Well, that's what everyone is trying to figure out. Would you mind me inspecting your telephone?"

"For what reason? I'm beginning to feel like I'm a suspect. Am I?"

"Well, we were looking at you as a person of interest because so many people around you have died or committed suicide, but now I have to admit, this murder throws a different light on this entire investigation."

"So am I a suspect or not?" Wendy asks to clarify.

After a moment, Jay shakes his head. "You are not a suspect. We had you here to clarify several points, which you have graciously done. I'd just like to go through your phone with you to see if there are any unusual calls or messages you've received in the last couple of days. I would also like you to call your service to see if anyone left you any type of weird message today."

"Okay fine, but the only calls I received today were from Sean, Jessica, and Mona and all of them were routine. Do you want me to dial my answering service now? I can put them on speaker phone so you can hear what they're saying."

"Please do."

The service answers and Wendy checks messages and all incoming calls. There are ten calls. Eight of them were referred directly to Pegge Peterson, one was a salesperson that was referred to Mona, and one was a message from Bonnie, wanting Wendy to call her about the next scheduled board meeting.

"Thank you. Are you sure that's everything?" Wendy asks the service person.

"Yes, ma'am, that's all."

"Did Connie Jackson call my office?"

"No, not that we are aware of."

"Thank you, that's all," Wendy says and hangs up. She turns her attention back to the agents. "It's possible that Mona received a call from Connie while Mona was still handling the phone in the office."

"Would you mind calling her and asking her if she did?" Steve asks.

Wendy nods and dials her number. When Mona answers, Wendy tells her she is on speaker phone with Agent Mather and Agent Davis.

"Did Connie Davis call the office today?" Wendy asks.

Mona says, "Yes, she called and wanted to speak with you, but I reminded her you were out of town, and she asked if I could connect her to Pegge, so I forwarded the call to Pegge's office. Why?"

"Apparently someone shot and killed her husband tonight."

"What? What the hell is going on?" Mona asks, surprise ringing in her voice.

"I have no freakin' clue," Wendy says.

"Mona, this is Agent Mather, did Connie tell you or anyone you know of where the spare key for her safe house is hidden?"

"I think she may have mentioned that it was under the rock in the dirt in the wine barrel planter or something, on the back porch. I don't know if she told anyone else."

"Thank you for your help, Mona," Mather says, then leaves the room to make another telephone call.

Wendy takes a moment to reassure Mona that things are fine, then ends the call.

Mather returns a few minutes later and tells Wendy, "I have a few more questions, and then I'll drive you to your hotel, since it's so late."

"That won't be necessary. I can call a cab."

"Absolutely not. You have flown to Boise at my request and have been here much longer than any of us expected. The least I can do is drive you to your hotel on my way home."

Wendy nods. "Very well, if you insist."

"I insist. I have to take Steve to his hotel by the airport anyway, so it isn't out of our way."

"Then let's finish this meeting up so I can open the mini-bar at the hotel and have a few drinks. After a day like today, I deserve it."

Mather nods his understanding and agreement. "I just want to recap and clarify our previous discussion, and bear with me if my thoughts are somewhat scattered. I'm trying to shift back to where we left off prior to our break. Did I understand you correctly when you said the only people you knew, or had several discussions with, out of the ten people we discussed were your brother, Mark, Tyler Crookshank and Jim Bush?"

"That's correct, with the understanding that my brother and I hadn't spoken to each other for several years prior to his murder."

"Just out of curiosity, why was that?"

"Because my brother was a lying, manipulative, person whose only thrill, besides his beautiful wife, was to control people with the use of his enormous wealth. In short, I always thought he was an asshole."

"Yet he left you over six billion dollars and some beautiful real estate in La Jolla?" Mather asks.

"Yes, but that doesn't make him any less of an asshole. It just makes him a rich asshole."

"I have one final question. Is there any reason why your fingerprints would be in Nancy Davis' house?" Mather asks and, with that, snaps the trap that he believes will be the snare for Wendy Stevens.

A GLIMPSE OF
UNANTICIPATED CIRCUMSTANCES
BOOK 4

The FBI investigation is turned upside down when another of Wendy's clients' husbands is clearly murdered while Wendy is unquestionably out of town. This begins a series of extreme political maneuvering between Jay Mather and Steve Davis as each man struggles to make sense of the facts of the case.
After Jay is convinced that Wendy is the target of an angry former client's spouse, rather than a killer herself, he abandons protocol and good sense and begins dating Wendy. Wendy flourishes in her relationship with Jay, as Jerry Summers provides details surrounding the unbelievable drama of a day in the life of a serial killer.

In this fourth book of the 'Un'missable Series, Jerry Summers builds on the readers' love/hate relationship with Wendy. Summers works to establish Wendy's humanity, reveal her tortured past and disdain for injustice, and soften her hard edges to reveal more of her incredibly complex personality. This more in-depth exposure of Wendy will keep you struggling with your own beliefs about good versus evil and right versus wrong.

The struggle is real for Wendy, and it will be very real for you, too. Watch for Book 4 in winter of 2016, and endeavor, with Wendy, to figure out where you draw the line.

The 'Un'missable Series includes: Uncontrolled Spin, Unmerited Favor, Unrestricted Behavior, and Unexpected Circumstances (winter, 2016).